Colorland

Other Books
by
Robert Rayner

The Ragged Believers
Defiant Island
Second Wind

Colorland

Robert Rayner

SPEAKING VOLUMES, LLC
NAPLES, FLORIDA
2015

Colorland

ISBN 978-1-62815-269-2

Colorland is for Nema, Tesfaye, Yalow, and
all other friends in Ethiopia.

Acknowledgments

Thanks to Bridget, Katie, Kaitlyn, and Heather for reading and responding to the opening pages of an early draft of Colorland.

Thanks, as always, to Nancy for putting up with my hours of silence and solitude.

And a special thanks to the band, Stepping Out, for recording 'Burning in Colorland', the song that derives from this novel. (Stepping Out is Tony on drums, John on guitar, Julie and David on vocals, and me on keyboard.)

Prologue

Isolde is crying again.

Wenden, waking, hears her through the thin walls of the old farmhouse. He rises and pulls on shoes and a warm jacket. They all keep their clothes beside them at night, ready to dress in a hurry. Across the room, Meru stirs and murmurs in her sleep. She'd been on first watch, until Ridge took over at midnight. Wenden tucks her blanket around her.

When Speed brought them here, and showed them the two spare bedrooms, they decided one would be for the girls and one for the boys. But Isolde comes to Ridge most nights, despite his aloofness, and Wenden goes next door and sleeps in Isolde's bed, in order to leave them alone. Sometimes Meru creeps in with him, for warmth and comfort. Only once has it gone beyond that. Wenden wonders if he should be offended by her lack of desire for him, but he understands, because he sees how Meru looks at Ridge. It's the same as he looks at Isolde.

He pauses in the hallway, listening to Isolde's weeping. He'd like to go in and comfort her, knowing she's alone, remind her that Ridge can't help how he is, he's like it because he saved them all, but she knows this. Besides, he fears how his friend would react, in his present state, if he found them. Even in Ridge's aloofness, Wenden knows the vestiges of his bond with Isolde remain, as responsibility for her, if no longer love, and he doesn't want misunderstanding to unleash his friend's ruthlessness.

He stands on the veranda. The morning sky is red and immense, and the plain stretches in shades of russet and brown as far as he can see. Speed is somewhere out there, checking the perimeter, as she does every morning. She promises they're safe here. No-one can approach without their knowing in plenty of time to flee, and the city can't afford aerial reconnaissance. Not yet.

The sun is just up and the air is cool. Wenden reckons it's late October, which means they've been there nearly a year. He wonders if that's cause for celebration or lament.

Ridge comes around the side of the house and stands beside him.

"Isolde's crying," Wenden tells his friend.

"She's always crying," says Ridge.

"She can't help it."

"I know."

"My watch," says Wenden. "Get some rest."

Ridge goes inside. He peers in his room. Isolde is grey. Like Wenden, like all of them, like everything. He's almost forgotten color, since he's been trapped on this side. Sounds are muffled, in harmony with the grey pall, except the sounds of danger, or of anything at which he directs his essential ruthlessness. It's what he'd learned to summon—what he'd needed—in the months before they found sanctuary with Speed. Now he curses his transcendence, at the same time as he knows that one day he'll need it again.

Isolde sits up in bed, a grey wraith, sniffling, wiping her nose with one hand, one shoulder bare as the baggy tee shirt she wears to sleep—one of his—slips down. She reaches her arms towards him. She rises from the bed like smoke. Her hands slither over him. Her voice comes from a distance.

"I want to feel you."

"You can't."

"What do I feel like to you?"

"I've told you over and over. Like nothing. Just a … a resistance."

She tries to smile. "I've never resisted you. Not for as long as I can remember."

"Sorry."

"Don't you feel anything in Colorland? I don't mean just touch, but feelings?"

He tries to summon feelings.

His coat round her shoulders, her hand in his, the day old trace of her scent on a borrowed shirt flit through his memory and are lost.

"You ask me that every day."

Outside on the veranda, Wenden rises from his seat on the steps to greet Speed. She says, "Everything okay?"

Wenden shrugs. "Isolde's crying again."

The bell for the end of class sounded across the playing field. Wenden opened his eyes. Had he fallen asleep? He'd meant just to close them against the sun for a few seconds.

Mr. Betts was still talking. "To sum up, the easiest foods to survive on if you're lost in the wilderness are berries, nuts and plants. Steer clear of mushrooms unless you're sure they're edible. That concludes the unit on outdoor survival. Don't forget there will be a test on it next week. Also don't forget there is a meeting of Teens4Progress after school today and the principal expects to see everyone there although attendance is, of course, voluntary. You may dismiss, except Ridge, to whom I would like to talk for a few minutes, please."

It was nice of Mr. Betts to take the outdoor pursuits class outside, appropriate, too, but it was difficult to concentrate on a warm Friday afternoon with the persistent hum of the city around them, the grind of trucks on the hilly road beside the school, a grade 12 phys. ed. class jogging around the perimeter of the field, and Isolde sitting beside him, leaning back on her arms, her legs stretched out and her dress pulled up above her knees to let the sun play on them.

On her other side Ridge lay full length with his eyes shut.

Isolde nudged him. "Mr. Betts wants to see you."

Ridge strolled across to the teacher while Wenden helped Isolde to her feet.

"I would appreciate it if you would at least pretend to pay attention," Mr. Betts told Ridge.

"I was paying attention," Ridge protested.

"You were asleep!"

"I concentrate better with my eyes closed."

Mr. Betts sighed. "So you could tell me, for example, some of the plants I mentioned to the class as good food sources in the wild."

"Hazelnut, elderberry, choke cherry, hawthorn, high-bush cranberry …" Ridge started promptly.

Wenden, overhearing, grinned. He didn't know how his friend did it.

"Okay," Mr. Betts muttered.

Wenden and Isolde sauntered on, out of earshot, as Ridge continued, "… Sea kale, wall pepper, wintercress, dandelion, arrowhead …"

One of the students from the phys. ed. class trotted up to Isolde and took Wenden's place beside her, forcing Wenden to follow a few paces behind.

He winked at Isolde. "Hey, gorgeous."

He was tall, with a high forehead that seemed to weigh heavily on the rest of his face, giving it a crushed appearance. He wore an armband: Teens4Progress. Captain.

Isolde said, "Piss off, Jay."

Jay put his arm round her shoulders and pulled her to him. "You know you don't mean that."

Wenden wondered how it would feel, to have her so close, her soft shoulders, her hair in his eyes, her smell filling him.

He put his hand on Jay's shoulder and said, "Leave Is alone."

Without removing his arm from Isolde's shoulders, Jay swung his other arm back, smacking his elbow into Wenden's face. "Go wank off some-where, fat boy."

Wenden fell back, clutching his cheek.

Isolde spun around, freeing her shoulders. As she completed her spin she punched Jay in the face.

He snarled, "Bitch. I'll …"

Wenden saw Ridge jogging across the field towards them. Jay scurried off. All the students were afraid of Ridge, even the older ones.

Isolde took Wenden's face between her hands.

He muttered, "Sorry, Is."

"Sorry for what?"

"For being so useless."

She stroked the red welt where Jay's elbow had landed on his cheek. "You're not useless."

Ridge called, "What's going on?"

Isolde whispered to Wenden, "Don't say anything to Ridge. I don't want him landing in trouble on a Friday afternoon for kicking the crap out of Jay." She told Ridge, "Just Wenden and Jay got in a bit of an argument."

"You okay, Wen?" Ridge asked.

"Yeah."

"Come on, then. Let's skip social studies, take off down town."

"There's that T4P meeting," Wenden said.

"So?"

"Jus' saying. And we skipped social studies last week. Got shit for it, remember? And my folks got a call from the school saying I'd have to make up time on Saturday morning if it happened again."

"The school didn't call my place," said Ridge.

"Nor mine," said Isolde.

"How could they, when you got no phone at home?" said Wenden. "And if you did have, you got no-one there to answer it."

"You can get out of Saturday detention easy," said Ridge.

"How?"

"Just don't go. What are they going to do if you don't show up—shoot you?"

"Easy for you to say," Wenden grumbled. "No parents to get on your case."

Ridge set off towards the road.

Isolde said, "If we're skipping school, I gotta get ready for the outside world."

She slipped out of sight behind a corner of the building and emerged seconds later with the green sweater of her school uniform discarded, revealing a white shirt untucked, two buttons open at the top, and her demure, knee length grey dress now a barely decent frill. Wenden thought she must have hiked it up nearly to her neck. He tried not to look.

Ridge nudged him. "Hey, Wen. Put your eyeballs back in."

"Sorry," Wenden muttered. "Can't help it."

Isolde linked arms with the boys as they walked towards the school entrance. Wenden glanced back. No teachers watching. He knew he'd regret goofing off when his parents got another call, but at that moment there was nothing he'd rather do than head down town with his friends.

As soon as they walked out on the street, a patrol van drove up the gentle hill that crested at the school gate. It stopped on the other side of the road and two guards, a man and a woman, climbed out, hurried across the road, and stood in their way.

The man eyed Isolde. "That's not a school uniform."

Isolde said, "That's because I'm not in school, dickhead."

"City Ordinance #321 states that you are required to wear your uniform on the way to and from school, as well as in it," said the woman. "Furthermore, City Ordinance #001 forbids rudeness and disrespect to any representative of city authority. Would you like to apologize, or shall we report you?"

"Sorry," said Isolde.

"And another thing," said the man. "City Ordinance #320 requires you to be in school between the hours of 8:30 and 3:30. You also have a T4P meeting after classes."

"We're allowed out because we're doing a social studies project," said Ridge. "It's on how people respond to what students wear."

"That's why I'm dressed like this," said Isolde.

"For the survey," said Ridge. "We need influential and important members of the community to take part. Would you be willing to answer some questions?" Without waiting for an answer he told Wenden, "Go on. Ask the questions."

Wenden was the only one of them who had brought a notebook and pencil to Mr. Betts' class. He still had them in his hand. He mumbled, "Right," and made a show of consulting his notebook before asking, "How do you react to the way my friend here is dressed?"

He nodded towards Isolde, who pirouetted, her shortened dress flaring up. She struck a pose, hip thrust out, knee bent, one hand on her shoulder and the other on her thigh.

She saw a flutter in Ridge's eyes and thought—He's going to do it. It's been a while.

The memory of the first time flickered through her mind.

Ridge and Isolde, on their way home from elementary school, have stopped at a playground in a park. Ridge is pushing Isolde on a little roundabout. Her face is back and she gazes dreamily at the sky as he propels her slowly around. A teenager who has been watching them, watching Isolde, comes forward and tells Ridge, "I'll give your girlfriend a ride she'll remember." The teen, who looks like a man to Ridge, pushes Isolde faster and faster. Ridge protests and tries to stop the roundabout. The teen-who-looks-like-a-man shoves him violently aside, sending him sprawling across the playground. The teen turns his back on Ridge and spins Isolde even faster. She is terrified. The roundabout is going too fast for her to jump off. She clings to it, afraid of being hurled off. Ridge, picking himself up, feels his eyes flutter, as if he's been reading too long. When he can see clearly, everything is grey. He blinks, thinking it's a trick of eyesight or light, color will return. It doesn't. He doesn't know what has happened, just that somehow he's transcended normal life, he's in Colorland, where his superb confidence hones his everyday abilities to their peak. Sounds are muted, except those he needs to hear in order to execute his goal. He takes a stone from his pocket and fits it in the cradle of the slingshot he always carries, a fifth birthday present from his father. It's made from black ash, and the wood is worn smooth from constant use, firing for fun at trees and flowers, and at raccoons and groundhogs that raid his mother's vegetable garden, as well as taking down rabbits for his mother to make rabbit pie. The stone nestling in the cradle sounds to Ridge like the thwack of a baseball into a glove. He could fire it at the back of the teen's head but he doesn't want this. He wants it to smash his face. Somehow he knows he can pitch it at nearly 80 miles an hour against the roundabout with no risk of hitting Isolde. The roundabout is travelling at 15 miles an hour, and —he calculates velocity and trajectory effortlessly—the stone will ricochet and strike the teen-who-looks-like-a-man in the face at a speed of nearly 50 miles an hour with a force of 250 pounds per square inch, which will inflict serious damage, causing severe laceration, possibly breaking teeth or nose, Ridge doesn't care. He pulls back the elastic and pitches the rock exactly as he envisaged. It rebounds from the roundabout and strikes Isolde's tormentor with a dull thud that seems to reverberate around the park. The teen-who-looks-like-a-man collapses face down under the raised arm of the teeter-totter. Ridge stops the roundabout. The teen rolls over, mutters something. Ridge sticks his toe under the lowered end of the teeter-totter and flips it up, sending the other end smashing into the teen's face.

Ridge stalks away. Isolde jumps from the roundabout and runs after him. She slips her hand into his. For a moment he looks at her as if unsure who she is. Then his eyes flutter and he says, "You okay, Is?"

The world returns to color. But he carries the knowledge of his transcendence in him. He is Ruthless.

Isolde did another twirl, her dress flaring up even higher.

"Well?" Wenden prompted the guards, his pencil poised over his note-book.

The man's eyes roved over Isolde. "Some may consider it attractive ..." His partner glared at him and he went on quickly, "But it's inappropriate."

"It's slutty and immoral," the woman said firmly.

"Slutty and immoral," Wenden repeated slowly, pretending to write.

Ridge had been standing apart with his hands behind his back. Isolde, watching him from the corner of her eye, knew he'd taken his slingshot from his back pocket and, holding it behind him, had loaded a stone and was aiming it at the patrol van.

There's a crack like a gunshot and a window in the patrol van shatters. The guards look at the van and back at the friends.

"Something flew past me," says Ridge. "It came from the field."

The guards run into the field. Ridge darts across the road and wrenches open the driver's side door of the van, scattering glass.

The guards ran back from the field. The woman said, "There's no-one there." She looked around and demanded, "Where's your friend?"

"He had to go home," said Isolde.

Wenden glanced across the road. The van door was shut and there was no sign of Ridge.

"If you're lying …" the woman started.

She broke off, staring across the road as the van started rolling backwards down the hill. She took off after it. Her partner followed. Ridge's head appeared above the edge of the ditch on the other side of the road. He climbed out and started running in the opposite direction to the van. Isolde chased after him. Wenden lumbered behind. Ridge and Isolde stopped to wait for him a few hundred yards down the road. As he caught up, Isolde was asking Ridge, "Are you back now?"

"'Course."

"I wish you wouldn't do that. It scares me."

"Couldn't pull off stuff like that without crossing over."

"Still—someone could get hurt."

Ridge bristled. "So what? I'm not standing by doing nothing while one power mad guard harasses you and the other leers at you. Anyway, all I did was release the hand brake, jump out the passenger door, give the van a push, and jump in the ditch."

"I don't know how you have the nerve," said Wenden.

"Don't encourage him," said Isolde.

Ridge's eyes glittered.

2

Bradford Glut, the Mayor of Bayport, squat and porcine, with thin, coarse, sandy hair and a florid complexion, rose in the city council media room, nodded to the nine councilors sitting alongside him, frowned at one, the only woman, who sat pointedly apart, and began, "The society we have so carefully nurtured together is under threat."

He looked up into the glare of video lights to make sure the crowd of invited guests and reporters was focused on him as he continued, "The City of Bayport has been independent for ten years. Through prudent financial stewardship we have achieved a stability that is the envy of other independent cities, as well as of the provincial government, which was only too happy to cede to us responsibility for all services and public institutions in the city and in a wide area around it, along with the power of taxation, when our citizens rightly balked at paying the disproportionately high taxes the province was forced to impose in order to preserve the traditional but outdated rural way of life of many of its citizens.

"Nevertheless we are under threat, not financially, but morally, because of the actions and behavior of a minority of our citizens, especially our young people, who seem increasingly to choose to ignore the rules that underpin a just, moral, and orderly society such as ours. By way of example, let me share with you some statistics, starting with the truancy rate at Bayport Regional High School, where 25% of the students are absent for more than 70% of teaching time. Cases of public drunkenness, drug use, rowdy and unruly behavior, vandalism and petty theft by our young people have risen by 30% in the last two years. The teenage pregnancy rate is the highest it has ever been, with no less than ten out of every 100 of our young women giving birth or getting abortions—illegally, I might add—before the age of 18."

The Mayor paused, shook his head, and sighed before displaying a parchment headed by the Bayport coat of arms. "Accordingly, I am signing into power Ordinance #667—In the Matter of Law and Order in the City, which states, Whereas in a democratic polity, the maintenance of peace and order assumes paramount importance; and whereas public order is synonymous with the peace, safety and tranquility of the community, the City of Bayport henceforth will increase the number of security guards provided to the city by the International Security Executive, and the number and frequency of security patrols undertaken by those guards, who are herewith accorded enhanced powers, including the power to enter homes and businesses, and the power of arrest and indefinite detainment, where reasonable suspicion of wrongdoing exists. Moreover, all I.S.E guards will henceforth be armed with the latest, extended range taser guns, as well as with the night sticks they have carried since council appointed the I.S.E to take over from the disbanded city police force. Furthermore and forthwith this Ordinance disbands the Court of Bayport, and in its place grants the I.S.E. Chief of Security the executive power to sentence miscreants to retraining, shunning, or banishment, in accordance with the seriousness of their crime, and removes the right of miscreants to appeal their sentence. These powers to take effect forthwith."

The Mayor finished reading and looked up. "Your Chief of Security is, as ever, hard at work, overseeing the extra security guards and patrols who, even as I speak, are on the streets and in the malls, acting on your behalf with ever greater zeal to maintain peace and order in your city. We urge you not only to co-operate with the Chief of Security and the guards, but also to assist them by sharing any knowledge you have of citizens, especially of young citizens, even if they are your neighbors or your family, who fail to observe our shared standards of behavior and morality, so that together we may help them become responsible and contributing members of our community."

As he spoke, three guards entered and stood at the back of the room. Androgynous in peaked caps and black uniforms, they had batons and tasers clipped at the waist.

Bradford Glut concluded, "Are there any questions?"

The councilor who sat apart rose and began, "I suggest rather than taking punitive action we look at the causes of the unrest among our young people, unrest caused in large part by the actions of this council. Moreover, you, sir, have no moral or legal authority to take these measures …"

The three guards came forward. Two of them took the councilor's arms while the third said quietly, "Amali Winter, it has been reported to the Chief of Security that certain irregularities occurred in your last election campaign, in the form of bribery and misuse of campaign funds. Please accompany us."

Amali Winter, small, slight, olive skinned, black hair coiled in a bun, said, "The Chief of Security knows as well as the Mayor that these accusations are totally unfounded."

As the guards led Amali Winter away, Bradford Glut said, "Thank you all for attending this morning. Let us hope these new measures bring peace and order to our city."

"Crap," said Ridge. "All they'll bring is a shit load more power to that fucking megalomaniac."

He was watching the media conference on closed circuit television in the Bayport Centre Mall with Isolde and Wenden. They were among a crowd of Saturday morning shoppers whose movement had been restricted by the sudden appearance of several guards, who had corralled them in front of the television. Ridge had started to push his way through, but Wenden cautioned, "Better stop and watch—just for a bit." Not stopping could be interpreted as showing lack of respect for the Mayor and the authority of the city, and it was always best, in any case, not to do anything that attracted attention. If the guards didn't see them, one of the security cameras would, or someone in the crowd would report them. Ridge had

10

taken no notice until Isolde, plucking at his sleeve, murmured, "Wen's right."

Wenden rolled his eyes toward one of the guards standing on the edge of the crowd. "Careful," he murmured. "He's watching us."

"Nah," said Ridge. "He's watching Is. Has been since we came in."

Isolde glared at the guard. She muttered, "Pig."

Ridge put his arm around her shoulders and his hand over her mouth as she went on, her voice muffled, "Can't I walk through the mall without some sleazy scumbag guard gawping at me?"

Ridge shrugged. "I've told you before. They think you're cute."

"So that gives them the right to leer at me—because they think I'm cute?"

Ridge gestured helplessly. Since they were in elementary school together, he'd been aware of the responses Isolde innocently provoked, the shifty leer, the accidental brushing against her, the furtive hand groping from the anonymous safety of a crowded place, the presumptuous, open stare that came with the arrogance of power.

And he'd watched her anger grow.

Isolde stared at the guard until he looked away.

"Just ignore him, Is," Wenden pleaded.

"Easy for you to say," Isolde snapped.

"But he's right," said Ridge.

He waited, watching her carefully, until her shoulders fell, and her fists unclenched, and her jaw relaxed, before saying, "Come on. Let's get a coffee."

He sauntered towards the escalator, heading for the Starbucks on the second level. Isolde, her anger shed, strolled dreamily beside him, humming to herself, occasionally pirouetting as she walked, lost in the tune in her head. Wenden shambled behind. He marveled at how his friends had no trouble moving through the crowd. People just seemed to part for them, while he had to shoulder his way through. He didn't know how Ridge did it—he hardly looked threatening, with his slight build, and pale blonde hair, and the serious expression that rarely left his face, thin lips set firm, jaw clenched, eyes slightly narrowed, hint of a frown creasing his forehead—but he knew why they made way for Isolde. Who wouldn't step aside for a slender fifteen year old girl with a heart shaped face, almond eyes, and long chestnut hair, in a cream leather jacket and a short, swirly, flowery flapper dress? He saw how people watched her and Ridge when they walked together, some oozing envy, as if recalling their own youth, some angry, as if insulted by their insouciant perfection. He felt like a clod as he slouched behind them, tall, heavy, nondescript.

A guard stationed at the foot of the escalator watched them approach and stood deliberately in their way. Wenden wondered what the excuse for harassing them was going to be. If this was a weekday, they could be detained for not being at school, and for not wearing their uniforms. As it was Saturday, the excuse might be for making excessive noise, or using bad language, or dressing inappropriately. He eyed Isolde's skirt, short enough for the guards, or anyone who cared to complain, to consider inappropriate, although it came over half way to her knees. His own black trench coat and battered leather hat, and Ridge's tattered military jacket and cap, might be considered provocative or subversive. You never knew.

The guard warned, "No fooling around on the stairs." His eyes slithered over Isolde before he moved slowly aside.

Wenden looked back from the top of the escalator. The guard was still watching them. Watching Isolde.

Wenden caught up with Ridge at the entrance to Starbucks. Isolde was on the other side of the aisle, gazing into the window of a vintage jewelry store. The boys crossed the aisle and stood behind her. She pointed to a ring of dull silver, a tiny butterfly with spread wings wrought into it. "It belonged to Grandma. Dad said he was going to give it to me when I was twenty-one, like she wanted him to, but he had to sell it a few months back when we didn't have enough for groceries after he got fired and just before they banished him. The guy in the store said it was worthless but he'd give him $5 for it. Dad said he knew it was worth more than that and the guy said to take it or leave it, he didn't care."

"Look what they're charging for it," said Wenden, pointing at the tag beside the ring. "$100."

From behind they heard, "Move along. There's nothing there for you."

Wenden and Isolde turned. The security guard had followed them.

Ridge didn't move.

Isolde said, "Come on, Ridge," and took his arm.

His hands were twitching. She caught Wenden's eye and nodded at Ridge's other arm. Wenden moved to hold it but Ridge said, "I'm okay." He sauntered back towards Starbucks, Isolde still clutching his arm, talking softly to him.

At the counter, Ridge said, "My treat."

Wenden and Isolde sat at one of the tables in the coffee shop's fenced area that projected into the aisle. Isolde gazed across at the jewelry store window, while Wenden pretended he and Isolde were an item. Ridge arrived with the coffee. Isolde was still gazing across the aisle. Ridge watched her for a moment, following her eyes. He sipped his coffee, handed his cap to Wenden, and said, "Wait here."

He headed across the aisle towards the jewelry store and stood before the display window. He felt his eyes flutter, and everything, everyone, was grey.

"Jesus—now what?" Wenden muttered, watching Ridge. "Should we go with him?"

"What did he say to do?" said Isolde.

"Wait here."

"Better do it, then."

Ridge looks around quickly. He's the only Transcender. No. A flash of color in the grey miasma catches his eye. A stocky woman with close set eyes is watching him from the crowd of shoppers. She's wearing a pale green trouser suit and has short, vivid red hair.

Why has she transcended? Is she on a mission of her own, or is it something to do with him? She's reading him. He can tell by the way her eyes are fixed on him, boring into him. She knows who—what—he is. She smiles and nods knowingly, as if amused by his use of the power of transcendence for this silly, show off exploit for Isolde. She moves behind a shopper before he can get a good, sustained look at her, to read her. He bristles. He's ready if she tries to intervene.

With a glance at the security guard to make sure he's looking away, Ridge sidles into the store and stands by the window. A shoulder high display cabinet, glass fronted, containing five shelves crowded with crystal glassware and porcelain figurines, stands against the wall beside him. Two counter clerks, a man and a woman, are on duty.

The man—thin face, tidy moustache—approaches Ridge. "Can I help you, sir?"

Ridge points to the window display. "That butterfly ring …"

"… Is very expensive, sir." The man looks Ridge up and down before adding, "Probably not in your—er—financial range, sir."

He says Sir with sneering irony. He puts his hand on Ridge's arm to steer him from the store.

Ridge shrugs him off and reaches into the display window. "Still—you won't mind if I take a look, will you?"

The man says, "The alarm …"

A loud, piercing buzzer sounds.

Ridge collapses. He writhes on the floor, his arms flailing, his fingers curled and rigid, like talons.

The man kneels beside him. He calls to the woman, "Get help." She runs to the door, where people are already gathering as the alarm blats. The security guard from the escalator is elbowing his way through the crowd. The woman calls to him, "We need an ambulance. Someone's collapsed. A young man." The guard stops and speaks into his radio. Ridge is still thrashing on the floor, his back alternately arching and slumping. A trickle of blood seeps from the side of his mouth. Several people enter and stand beside the still kneeling clerk, who is leaning over Ridge. The clerk flutters his hands over and around Ridge without touching him, as if he's afraid the fit is contagious.

As everyone gazes at Ridge's face, now flecked with blood, he hooks one foot under the display cabinet and lifts.

A woman says, "The poor boy's bleeding at the mouth. Do something."

The man looks up at her. "Like what?"

The security guard enters and pushes his way to the front of the group, where he stands, peering down at Ridge.

Ridge raises his foot higher, toppling the cabinet sideways into the aisle, showering broken glass and fragments of china across the store. People scream. The crowd surges backwards at the same time as more people push their way in. Another security guard is among them and demands, "What's going on?"

The woman counter clerk says, "It started with this young man on the floor having a fit ..."

They all look towards the young man.

He's not there.

Outside the store, Ridge has risen, after crawling through the distracted crowd and past the inrushing guard. He walks quickly to the escalator and presses the button for the lower floor. As the doors close, and just before he relaxes enough for everything to return to color, he sees the woman again, watching him. She smiles, not a smile of comradeship or affinity or complicity, but a knowing smile that seems to say—I will remember you.

Ridge doesn't care. She can't do anything.

He is inviolable.

He is amoral.

He is Ruthless.

He crossed the lower level of the mall and ran up the back stairs, emerging on the second level on the other side of Starbucks. He slipped into his seat. Wenden, who was sipping coffee as he watched the commotion across the aisle, started and spilled his drink down himself.

"Jesus," he spluttered. "Where did you come from?"

Ridge grinned. He took his cap from Wenden and pulled it low over his face.

Isolde demanded, "What was that all about? I was worried sick."

Ridge took her hand. "Sorry."

She pulled her hand away. Stared into it.

Ridge reached over and closed her fingers over the butterfly ring. "Better keep it hidden."

She launched herself from her chair and flung her arms around him.

Wenden shook his head. "I can't believe you did that."

He raised his cup to his mouth again but his hand was shaking so much it slopped more coffee down his front.

Ridge thought—Poor old Wenden.

Isolde, back in her chair, told Ridge, "Your lip's bleeding."

She leaned towards him and wiped his mouth gently with a Starbucks napkin.

"Not my lip—my tongue," said Ridge. "I bit it to make it look like I was spitting up blood."

Wenden shook his head again.

Isolde was staring at Ridge.

He said, "What?"

She said, "Idiot."

He grinned.

Across the aisle, a patrol of three guards arrived at the jewelry store.

"Time to go," said Ridge.

They left the mall by the back stairs. Half way down, Isolde grabbed Ridge by the arm.

He stopped. "What's up?"

She backed him into a corner of the stairwell and stood close to him, her eyes fixed on his. He'd been her best friend, more than that, since they discovered one another in kindergarten, two misfits always in trouble, Isolde for her dreaminess and flightiness and outbursts of anger, Ridge for his surly prickliness, each recognizing in the other a strangeness that would always set them apart from others at the same time as it bound them together. She remembered her father once describing Ridge as her boyfriend, and telling him, "He's not my boyfriend. He's Ridge." She'd always thought she knew him as well as she knew herself.

She demanded, "What's going on with you?"

"What d'you mean?"

"I mean—back there in the mall, and yesterday when the guards stopped us at school, it was like you crossed over into another world, some kind of parallel universe. I know you were doing it for me—but I felt like I'd lost you for that time."

"You're not going to lose me, Is."

"But it felt like you were somewhere … where I couldn't be with you."

Ridge looked away.

Isolde took his shoulders, shook him. "Tell me! The way you got just now in the mall, it was like when those drunks were bothering me outside the movie theatre—right?"

She'd been waiting while he went to the washroom when they started to bother her, moving quickly from beery talk to pawing at her. When Ridge came out, he said, "Hey, guys, I know this chick. Want to know what she likes?" Held his arms wide, inviting them into his confidence. They moved to him, one each side. He took them each by the neck, slammed their heads together, and pushed them bleeding into the traffic.

He shrugged.

Isolde went on, "And that time last summer at the convenience store …"

She'd been working evenings, usually alone. Ridge had come by to walk her home. He was sprawled on the floor at the back of the store, browsing through magazines while she cashed up. A man entered, locked the door, turned the sign on it to Closed, and said, "I'll have the money from the till." The first stone from Ridge's slingshot hit him on the side of the head, the second, bigger, between the legs. As the man doubled over, Ridge strode forward with a can of pineapple juice, family size, and swung it underarm up into the man's face. He staggered backwards. Ridge spun him around and pushed him face first into the door, breaking the glass and sending him sprawling across the sidewalk.

And now the silly, careless, single minded pursuit of a ring for her.

Each time he'd seemed beyond her, lost to her.

She repeated, "Tell me!"

Ridge shrugged again.

Wenden muttered, "Want me to go away, leave you alone, you two?"

Ridge shook his head.

Isolde pleaded, "Please, Ridge, tell me."

He said slowly, "You know how sometimes something happens, and afterwards you think what you could have—should have—done, if only you had the nerve and the confidence to do it, but of course by the time you think that, it's too late."

Isolde nodded.

Wenden mumbled, "Only, like, all the time."

"Well—it's like having the nerve and the confidence to do it straight off, at the moment you need to do it," said Ridge. "It's like transcending what you can usually do, and going into overdrive, and having super confidence, jus' knowing you can do what you want to do, like when we used to go skiing, before the hills went out of business, and we'd stand at the top of a really steep run, and the more nervous we got, the more likely we were to crash, but if we just took off, thinking, this is going to be easy—then we did it!"

"Where d'you get this super-confidence from?"

Another shrug. "Dunno. It's just … when I transcend—get on the other side of what we usually think is normal, in that space you're talking about— it's like who I really am gives me the confidence to do what I need to do."

"So who are you, really?" Isolde asked.

"Doesn't matter. But I've learned to sort of call it up—to transcend to Colorland—when I need to."

She said heavily and slowly, emphasizing each syllable, her head cocked, "Transcend to Colorland."

"It's what it's called."

"How do you know what it's called when you don't really know what it is?"

"I just sort of knew from the first time it happened."

"That time in the park, years ago."

"Right."

"But it's like when you're there—in Colorland or whatever—I don't matter. Almost like, for you, I don't exist."

He looked down.

She shook his arm. "I said I don't even exist when you're in Colorland—right?"

"It's not like you don't exist. It's just there's no room to think of anything except what I've transcended there to do."

"If you're so super confident and all when you're in Colorland, why don't you stay there all the time?" Wenden asked.

"'Cos being in Colorland, it's like an addiction, and you risk getting stuck there, trapped in the thrill of it. You're cut off from normal life, and you can't feel anything 'cept what you need to, and no-one can feel you, and everything and everyone goes grey—everyone except other Transcenders—because you're putting all your energy and concentration into whatever you crossed over to do, and there's no room in your consciousness for anything else, and being on that high, so sure of yourself, like you never are in normal life, you don't want to let it go."

"What happens when you get trapped?" said Isolde.

"Not much. Just everything stays grey, and sounds are muffled, and you can't feel, not feelings or touch, and no-one can feel you, like I said."

"No-one can feel you when they touch you, but they can still have feelings for you—right?" Isolde pressed.

Ridge didn't answer.

"Why's it called Colorland when everything's grey?" Wenden asked.

"It's, like, ironic. It means the opposite of what it says. Like saying break a leg when someone's going on stage."

"How long does it last, if you get addicted and trapped?" said Isolde.

"Dunno."

"For ever?"

"I said—dunno." Ridge shrugged. "Okay? Interrogation over?"

Isolde leaned against him. "You better not get yourself stuck in Colorland, Ridge. I couldn't bear it."

They walked on down the stairs.

3

Outside, Isolde stood between Ridge and Wenden, surveying the scene on Water Street, wan June sky, bright shop windows, four lanes of stalled traffic, pedestrians edging their way cautiously along each side of the road, flattening themselves against the buildings whenever the traffic moved. There were no sidewalks because the city council had taken them up to make room for the extra cars entering the city after the council had also done away with public transport in its efforts to save money.

Three guards, two men and a woman, were stopping cars to check registration and inspection certificates, while three more, all men, stood in a shop doorway further along the street, eyeing the passing pedestrians, stopping some and asking for ID. A surveillance camera mounted on a street light caught Wenden's eye as it panned in a slow arc.

Ridge, following his gaze, said, "Give the snoops the finger, Wen."

"Not worth it," said Wenden, wishing he had the courage to do so.

Ridge shook his head in disgust. "We got guards and surveillance cameras all over creation just because Glut's a megalomaniac."

"Well—and because of all the student riots and union demonstrations getting out of hand last few years," Wenden pointed out.

Ridge turned on him. "Do you blame people for being mad? Student fees going through the roof, and the pulp mill and the steel works and the docks closing and all those guys getting laid off ..."

"But smashing shop windows, and looting, and burning cop cars," said Wenden. "The city had to do something."

"It didn't have to disband the city cops and put power mad guards and surveillance cameras everywhere," Ridge insisted. "Whose side are you on?"

Wenden shrugged. "I'm not saying Glut's right."

"What are you saying, then?"

"I'm jus' saying is all."

Wenden thought of reminding Ridge that most people had been glad when the city took those measures, but decided to keep quiet.

"And having people shunned," Isolde added. "And sent for retraining, and banished, like my dad. That's way over the top."

"Right," Wenden mumbled. "Sorry."

"And now it's going to be all out war on kids," said Ridge.

"Just 'cos of a few screw ups who don't know how to behave," Isolde added.

"Quite a few screw ups," Wenden couldn't help putting in.

Ridge turned on him again. "So you've been out of school for, like, three quarters of the time, have you?"

"No—but I have been known to skip the odd class with you guys," said Wenden mildly.

"That doesn't count," said Isolde.

"And how many times have you been arrested for being drunk in public, Wen?" Ridge demanded.

"I haven't. You know that."

"… And for being rowdy …"

"That neither."

" … And vandalizing stuff?"

"I'm just saying is all," Wenden protested again. "I don't agree with what Glut's doing, but I can sort of get where he's coming from."

"Only place he's coming from is he hates anyone who's not like him, him and his pure and holy friends, and who doesn't live like him, and doesn't agree with him," Ridge scoffed. "We haven't done any of those things he talked about, but you can bet your life we'll get harassed all the same, jus' 'cause we're kids."

One of the guards blew a whistle and pointed at the friends.

"See what I mean?" said Ridge.

"What's he want with us?" said Isolde.

"He's going to say you're wearing inappropriate dress," said Ridge.

"Do you want my coat, to put over your dress?" Wenden offered. "Then he might not bother us."

"Nah. Fuck him," said Isolde.

She knew if she pretended to be demure and apologetic, and promised to dress appropriately in the future, the guard would let her go with just a warning, but her anger took over and she couldn't help herself. She smiled at him and raised her middle finger.

He blew his whistle again and shouted, "You kids—stay there."

"Oops," said Isolde.

"Better take off," said Ridge.

"Where?" said Wenden. "Look at all the people along the side of the street. There's no room to move."

"No problem," said Ridge.

He strolled into the middle of the road, setting off a chorus of horns.

Isolde skipped after him, laughing and saying, "Now they can come after us for jaywalking as well as inappropriate dress."

Wenden, watching the three guards draw their clubs and set off towards them, sighed, "Oh Jesus," and followed.

Ridge took Isolde's hand and they ran up the middle of the road, heading for Central Park at the top of Water Street, where an outdoor market was held on Saturdays. Wenden lumbered behind. The guards checking traffic moved to intercept them, but the friends dodged around the slowly moving vehicles and kept going. When they reached the park, Ridge, still holding Isolde's hand, plunged into the maze of stalls, pausing at each turn to make sure Wenden was not too far behind. When they came out on the other side of the market, they sat on a bench set back from the street and surrounded by shrubs.

Wenden, peering behind, said, "I think we lost them."

A blare of horns erupted from Central Park Avenue in front of them, followed by the shrilling of whistles. They peered through the shrubs. A man stood at the edge of the line of traffic. He darted forward, retreated, darted forward again.

Wenden said, "It's just some guy trying to cross the road."

As he spoke, the man slipped and fell. A car with the insignia, Bayport City Council—Traffic Inspector, drove over his leg.

Isolde said, "He's hurt," and ran towards the street.

Ridge and Wenden followed.

The pedestrian lay on his back between the front and rear wheels of the car, one leg tucked under him, the other extended. He had a curious scar, in the shape of a cross, on the right side of his forehead. The driver opened his window. He looked out at the fallen man and said, "That'll teach you to jaywalk." His companions, a man in the passenger seat and a woman in the back, both guards, laughed. The line of cars crept forwards. Ridge and Isolde grabbed the pedestrian by the shoulders and tried to drag him to the side of the road but his toe was caught on something under the car. The rear wheels were almost on his leg.

Ridge felt his eyes flicker. Should he transcend again, so soon after crossing over at the mall? He was stupid to have used his power just to show off to Isolde. If he entered Colorland again now, would he have the resolution to get back?

He had no choice.

Everything is grey and sounds are muted again. He bounds forward and leans in the car window. Shuts off the ignition and pulls out the key. The driver, thickset, with black, slicked back hair, says, "What the fuck?" He opens the door, plants one foot on the ground, and starts to climb out. Ridge leans his shoulder against the door as the driver rises, trapping him by the leg and at the same time squeezing his neck between the top of the door and the roof. The driver makes a gurgling noise. Ridge presses harder. The guard in the passenger seat runs around the side of the car and throws himself at Ridge, who stabs him in the eye with the car key. The guard reels back, his hands covering his face. Wenden has reached under the car to release the pedestrian's foot and is helping Isolde pull him to the side of the road. The woman guard opens the rear door and gets out, night

24

stick in hand. Ridge stabs upwards with the key, slashing her nostrils. She bends over, holding her nose, blood dripping through her fingers. Ridge pushes her away from the open rear door as he tells Isolde and Wenden, "Put him in the back. Then run." Patrols armed with tasers are approaching from up and down the street. The nearest guard stops and aims at Ridge. Isolde and Wenden are heaving the pedestrian on to the back seat. Ridge says, "Keep down." He pulls his slingshot from his back pocket and fires, hitting the guard on the chest. The guard and his companions duck behind a car. Ridge fires again and the windshield shatters. The driver of the city car, who slumped to the ground when Ridge took his shoulder from the door as he armed his slingshot, rears up groggily. Ridge pushes him back down. He puts one foot on his ankle and with the other kicks the side of his knee. Something cracks. Isolde and Wenden have bundled the injured man in the back. Wenden slams the door. Ridge repeats, "Run!" He gets in and starts the car.

Isolde says, "I'm coming with you."

Ridge says, "No. I'll get him to hospital, then call."

He accelerates into the space that has opened in front of the car. He glances in the mirror and sees Wenden holding Isolde by the hand, pulling her into the crowd as she looks after Ridge. There's a flash of color among the grey. The Transcender, the red haired woman from the mall, is watching him from among the crowd that has gathered at the scene of the accident.

4

Wenden was at home that night when his cell phone rang. His mother was in her office upstairs and he was watching television with his father. It was one of the few things they could do together without arguing. Not like when he was a kid, when they played baseball and basketball in the yard, and went hiking in the countryside around the city. Now the distance between them seemed greater every day.

It had started when his parents joined Bradford Glut's People for Progress Party, and started pressuring him to join Teens4Progress, its youth division, before it became compulsory at school. They got mad with him when he refused and said he could care less about Mayor Glut. All city politics meant to him was the guards harassing him and his friends, and having to listen to the Mayor's Message for Young Citizens every morning at school, only shreds of which penetrated the fog of the automatic daydream he fell into as soon as it came on the PA, proclaiming stuff like they had no rights without responsibility, and the shared morality of citizens outweighed personal inclination, and submission to the authority of home, school, and city was a necessary step on the way to adulthood, and blah blah blah.

Then his parents became part-time guards, and started going out with patrols, and warned him he could expect no favoritism if they or their fellow guards caught him transgressing the Mayor's Code of Conduct for Young People.

It had been downhill ever since.

He glanced across the room as he snatched up the phone. His father was asleep. A game show was on TV.

Before Wenden could speak Isolde said, "I'm outside, round the back."

Did she have news of Ridge? The last Wenden had seen of him was as he swung the city car into a side road, while Wenden led Isolde back into the park, where they'd hidden from the guards among the crowd. On the other side of the market, Isolde had said, "We'll split up. We'll be less noticeable," and disappeared back into the crowd, leaving Wenden to wander home alone.

He slipped out the back door and moved quickly away from the light of the kitchen window. Street lights went out at 8:00 p.m. to save money, and the curfew for anyone under eighteen started at the same time. The residents in the subdivision of comfortable homes where he lived were keen members of the Mayor's Neighborhood Watch. If they saw him out after curfew, even if he was just in the yard, they'd report him, and a patrol would be knocking at the door within minutes.

He peered into the darkness of the back garden, waiting for his eyes to adjust to the dark. He heard a whispered, "Wen," and Isolde appeared beside him. She leaned close and whispered, "Where can we talk?" The light from the kitchen window glinted on the stolen ring on her finger.

He took her hand and led her through the back garden. They sat between the compost pile and the garden shed, out of sight and hearing of neighbors and patrols.

"Ridge?" Wenden whispered.

"Haven't heard from him, and he isn't home, which means he's in trouble."

"What should we do?"

"Find him. We'll try the hospital first."

They slunk back through the garden and past the house. Wenden looked in the window and saw his father still asleep, his mother leaning over his chair, about to wake him. They'd wonder where he'd gone but that was too bad. He walked with Isolde through the subdivision, staying in the darkness in the middle of the street, away from the light spilling from houses. They stopped when they came to City Road, a busy four lane throughway with no sidewalks.

"Now what do we do?" said Wenden.

"We run," said Isolde.

"Someone will report us for being out after curfew."

"That's why we run."

They jogged along the side of City Road. A transport, horn blaring, roared towards them. As it swept past, just missing them, its tailwind sent them staggering sideways. Wenden grabbed Isolde by the arm to steady her. She fell against him as she was spun around by the wind. He put his arms around her to stop her falling. For a moment her hair was in his face and her body pressed against his.

She muttered, "Thanks."

He mumbled, "Sorry."

"What for?"

Wenden looked away.

She said, "Poor old Wen."

They stood close and surveyed the road ahead. It was lined with brightly lit businesses and bars that threw pools of light, leaving patches of darkness in between. Bubba's Joint, Troy's Hardware, Murphy's Bar, All-Nite Grocery.

"'Spose we can make it to Bubba's?" said Isolde.

Wenden nodded.

They waited for a gap in the traffic before setting off, Isolde in the lead. They threw themselves into the parking lot beside Bubba's Joint just before a line of vehicles roared past. They crouched in the darkness between parked cars until there was another lull in the traffic, then took off running. Two cars passed in a glare of headlights and wail of horns. They dodged into the All-Nite Grocery's busy parking lot, Wenden breathing heavily. They waited for another break in the traffic before venturing out into the road again. Two cars passed. Then a slow moving vehicle approached, its headlights on full beam. Isolde stopped. Wenden stumbled into her. A spotlight snapped on, its beam sweeping along the side of the road towards them.

Isolde said, "Patrol. Back!"

They turned and ran towards the grocery store. Before they reached it the spotlight caught them. A voice, metallic through a loud speaker, ordered, "Stand where you are."

They veered into the parking lot. The patrol van pulled in behind them and two guards jumped from it. Isolde and Wenden raced for the store entrance and crashed through the doors as more guards jumped from the van, tasers in hand. Isolde, ahead of Wenden, wheeled into the crowded produce aisle, pushing shoppers and carts aside as she ran, Wenden close behind. They turned into the cereals aisle, where only a few shoppers stood at the far end. They scattered as Isolde ran through them and burst through a door at the end of the aisle marked Staff Only. Wenden heard the guards charge into the aisle behind him. A fire extinguisher hung on the wall nearby. He wrenched it from its bracket, pulled the lock pin, squeezed the trigger, and hosed them. They slowed, clutching at their eyes. He pushed through the door behind Isolde. He was in the meat cutting department. He ran through hanging carcasses towards an exit sign. He pushed through the door, at the same time hearing guards burst into the meat room. He heard a warning shout, "Stand!", and a second later the zap of taser darts hitting the door as it swung closed behind him. He flinched. What was it like to be tasered? What kind of pain would it cause? If he stopped, gave himself up, said sorry for running away, would they still taser him? He saw Isolde at the line of cars waiting for grocery pick up. She was loading bags for a woman who was talking on a cell phone as she paced beside her car. Isolde finished loading and slammed the trunk. The woman, still on her cell, tipped her. Isolde said, "Thank you," climbed into the car and drove away. She swung around to where Wenden stood and said, "Move your arse, Wen, for Christ's sake." He jumped in and she accelerated out of the parking lot as guards ran from the store and headed for their van.

"They shot at me," Wenden gasped. "They fucking shot at me." He was shaking and he was afraid he'd wet himself.

Isolde didn't answer.

Wenden said, "Did you hear me, Is? They fired their tasers at me, like I'm a criminal."

Isolde, eyes fixed on the road as she overtook a transport, said, "You are a criminal to them, dummy. We're both criminals."

"What d'you mean—criminals? What are we supposed to have done? We're out after curfew. That's all."

"We're out after curfew, and we didn't stop for them, and we've stolen a car, and likely they're on the lookout for the kids who stole a car on Central Park Avenue after beating up three of their friends."

"We didn't beat up anybody, or steal a car."

"Ridge did—and we were with him."

Wenden felt something slipping away, something to do with inconsequential stuff like walking home from school with Isolde and Ridge, and hanging out at the mall, and going to the beach. He murmured, "What are we getting into, Is?"

Again she didn't answer. A mile up City Road she waited for a break in the traffic and stopped broadside in the middle of the road, headlights on high beam and hazard lights flashing. She ran into the darkness as traffic backed up. Wenden, glancing behind as he followed her into a patch of woodland beside the road, saw the patrol pull up twenty vehicles back.

He called to Isolde, "Where are we?"

She waited for him to catch up. "Hospital grounds. I was up here all the time because of my asthma when I was a kid. Dad used to park near here and carry me the rest of the way because he thought it was immoral for the city to charge for parking on the grounds." She grinned. "He knew all the short cuts."

She led the way through the trees to the back of the hospital. With a glance around, she ran down a ramp, past a sign that warned, Keep Out! Staff Parking Only! They were in a cavernous space half filled with cars. Isolde ran to an elevator in a dimly lit corner. The elevator arrived and a man and woman in nurse's uniform stepped from it, engrossed in conversation. Wenden nodded to them as they passed and the man nodded back. Isolde and Wenden entered the elevator and Isolde pressed the ground floor button.

The man, frowning, turned and said, "Wait. You can't come in this way."

The elevator doors closed.

"'Spose he'll call security?" said Wenden.

Isolde shrugged.

They lurched to a stop at the ground floor. The doors opened on to a hallway. A hospital security guard stood with arms folded, watching the elevator. Isolde collapsed against Wenden. He struggled to hold her upright as they staggered out.

"My sister's having a fit," Wenden gasped, hoping that was what Isolde intended. "Have to get her to casualty."

The guard swept Isolde up in his arms and carried her to the reception area at the end of the hallway. He deposited her on a chair and, with a careful look and a nod at Wenden, returned to his post.

At the reception window, a young woman not much older than the friends asked Wenden, "What's up?"

He glanced quickly around. Only a few people were waiting for treatment, an old man in tattered clothes who seemed to be asleep, a woman nursing a crying baby, a couple sitting close together, the woman with a black eye, the man with a dirty bandage on his hand, oozing blood. No-one was near Wenden.

He asked, "Did someone my age bring in a guy who got run over by a car?"

"What's it to you?"

"It was my friend who brought him in. We haven't seen him since. We're looking for him. Worried something happened to him."

The receptionist's eyes flickered towards the door. "Better watch it."

Wenden looked around. The security guard had returned and was moving towards Isolde as he talked into his radio. He stood in front of her, put his hand on her shoulder, shook her, and said, "Thought I recognized the two of you from the description Control sent out. You and your friend are wanted for assaulting guards and stealing a car owned by the city."

Isolde was sprawled in her chair, eyes closed.

The guard leaned over her, shook her again, and said, "Time to stop play acting, little miss."

Isolde opened her eyes and sighed. "Yes, sir. Sorry, sir."

She stood quickly. The top of her head caught the guard under the chin. He tottered backwards and she punched him in the face. He tripped over a chair and fell beside the reception window, his head thudding against the wall.

The receptionist pressed a button and spoke into a microphone on her desk. "Code red. Casualty reception."

Wenden looked round at her.

She said, "That'll cause a ruckus. Use it to get the hell out of here."

"But my friend …"

"They took him in."

"Who?"

"Guards. A woman in charge."

Nurses and paramedics were pouring into the room. The receptionist pointed them towards the guard, who was still on the ground. As the medical staff crowded around him, she spoke quickly into a phone, then told Wenden and Isolde, "Run through casualty to the ambulance bay. Someone'll be waiting." She pointed to a door beside her window.

Wenden muttered, "Thanks," and slipped from the room with Isolde.

5

The woman from the mall, the Transcender, leaned close to Ridge and said quietly, her voice like the serrated blade of a knife, "You assaulted three security patrols, two off duty guards, and a city official. You stole a car that belongs to the city. You disturbed the peace on Water Street and on Central Park Avenue. You drove in a dangerous manner and with reckless disregard for the safety of others. You refuse to identify your accomplices, although that is not a problem because their description has been circulated to all patrols and you can expect them to be brought in at any moment."

Ridge shrank from her. She reminded him of Mrs. Harpic, his grade one teacher at Bayport Primary, who foolishly confided in the course of teaching the curriculum mandated unit on spiders that she was arachnophobic, and who thereafter suffered the almost daily discovery of spiders in her desk drawer, in her shoes, even in her lunch bag, until driven to become a scowling, vengeful force of malice, specializing in the sudden slap on the back of bare legs, preferably with a steel ruler. She'd terrorized his days and haunted his sleep for the rest of that year. Now, looking at the woman from the mall, he saw Mrs. Harpic, and felt the helpless terror of his six year old self.

"Do you have anything to say for yourself?" she concluded. She spoke slowly and carefully, as if assessing the effect of every word.

He recovered enough to mumble, "Screw you and the guards."

He felt the stinging slap on the back of his legs, though she hadn't moved. He bit back tears and the urge to apologize for his truculent defiance.

He was standing between two guards in a room that was bare except for a desk and a chair and a filing cabinet. A nameplate on the desk read Leigh Dirk—Chief of Security. Two more guards stood on each side of the door. Leigh Dirk stalked behind the desk and sat down.

Ridge had driven the man with the strange scar to hospital and had just made him comfortable in casualty when six guards, led by the Chief of Security, had arrived. He'd contemplated transcending again, but remembered he'd crossed over twice in the last few hours and decided against it. The woman, watching him carefully, had said, "Good decision—unless you want to get trapped in Colorland." She'd nodded to the guards and they'd taken him down town to Security Control.

"Send him for retraining," Leigh Dirk told the guards. "Six months."

"Bayport Education Centre?" one of them asked.

"Right."

"And his accomplices, when they're brought in?"

"Same charges, same punishments."

She leaned back in her chair and contemplated Ridge. "Call your mother and tell her you are being sent for retraining."

She pushed a phone across the desk. Ridge punched in the numbers for his mother's cell, knowing she wouldn't answer because the phone was lying in a drawer at home, its battery dead and its credit exhausted. Six months ago she'd moved away to live with her new man. She'd wanted Ridge to go with her, but he didn't like the man, and didn't want to leave Isolde, so told his mother he'd stay and look after the house, in case she wanted to come back. He'd been living alone since then, keeping it secret to prevent social services taking him in. He had little memory of his father, who had moved on shortly after presenting Ridge with the slingshot on his fifth birthday, and had returned only occasionally during the next few years, and not at all for the last five.

Ridge tucked the phone close to his shoulder, shielding it so that Leigh Dirk and the guards couldn't hear the automatic Customer Not Available response at the other end. "Ma, I'm in trouble with the guards." He pretended to listen, and to interrupt. "Yeah. I know. It wasn't my fault ... Yeah. Sorry. They're sending me for six months retraining ... No—you can't

visit me, you know there's no visitors. I'll get in touch when I get out …
Love you too, Ma."

He put the phone down.

Leigh Dirk told the guards, "Put him in the holding room for transfers.
We will send him to the Centre tonight." She looked back at Ridge. Stared
intently into his face, her eyes like lasers. "You have a lot to learn about
Colorland, young man, starting with—Ephebiphobia trumps Ruthless." He
looked blank and she said, "You do not know what Ephebiphobia means,
do you?"

He shook his head.

She smiled. "You will find out. Meanwhile I will tell the Transcenders
on my staff to keep a careful eye on you while you serve your sentence. You
will remember that, if you know what is good for you."

6

Isolde and Wenden ran through the casualty ward, between curtained beds and past a nursing station where only one nurse remained. A paramedic stood at the exit ahead of them, holding the door open. She waved them into a short hallway leading outside to the ambulance bay, where an ambulance was parked, its rear doors open. As they ran past she said, "Get in and stay low." She slammed the ambulance doors behind them. They heard her climb in the front. A few seconds later the radio hissed and a voice said, "Come in, Kay."

The driver said, "Gotcha."

"Union Avenue at Orange Street. Stabbing."

"On my way."

The engine roared and the ambulance surged forwards, siren wailing.

Kay shouted over the noise, "What have you two been up to?"

"Trying to find a friend," said Isolde.

Kay braked sharply and said, "Guard. Get on the floor."

She stopped. They heard her window slide down and a voice demand, "Where are you going?"

"Out on an emergency, piss brain, and if anyone dies because you're delaying me I'll make damn sure you get the blame."

Without waiting for a response, Kay gunned the ambulance ahead. They felt it turn sharply and pick up speed.

"We're clear," said Kay over her shoulder. "But stay down."

As she spoke they heard the wail of a patrol van approach and recede.

A few minutes later Kay said, "My stabbing scene's coming up. You're on Union, near the junction with Orange Street. There's an alley just before the junction. Goes down to the old industrial estate. You can hide there but watch yourselves. When I slow, open the back, jump out and run. Get ready now."

They crouched by the rear doors. Peering ahead past Kay, they saw the flashing lights of two patrol vans, their spotlights cutting a wide swathe of light. A body, covered, lay beside the road. Traffic was held up both ways.

"I'm going to cut along the shoulder," said Kay. "As soon as I tell you—go. Good luck."

They chorused, "Thanks."

Wenden grabbed the handle of the rear doors.

Kay slowed and swerved onto the shoulder. "Now!"

Wenden wrenched the doors open. They jumped out. He slammed the doors. The alley lay a few yards ahead. They turned into it, ran into the darkness, Isolde leading the way, their footsteps echoing from the metal walls of high buildings on each side. Wenden collided with a garbage can and sent it clattering into the darkness. Something—raccoon, rat, possum—scuffled away before them. Their footsteps suddenly no longer echoed. Isolde stopped. She grabbed Wenden's arm. He stopped beside her, breathing heavily.

He felt her lips brush his ear as she whispered, "What's at the end of the alley?"

"The old industrial estate."

"But we're in open space."

"There isn't any. It's all warehouses and factories, empty since the economy went down the toilet. Dad used to come down here for work. Used to bring me with him sometimes."

Headlights suddenly appeared a short distance to their right. They flung themselves back into the alley as a car, travelling parallel to them, shot past, briefly illuminating their surroundings. They were in a square, cloisters on each side and a dried up fountain in the centre.

"Got it," Wenden whispered. "We're in what they called Market Square. It's on the edge of the estate. It was meant to give it an old fashioned, community feel. Used to be a nice fountain in the middle. They had a market here at weekends, and concerts and stuff."

"What's a car doing down here?"

"Probably going down Orange Street to the old docks. Good spot for screwing or shooting up. We better watch it. The patrols like to come down here, too. It's what they call a Designated Clean-Up Area, meaning they harass anyone they find here."

"How d'you know?"

"Mom and Dad got a load of stuff about the patrols when they applied to be part-time guards. It was all marked confidential. I read it one night when they were out."

"It's not safe to stay here, then."

"Can we go home, d'you suppose?"

"They'll be watching for us, after what happened this afternoon."

"Shall I call my folks? See if they can help?"

He spoke hesitantly. He didn't like to mention his parents when he was with Isolde and Ridge. It seemed too much like flaunting the security and comfort of his home while they lived on their own, Ridge's mother off somewhere with her new man, Isolde's father, a journalist, banished for a year for writing articles critical of Mayor Glut, her mother long gone. Wenden had never seen her. He wondered how his friends coped without parents, even ones as unsatisfactory as his.

Isolde muttered, "You can try."

Wenden tapped his home number into his cell.

His father answered immediately. "Where are you?"

Wenden had planned to tell his parents everything, thinking they'd somehow get him and his friends out of the mess they'd fallen into. But he heard only anger, not concern, in his father's voice, and was instantly on his guard.

"Down town. Why?"

"You know damn well why. Your mother and I have had a visit from the guards, looking for you and your friends. There's a patrol parked outside, waiting for you. You can either get yourself home right now, or tell me where you are so I can send them to pick you up."

"But Ridge is in trouble."

"I know he's in trouble. The guards told us what he's been up to. He's already been sentenced to six months retraining at the Bayport Education Centre. And that's what will happen to you unless you give yourself up, apologize for all the trouble you've caused, promise never to see your friends again, and hope the Chief of Security goes easy on you."

"But I've done nothing wrong. Neither has Ridge. Or Is."

"It doesn't sound that way to me. Now come home before you get yourself even deeper in trouble and do your mother's and my reputation even more harm. Don't you see how embarrassing this is for us, what an impossible situation you've put us in? We're members of People for Progress, for heaven's sake, and we're guards—and we have a delinquent son!"

Wenden said nothing.

His father barked, "Well?"

"Well what?"

"What's it to be—come home, or tell me where you are and I'll send the guards to you?"

"Neither. Guess I'll take my chances."

The feeling of things slipping away was back, stronger than before.

"You do that—let us down, humiliate us, embarrass us—and you can consider yourself without parents."

Wenden stayed silent again, thinking of his home, his room, his stuff.

His father said, "Do you hear me? Carry on like this and your mother and I will formally renounce you. That means …"

Wenden shut the phone off.

He felt Isolde's arm creep around his shoulders. "All right?"

"Looks like I'm on my own."

He was homeless. Parentless. Felt suddenly desolate.

"Join the club," Isolde murmured. "But you're not on your own. You've got me and Ridge, when we find him."

"He's been sentenced to six months retraining at the Bayport Ed Centre. Dad said."

"So they caught him. Wonder how they managed that."

Wenden took her hand and led her through the pitch black. He sat. Pulled her down beside him. They were on a low stone wall.

"Where are we now?" Isolde asked.

"On the fountain surround."

"In the middle of the square?"

"Best place. We'll see a patrol long before they see us, and we'll have plenty of time to go in any direction."

They sat in silence.

Isolde rested her head on Wenden's shoulder. He wished he dare put his arm round her shoulders.

He said, "What are we going to do?"

"Find Ridge, of course."

"But even if we find him …"

He felt Isolde's hand slide across his mouth. Her lips brushed his ear again. She breathed, not even in a whisper, "Listen."

He sat motionless, straining to hear. He grew dizzy. Realized he wasn't breathing. Took in a shuddering gulp of air and instantly cut it off, afraid it would be heard. His finger tips and toes were tingling and his chest felt as if a steel band was being tightened around it.

Movement. Too heavy and clumsy for an animal.

A dim flashlight played briefly over him. Moved on to Isolde. Snapped off.

A voice from the darkness, guttural. "Kids."

Another, surly and harsh. "You got money?"

Both men.

Wenden and Isolde answered simultaneously.

Wenden said, "Not much. Sorry."

Isolde: "Not for you, arsehole."

Wenden, still sitting close to Isolde, felt the heat of her gathering fury radiating from her and prepared to follow her in whatever she did, at the same time as he wished she was more placid, more conciliatory.

A man's laugh from somewhere to the side.

That made three of them. At least.

Guttural voice ordered, "Put your money and watches and cell phones on the wall. Then run along home to mommy and daddy."

Isolde was a furnace. She was still pressed against Wenden. He felt the muscles in her arm and thigh tense. She stood. Wenden followed.

Surly, harsh voice: "So what's it to be, kiddies? Act nice and do as you're told? Or do you want us to take your stuff off you?"

Isolde's arm shot out in the darkness. Wenden felt it jar as it connected with something. A sound like a pumpkin flattened on Halloween. Was it luck, or could she see?

The voice muttered, "She fucking hit me."

Laughter.

Rapid movement towards them.

Headlights and flashing lights on Orange Street. A spotlight sweeping left and right, silhouetting two figures in front of them. Where was the third? One of the shadows closed in on Isolde. Wenden took a half step to put himself in front of her. A fist slammed into his kidneys from the side, another from the front into his stomach. He bent double, gasping. Isolde's attacker slapped her face. As her head jolted sideways he slapped her, backhand, on the other side of her face. Her head snapped back the other way. She slid to the ground. The vehicle pulled out of Orange Street and turned towards Market Square, its spotlight roving from side to side. The assailants ran into the darkness. The spotlight caught and stayed on one running figure. An amplified voice ordered, "Stand!" The man kept running. A taser fired from the van. The man dropped, writhing in the spotlight. The van pulled up beside him. The rear doors opened. Two guards pulled him inside and slammed the doors.

Wenden, still trying to draw breath, groped on the ground for Isolde. He lifted her and rolled her over the wall into the dried up fountain. He pushed her under the overhanging lip of the surround and pressed his full length against her to keep her there as the spotlight played over them. His face was in her hair. It smelled of apples. She was as soft as she'd felt in a thousand daydreams. He hoped Ridge wouldn't mind.

She whispered, "Are we getting it on or what, Wen?"

He felt himself color. "Sorry. Just trying to keep you out of sight. Thought you were unconscious and you might come round and try and get up."

"I'm kidding. I think I was out for a second or two."

"If the van moves, we have to move with it, keep in the shadow of the wall. Like—now!"

They slithered around the inner wall as the spotlight swept across the fountain from a new direction, illuminating where they'd been a few seconds before. They kept moving as the van completed a slow circuit of the square. When the lights stopped moving Wenden peered over the wall. The van was moving slowly out of the square. It stopped at Orange Street before suddenly accelerating towards Union.

Wenden whispered, "Are you okay to walk?"

"'Course."

"Then we better go."

"Where?"

"Follow me."

"I can't see you."

She slipped her hand into Wenden's. He led her back towards the alley, then veered left, murmuring, "Better stay in the open. Less likely to meet up with those characters. Wonder who they were, anyway."

"They're like us."

"What d'you mean—like us?"

"On the run. Desperate."

They turned left onto Orange Street. Lights glimmered ahead of them.

"What are we looking at?" Isolde asked.

"City centre lights reflecting on the harbor on the other side of Long-Wharf."

A few minutes later they were standing on the wharf, gazing across the harbor.

"At least we can see a bit now," said Wenden.

"And be seen," Isolde warned.

Wenden led the way along the wharf until they came to a warehouse.

"Dad used to come here to do the company's accounts," he said. "We'll be safe here while we decide what to do, if we can get in."

He walked past the warehouse and turned into a wide alley that went between the warehouse and a row of sheds. He thought he saw a flickering light in the first of them. He froze, staring at the dilapidated building. He could make out a door, a faded sign over it, Dawkin's Machine Shop. If there was a light inside, it had been quickly extinguished. He listened. Nothing. Turned his attention to a door on the side of the warehouse. He tried it. Whispered, "Locked. Wonder if the entry code still works." He felt for the panel beside the door, picturing the numbers his father used to let him press. He pushed keys and tried the door again. It opened.

"Brilliant," said Isolde.

They slipped inside and Wenden closed the door silently behind them. Without the distant lights of the city centre, the darkness seemed impenetrable, but Wenden, holding Isolde's hand again, felt his way along the wall. He muttered, "Careful. Stairs." He climbed slowly but steadily. At the top he walked along an iron platform until he came to a door. He opened it and stood back to let Isolde enter first, then thought better of it and said, "Wait." He tried the light switch beside the door. Nothing. Crossed the room to a desk. Pulled open the top drawer and felt around. A moment later a match flared. He lit a candle and stood it on the desk, saying, "They used to get lots of power outs down here. They always kept a supply of candles."

He looked around. The office was exactly as he remembered from his visits with his father years before. Just a desk, a couple of chairs, a couch, two doors. The one they'd entered by led to the stairs as well as to the platform that continued past the office and all around the interior, ending at another set of stairs that went to the floor on the other side. The second door opened onto a platform at the top of the fire escape at the back of the warehouse, where he used to play while his father worked.

No-one could get in the warehouse, and even if they did, they had two escape routes.

He turned to Isolde. She stepped forward into the candlelight. Her right cheek was blotchy red and purple and blood was pooling under her left eye.

He muttered, "Jeez, Is."

She said, "What?"

"Your face …"

She contemplated her reflection in the window that looked out at the black interior of the warehouse.

Wenden mumbled, "I should have moved quicker, stopped him …"

Ridge wouldn't have let the man hit her. Wenden wished he had his friend's unthinking ease of action. Wished he could transcend, or whatever Ridge called it.

7

Waking, his first thought was—I am Ridge.

Just Ridge. His mother had named him Rowan Ridge, for the type of tree under which she claimed he was conceived. But he insisted on just Ridge.

The morning he thought, I am #010763, he knew he would be defeated. They would have taken away his identity, turned him into a cipher, the way they wanted.

He would have said it aloud—I am Ridge!—but retrainees were not allowed to speak, except in class, and then only to the instructor, or to chant the required mantras. If he spoke, he would be caught on one of the security cameras and the guards on duty in the control room would fire one thousand volts into him through the stun belt he had to wear throughout his sentence at the Education Centre. If the guards couldn't determine who had spoken, they would punish randomly by firing a charge through the belts of six of the two dozen retrainees in the dormitory.

There were three interlinked sleeping quarters in the compound, each with classrooms attached. The retrainees attended class and went to work like monks and nuns who had taken a vow of silence. Their ages ranged from fourteen to thirty. Miscreants older than that, they'd been warned in their first class, were considered too hardened in their ways for retraining and were shunned or banished.

The youngest retrainee was a girl who looked even younger than the minimum age, and who watched Ridge with the eyes of a disciple, or a predator.

He had been sent not to the Bayport Education Centre, but the Hinterlands Centre. He didn't know where it was located. Rumor had it that it was remote and impossible to find unless you knew where you were going. Leigh Dirk had appeared as he and a dozen others were lining up in the transfer room. She'd plucked him from the line and told the guards, "I do not trust this one. Send him out to the Hinterlands."

One of the guards said, "But the paperwork says the Bayport Education Centre, and he told his parents …"

"I will take care of it. I think his retraining will go better if we get him out of the city, away from his friends."

Then he, and three others, had been loaded into a covered truck and driven through the rest of the night and through the next day until late in the evening, out of the city, through the urban outskirts of more and more widely spaced houses, and into the Hinterlands, the huge area around Bayport that the province had required the city to take responsibility for as part of the deal granting its independence. The agreement stipulated that the city would take over upkeep of infrastructure and provision of services in the Hinterlands. In practice it meant the steady erosion of those things, ameliorated by the provision of cheap housing and apartments in resettlement areas within Bayport. The result was a prosperous city core, and Hinterlands of crumbling blacktop or dirt roads, abandoned farms, occasional deserted hamlets, and a burgeoning wild life of moose, deer, bear, coyote, horses, feral dogs, foxes and wolves.

Ridge shifted on his cot, settling himself less uncomfortably on the thick stun belt. It was a symbol of his subjugation, as well as a disciplinary tool. Leigh Dirk had snapped it around his waist while he waited in the transfer room. As she buckled and locked it, he felt the guards on each side of him relax their grip on his arms, and he transcended, planning to bolt from the room and through the exit he'd noted as he was marched from Leigh Dirk's office, sure he could outrun them all. He'd never experienced pain and helplessness like it. Could never have imagined it. The worst he'd experienced up to that time was when he hammered his finger doing repairs in his mother's cabin. He remembered the agony in his finger. But this pain was everywhere, invading his whole body, instantly morphing him into a useless, convulsing, juddering mass as the belt pumped a thousand volts through him.

Leigh Dirk, standing over him, had smiled. "I knew you would do that. I programmed the sensors in your belt to fire the moment they picked up the electrical impulses in your brain that intensify as you prepare to transcend. If you do not behave, I will programme them permanently. So—would you like to try again?"

He forced the memory of that humiliation and pain from his mind, and closed his eyes, willing himself back to sleep.

A bell rang.

He was in school, mathematics, last class of the day, Wenden in the desk behind him, Isolde in the next row, gazing out of the window. She had choir practice after school. He and Wenden would goof around outside until she finished. Then they'd walk down town, probably stop at Starbucks in the mall. She'd want to sift through the bins at ValueVillage. He and Wenden would follow, commenting on the clothes she held against herself for their approval.

The bell stopped.

Sounds of stirring around him.

She'd be waking now, on her own in the trailer park. If he hadn't been stupid enough to get caught, she'd probably be waking with him, in his mother's cabin near the river, just the two of them, his mother off somewhere beyond the city limits with her new man, good luck to her, he hoped this one lasted. Wenden would be getting up in his nice house, his folks preparing breakfast.

He opened his eyes.

I am Ridge.

Overhead lights glared. The trainees rising like automatons. 6:00 a.m. Fifteen minutes to wash and dress and report for breakfast. He stood and shuffled the red jump suit more comfortably on his shoulders and settled the belt on his hips. The only time belt and uniform came off was for the weekly shower.

He glanced across the dormitory. She was standing beside her cot, too. Olive skin. Black hair, short and spiky and disheveled. Sharp features. Elfin.

Watching him.

He joined the line of identically dressed retrainees shuffling to the washrooms in silence. The red lights on the security cameras mounted high on the walls blinked. The days had a numbing sameness, each as devoid of originality and individuality as the ones before and after, as devoid of originality and individuality as the Centre intended the retrainees to become.

They walked across the compound to the canteen in pairs, like penitents on their way to pray. The compound was surrounded by an eight foot high wire mesh fence, barbed wire strung along the top.

The girl had maneuvered to walk beside him again.

Roll call.

"#010763."

He stepped forward.

I am Ridge.

Breakfast of oatmeal and toast. Morning exercises among the canteen tables, half an hour of stretching and twisting to music under the impassive eyes of the black clad guards.

Classes started at 7:00 a.m. One hour of workbooks with fill-in-the-blank answers, #010763 on the cover. Today was language arts, The Persuasive Letter. Then a lecture on City Governance and Civic Responsibility, followed by Intensive Therapy, which involved the monk-like chanting of the Four Principles of Good Citizenship, each statement repeated for five minutes.

Co-operation and Compliance are the Keys to Social Harmony.

Respect for Authority, and Submission to Authority, are the Cornerstones of Good Citizenship.

The Complexities of Modern Governance Require that Responsibilities Outweigh Rights.

Civic Morality is Founded on the Values and Beliefs of the Majority, and on Respect for, and Compliance with, those Values and Beliefs, as represented by the Security Guards of the International Security Executive.

Then it was time for the road.

They formed up in the dusty compound, six gangs of twelve, each gang accompanied by two guards, both armed with tasers, one with the stun belt monitor. They set out in single file, two in each gang taking turns in harness, one attached to a cart bearing a cauldron of blacktop kept hot and molten by a propane fed fire, the other to a wheeled pallet of gravel. They walked on a narrow, twisting, dirt road through the dense woods that surrounded the compound and kept its location hidden. The dirt road joined a paved road and they followed it out of the forest and through a stretch of bog. Gangs broke away as they reached their assigned stretch of road until Ridge's gang was on its own. They walked gradually upwards for two hours into rolling hills of alternating forest and meadows, passing occasional derelict houses, until they came to their assigned section, where they fanned out and walked slowly, their eyes on the pavement, stopping to fill fissures and potholes with blacktop and gravel, knowing that one step off the road, or one spoken word, or one moment of slacking, meant a jolt from the belt monitor.

Ridge daydreamed as he worked, of bicycling out of the city with Isolde into hills and meadows like those around him now, of days on the beach with her, of quiet evenings with her in his mother's cabin.

At noon they stopped to rest and eat the packed lunch that had been handed to them as they left the canteen. They ate sitting or stretched out on the road. Ridge watched one of the retrainees, a skinny man with wild eyes, maybe in his mid-twenties. He was sitting and staring at a narrow lane that led between an abandoned house and a tumbledown barn. He edged towards it on his butt when he thought the guards were looking away. Ridge wanted to tell him not to do it but couldn't speak without the stun belt shooting a thousand volts through him, more if the guard felt like it. With a final, wild glance at the guards, the man jumped up and sprinted for the lane. He took only a few steps before he collapsed and lay in a twitching mass.

One of the guards spoke into his radio. "Patrol 6. Guard 87. Oak Hill. One attempted escapee, male, down."

A voice crackled in response. "Garbage patrol here. We'll be along shortly. Give him another shot to keep him there. Maximum force."

The guards looked at one another. The one with the belt monitor raised his eyebrows. The other shrugged. The first guard adjusted a dial on the monitor, hesitated, and threw a switch. The fallen retrainee flopped like a landed fish, then lay still.

They returned to the Centre at 5:30 p.m. Supper, meat loaf, was at 6:00 p.m. Lights went out at 8:00 p.m. Before then, showers at 7:00 p.m.

They lined up in two rows, men and women. The showers were single cubicles, men's and women's set back to back, a screen between them affording some privacy. They were allowed two minutes each. Ridge was fifth in line. He saw the girl jostling for position in her line, dawdling one moment, elbowing a girl aside the next. She ended up fifth, too. The lines crept forward. When it was the turn of Ridge and the girl to step behind the screen, she caught his eye and pointed surreptitiously at the ground. He glanced down. Nothing.

A guard deactivated his belt at the door of the shower. He threw off his tunic and stepped into the cell like cubicle. The guard locked the door behind him. The water, cold, came on. He treasured his two minutes of solitude and freedom from the belt and uniform.

A whisper. "Down here."

He thought he'd imagined it.

Again. "Down here."

He looked down. Tiled floor and square drain.

"The drain."

He kneeled. Put his ear to the drain. It was as wide as his head.

"Lift the grille. Stick your head in."

He lifted the grille. It opened on to a deep channel that ran between the two showers. He stuck his head in the drain and saw her face, upside down, like his.

She grinned. Brilliant white teeth against olive skin. "I'm Meru. Who are you?"

She had the kind of voice you heard from kids who went to Bayport Collegiate, the only private boarding school in the city. What had a cosseted and protected kid like her done to get sent for retraining?

"Ridge."

"We're going to escape."

"We?"

He'd thought of nothing but escape, but hadn't come up with anything yet. When he did, he'd be alone.

"Just you and me. I know how to get out, but I need your help."

"I don't want anyone with me when I get out."

"I won't slow you down."

"Maybe. But still—I'll go alone."

"So how are you going to do it?"

He didn't say anything.

She said, "Thought so. I'll tell you the plan next shower time. Make sure you're fifth in line."

The water stopped. The lock on the door snapped back. He replaced the grille and scrambled up just before the guard opened the door and ordered, "Out!"

A week later at shower time Ridge made sure he was fifth in line again. Meru was beside him. He didn't look at her. The guard locked the shower door behind him. As soon as the water started he lifted the grille and put his head in the drain.

Meru spoke quickly. "There's only one guard monitoring the security cameras tonight. His partner's sick and they're short staffed."

"How d'you know?"

"He told me. Said he'll shut the cameras off at midnight when he comes to my cot."

"Why's he coming to your cot?"

"Why d'you think, dummy? 'Cos he's got a bad case of the hots for me."

"But you're only ..."

"... Old enough. He says he'll recommend me for early release because of my exemplary behavior if I let him do it."

"So what am I supposed to do?"

"Take care of him, and any others we meet on the way out. But wait until he's really going at it."

"I won't let him hurt you."

"He doesn't want to hurt me. He wants to ... you know."

"'Course I know, and I'm not letting him do it."

"Just give him time to get going, then move in."

"But we don't know the security code to open the gates, even if we get that far."

"That's why we take a blanket, for when we go over the top."

The water flow dwindled and he replaced the drain cover.

8

Wenden, waking on the floor of the warehouse office, found Isolde where she'd fallen asleep the night before, her head burrowed in his shoulder, one hand, the one with the butterfly ring on her index finger, flung across his chest. She'd fallen asleep crying over Ridge. She veered between despair and a rage at the city and the guards that frightened Wenden. He didn't know what it might lead her to do.

For six weeks they'd been searching for their friend. All they knew was what Wenden's father had revealed, that Ridge had been sentenced for retraining at the Bayport Education Centre. Their only plan was to find him, make contact, hope they could come up with some way of freeing him.

Wenden had asked tentatively, a few days after they'd started searching, "How long shall we do this?"

"'Til we find him," Isolde snapped. "What else are we going to do?"

"We could wait for him to be released. Keep hidden meantime."

She'd flown into a rage. "Yeah, sure. We can wait for him to be released—provided he doesn't shoot his mouth off first and get himself in even more serious shit, or try and escape and get himself hurt, or worse. You know what he's like. Got any more smart ideas?"

She woke and said, "Sorry about last night, the crying. Hope you didn't mind me using you as a comforter."

Wenden said, "'Course not."

It was more than he'd ever dreamed of, having her so close to him at night, spending day after day with her, just the two of them.

They'd each bought a spare set of clothes at ValueVillage, and Isolde a red beret. She wore it, and Wenden his old leather hat, pulled low to keep their faces hidden from security cameras and patrols. They washed—themselves and their clothes—in public washrooms. They'd emptied their bank accounts at a cash machine, but wanted to eke out the money, so stole food, usually at the weekend market in Central Park, where there were no security cameras and it was easy to hide in the crowd. They separated to steal, so that if one was caught, the other could keep searching, for Ridge as well as for the other. Each time Wenden got away with taking something he marveled at his audacity, as well as his disregard of an upbringing that forbade flouting of the law. He felt bad for the vendors from whom he stole, knowing they struggled to make a living, but told himself he had no choice, that they would do the same. He and Isolde bought food, when they had to, from corner convenience stores, which were less likely to have security cameras than the big supermarkets. They knew if they were caught on one of the surveillance cameras they would be recognized by the guards who monitored them, and their whereabouts reported to all patrols, so they never shopped twice at the same store. They saw men and women lurking around the abandoned warehouses and factories that surrounded their hiding place, and were always careful to return to their hideout before dark, fearing another attack. The bruises on Isolde's face, and the black eye, had lasted for nearly two weeks, changing through hues of red and purple. Wenden mentally rehearsed what he would do if they were attacked again, but knew what he imagined was himself as some kind of impossible comic book hero, feared in reality he would be just as helpless again. He'd simply never learned street survival, never had to, especially with Ridge always around to step in.

They shared a granola bar for breakfast.

Isolde, pacing as she finished her portion, said, "Let's go."

They took the stairs to the warehouse floor. Wenden eased the side door open and peered out. No-one in sight. He went to the corner of the warehouse and looked around. Still no-one.

He called to Isolde, "Clear."

She joined him, after making sure the door locked behind her. As they set off two women turned from Orange Street onto LongWharf, heading for their home in Dawkin's Machine Shop, opposite Wenden and Isolde's warehouse. They often saw the women strutting and preening on Union, from where they brought a succession of men back to a dilapidated shed at the end of the wharf furnished only with a filthy mattress on the floor. The women had stopped the friends soon after they took refuge in the warehouse, introduced themselves as Liz and Sadie, and demanded to know what two kids were doing hiding out in the industrial estate. They had an air of confidence that reminded Wenden of Ridge.

The women waved, and Sadie, who had a crooked nose and bright orange hair cut mannishly short, called, "'Morning, kids."

Wenden and Isolde waved back.

Liz smiled at Isolde and said, "Hey, gorgeous."

Liz's black hair was cut even shorter than Sadie's. Her face was ravaged by acne and she had a drooping eyelid.

Sadie winked at Wenden and crooned, "Hi, big boy."

He blushed.

Liz and Sadie were dressed like twins in tight red jeans, green high heeled boots, and short jackets of white faux fir. Wenden, aware of the increasing shabbiness of his two sets of clothes, wondered how they managed to look so smart every day.

"You kids take care," Sadie said as they walked on while Isolde and Wenden made their way towards Orange Street. The July morning was cool and they were glad they'd remembered to include some warm clothes among their purchases at ValueVillage. Isolde wore a navy pea coat and Wenden a fleece under his trench coat.

They turned into Orange Street and passed an old man with frizzy grey hair and a weeping eye, who nodded to them and lifted his hand in a little wave, as if they were all setting off for work, he to Union Street, where they'd seen him begging for food or money, Wenden and Isolde on their search for Ridge.

As they headed for the alley by which they'd first arrived at the industrial estate, a patrol van turned into Orange Street. They threw themselves behind a stack of wooden crates and peered between them. The van passed them and nosed slowly down the street towards where the old man shuffled on, head down, oblivious of it. The van stopped thirty meters behind him and an amplified voice ordered, "Stand." The old man didn't seem to hear. The command came again. "Stand!" He shuffled on. The van stopped and the rear doors opened. Two guards jumped out, armed with tasers.

Isolde said, "Bastards," and started to rise.

Wenden pulled her down.

The old man stopped and turned around. He looked up. Saw the guards. Lifted his hand to wave. A guard fired. The man dropped and lay without sound or movement.

Isolde repeated, louder, "Bastards."

Wenden was afraid she was going to confront the patrol. He grabbed and held her. The guards threw the old man in the back of the van and climbed in. The van turned around and moved slowly back along Orange Street. It braked as it approached the crates. Wenden and Isolde prepared to run. The van stopped alongside them. Wenden looked for a weapon. Wondered if he could rip a length of wood from a crate. Nearly laughed at the thought of confronting a taser toting guard with a piece of kindling. The van crept ahead. Wenden and Isolde moved to keep the crates between themselves and the van. Suddenly it accelerated towards Union.

Isolde and Wenden emerged from behind the crates.

Isolde's fists were clenched and she muttered, "Bastards," over and over again.

Wenden said, "There was nothing we could do. It could be us next time." He hustled her across Market Square, saying, "We can't stay here in the open." He thought he heard footsteps behind them. He looked back. Nothing. They walked on, Isolde crying, and still muttering, "Bastards." Again Wenden thought he heard footsteps, running now. He turned and walked backwards, his eyes sweeping from side to side. He collided with Isolde, who had stopped. He felt the tension in her body, her clenched muscles, even through her jacket. He turned. A man stood in front of them, feet planted, a length of steel pipe in his hand.

Isolde snarled, "What do you want, arsewipe?"

The man, bullet headed, face a leering scowl, said, "The money you should have handed over a few weeks back."

He slammed the steel pipe twice into his hand.

Isolde runs at him. With her eyes still clouded with tears she doesn't notice that color has drained from him and from everything around her. He lifts the pipe and swings it at her but before it lands she cannonades into him, still gathering speed, dipping her shoulder and launching herself into the air at the last second so her shoulder smashes into his chin. He steps back, stumbles on the uneven ground, and falls. Isolde is over him before he can move. She drives her heel into his face. Kicks him in the ribs and testicles. Stamps on his face. He grabs her leg and tries to pull himself up but she shucks him off and kicks him under the jaw, snapping his head back against the pavement. She kicks him repeatedly in the neck. He's gagging and groaning. She puts her foot on his head and grinds his face against the road. All the time she's crying and muttering, "Bastards bastards bastards." She's aware of Wenden dragging her away, saying, "Don't kill him, Is."

They ran across Market Square, slowed as they made their way up the alley towards Union, Isolde still muttering and crying. Wenden put his arm round her to try and calm her but she shook it off.

She realized he was watching her from the corner of his eye and demanded, "What the fuck are you looking at?"

He said, "Nothing."

They emerged from the alley on to Union. The hardest part of every day was crossing the busy street, where patrols were a constant presence, and security cameras monitored vehicle and pedestrian traffic. They walked briskly to an apartment block and lurked near the entrance until a crowd had gathered on the side of the road. It was one of the few places in the city where there was still a pedestrian crossing light. They eased themselves into the middle of the group and kept their heads down as they crossed under the security cameras mounted on the traffic lights. On the other side of

Union they cut between a busy Quickmart and a Tim Horton's and made their way behind a succession of businesses and stores until they came to a parking lot. The first time they'd come this way, seeking a means of moving safely along Union, they'd seen two deer grazing on a strip of grass at the foot of an outcrop of rock at the back of the lot. The deer disappeared as they approached, and when they investigated they found a fissure in what they'd thought was solid rock.

They glanced around. No-one was looking their way. They squeezed through the gap and followed a winding trail that went up and over the outcrop of rock before passing through a patch of woodland and emerging on a cliff from which they could look down on the Bayport Education Centre. It was housed in a block of offices fronted by the busy Portage Avenue.

They inched to the edge of the cliff, where they flattened themselves among windfall, long grass, and ferns, and watched one end of the Centre, where a ramp sloped down to a metal door. After ten minutes they heard a rattle as the door rolled up.

Isolde breathed, "Here they come."

A line of red clad figures marched up the ramp, guards each side of them. Some of the retrainees were harnessed to pallets of gravel, others to carts loaded with steaming cauldrons, low fires flickering beneath.

Isolde and Wenden scrutinized the faces of the retrainees as they emerged. They missed many because they walked with drooping shoulders and their eyes fixed on the ground, or their faces were masked by the shadows thrown by the low morning sun. As the last in line shuffled out, Isolde looked at Wenden. He shook his head. She did the same. They edged back from the cliff until they were hidden in the trees.

"Are you sure you didn't see him?" Isolde demanded.

Wenden nodded. "But I couldn't see all their faces. Some had their head so low …"

"Ridge would have kept his head up," Isolde insisted.

They'd watched every morning. Then they'd scrambled down the cliff in order to follow at a safe distance until the line broke into gangs of twelve. After that they'd haunted the city, searching out the gangs, surreptitiously examining faces when they found one, moving on to search for another when they failed to spot Ridge among the retrainees, all the time on the watch for security cameras and patrols.

Isolde set off for the cliff edge, to follow the gangs.

Wenden asked, "Is it worth looking for him?"

She stopped. "What d'you mean?"

"I mean we've been looking for six weeks. I don't think he's here, Is."

She turned on him. "'Course he's here. He was sentenced to six months retraining at the Bayport Education Centre, wasn't he? We just have to spot him among the retrainees, follow him, find a way of getting a message ..."

"Maybe he got sent to the other one, the Hinterlands Centre."

"That's just for, like, serious cases. Anyway, your dad told you he was sentenced to six months here."

"He might have got it wrong. Or they could have changed their minds. And if Ridge isn't here, that's where he's got to be."

"You're just being defeatist."

"I'm trying to be realistic."

She marched back to him and put her face inches from his. He braced for her anger. Instead she fell against him. "What are we going to do, Wen? We'll never find him out there. No-one even knows where the Hinterlands Centre is, for a start."

He put his arms round her. "We will find him. We just have to get out to the Hinterlands, find a gang at work, and follow it to the Centre."

She sniffed. "Easy, eh?"

He shrugged. "What else we gonna do? Let's get our stuff from the warehouse and start out today. At least there'll be less chance of getting caught by the guards out there."

"What'll we live on?"

"We'll take all the food we've got, maybe lift a few things on the way out of town …"

"And when we run out?"

"I dunno. Find stuff, like old Betts taught us in Outdoor Pursuits. It'll be like the course practical."

She rolled her eyes.

They were crossing Union on the way back to the hideout when Isolde glimpsed the man who had confronted them that morning. He was skulking at the side of the apartments, watching them. She glanced back as they walked along Union. Thought she saw him at the side of the road, still watching. They'd nearly reached the alley when two guards walked from it, barring their way. They turned and saw the man, accompanied by two more guards. He pointed to them.

Isolde tugged at Wenden's arm. "In here."

They were beside a strip mall. They ran into Jazmin's Cutz 'n' Stylz, past four chairs where hairdressers were at work, and through a door at the rear. They were in a tiny yard, a low fence on their left. They climbed over it, ran across another yard, and turned into a narrow passage. They saw Union Street ahead of them. Peered out. They were at the end of the strip mall. The guards were outside Jazmin's.

"The apartments," said Isolde.

They ran towards them. Heard a shout from behind. "Stand!"

They burst through the entrance to the apartments and ran the length of a hallway to doors marked Fire Exit Only. Alarm Will Sound. Wenden shouldered them open. An alarm wailed. They heard the guards start up the hallway. They angled left outside the building and ran through gardens. They came to another block of apartments and ran along the side of it and through more gardens that ended at a wire mesh fence. They crawled under it and found themselves at the edge of a strip of shallow, dirty water.

"It's the canal," said Wenden. "Goes alongside the industrial estate. We're not far from LongWharf once we're across."

They jumped in and waded through debris and garbage. They heard the guards running through the gardens. Isolde ducked under water behind a shopping cart, Wenden behind a truck tire. They held their breath for as long as they could. They raised their heads. The guards were moving away. They waded the rest of the way across the canal and trotted, dripping, through the maze of warehouses on the other side until suddenly they were at the end of LongWharf. They peered along it, toward their hideout.

Isolde muttered, "I think we're clear."

They ran to the warehouse. As they turned towards the side door a patrol van pulled out from Orange Street on to LongWharf and accelerated towards them.

"Upstairs, grab the stuff, then out the fire escape," said Isolde.

They slammed the door, hoping it would stop the guards for a few seconds. Raced across the warehouse floor in the dark and up the stairs. They locked the office door, hoping it would give them a few more seconds. Grabbed their backpacks and stuffed them with food and clothing and a small quilt that hung on the back of a chair. The warehouse door below them burst open. Wenden swung his hip against the crash bar of the door to the fire escape and barged through. He felt the door hit something. He stepped out on to the platform at the top of the steps in time to see a guard totter backwards, grab for the railings that went alongside the stairs, miss, and tumble down, taking with him another guard who was following. The guards scrambled up and resumed climbing.

Isolde joined Wenden on the platform. She glimpsed Sadie and Liz watching from across the road, and the man, the informer, peering from behind the patrol van, which was parked at the end of the alley. As the fire door closed behind her, she heard the inner door of the office smash open. The guard leading the way up the fire escape held his taser at the ready and called, "Both of you, turn around and stand with your hands against the wall." The door behind Isolde started to open. She braced herself with her feet against the railing that went around the platform and pushed back on it.

Below her, she saw Sadie and Liz start across the road. They held their arms behind them, as if out for a stroll. One of the guards, seeing them, shouted, "You two—keep out of this." The office door pushed against Isolde. With her feet still braced, she held it closed. The pushing eased and footsteps inside retreated, then advanced, gathering speed. Isolde pictured a guard barreling towards the door, shoulder down, preparing to barge through.

She blinks. Wenden is grey. The warehouse, the fire escape, the sheds, the road, the guards, too. She realizes the same thing happened when she rushed the man with the steel pipe. She sees only Liz and Sadie in color, their clothes garish in the sombreness.

She remembers Ridge talking about Colorland and thinks—I've transcended, and Liz and Sadie are Transcenders, too.

Sounds are muted, except the footsteps of the guard rushing the door behind her. She feels pared down, the trappings of her everyday self shed, the concerns of the last six weeks discarded, every particle of her focused on escape. She smoulders with anger. The guard on the fire escape warns, "I said turn around and put your hands against the wall. Do it—now!—or we taser you." She drops her feet from the railing and moves into a crouch, head tucked, leaving room for the fire door to swing open. A guard bursts through, running full tilt, his shoulder still down for the expected resistance from the door. He trips over Isolde and his momentum sends him crashing into and half over the railing at the edge of the platform. Isolde grasps his ankles and heaves him the rest of the way. He soars soundlessly head first to the ground where he lands with a liquid smack.

Wenden mutters, "Jeez, Is."

Her eyes glitter.

The guard leading the way up the stairs calls to his partner, "You take the boy. I've got the girl."

He aims his taser at Isolde. She tries to shelter behind the railings at the same time as she sees Sadie in one smooth movement swing a taser from behind her and fire. The guard shudders and collapses on the stairs. Sadie aims at the second guard, who has time to look behind him before she fires. He collapses and rolls down the fire escape. Liz produces a taser and fires past Isolde through the open office door. A guard falls in the doorway. The informer bolts from behind the patrol van. Sadie tasers him. She watches him fall, says, "Scumbag," and tasers him again.

Liz calls, "Now, kids, get the hell out of here."

Isolde and Wenden clatter down the stairs.

Sadie greets Isolde with, "Welcome to Colorland, Rage."

Isolde is aware of Wenden staring at her.

She ignores him and nods to Sadie. "Vendetta." Turns to Liz. Nods again. "And Revenge. Cool."

Wenden, looking from Isolde to Sadie and Liz, mutters, "What's going on?"

Sadie says, "Go!"

Wenden says, "But the guards will identify you. They'll come back with reinforcements."

Liz looks levelly at him. "We haven't finished with them yet."

Isolde, setting off at a run across the wharf, with Wenden lumbering behind, calls over her shoulder, "Thanks. See you."

Sadie calls, "Hope so."

Isolde stopped at the edge of the wharf, looking down at the water. Color had returned as she ran. She'd had to blink a few times to adjust to it, and to clear her head of the fury that had consumed her. As Wenden arrived beside her, panting, she pointed to an old rowing boat tied nearby at the foot of a ladder of iron rungs set into the harbor wall. She climbed down, surveyed the water mark on the wall and said, "Tide's going out." She stepped into the boat.

Wenden clambered down and followed her.

"Untie us," she ordered.

After a few seconds they started to drift away from the wharf and out into the empty harbor.

"'Spose someone sees us," said Wenden.

"They won't," said Isolde, as she lay flat on the bottom of the boat. "All they'll see is an old dinghy drifting on the tide. Get down here with me."

"Where d'you think we'll end up?"

"Doesn't matter. As long as it's out of the city."

By dusk, the tide had carried them beyond the reach of the lights of the city centre, and they were lying in six inches of water.

Isolde sat up and said, "We need a bailer."

Wenden pulled off his hat and started shoveling water. As he bailed, he said, "Back there, Is—what was that about? It was like you were in some kind of sisterhood with Sadie and Liz. And the way you dealt with that guard …"

"Bastard," she interrupted. "They're all bastards."

"I know, but … throwing him over the railing."

"He deserved it."

"It was like you were some kind of action hero. Sadie and Liz, too."

Isolde grinned. "Yeah. It was a trip."

Her eyes glittered again.

Wenden didn't know whether to admire or fear her.

9

He lay rigid, eyes and ears straining into the dark. He had no way of knowing how near to midnight it was. He'd hoped the moon would shed a little light through the high, narrow, barred windows, enough to see the guard come to Meru's cot, but tonight it was just a sliver.

He pictured her lying in the dark, like him.

Waiting.

He heard movement. A retrainee turning over in bed? Or a rustle of clothes, a blanket being pulled back?

He held his breath, listening.

A sigh.

Meru, letting him know the guard was there, at her cot.

In her cot.

Did anyone else hear? Was anyone else awake?

He slithered from his bed and felt for his shoes. Pulled them on and snaked across the floor on his stomach to the foot of Meru's cot, careful not to let the buckle of his stun belt scrape on the ground. Now he could hear movement, the guard's hands whispering against her blanket as they slithered across her. How long should he—could he—wait while the guard assaulted a fourteen year old girl? Despite what she'd told him, he didn't want to wait until the guard got too far. She was too young, no matter what she said, how she acted. It was just bravado.

He slid alongside her cot. Stopped when his head bumped against her shoes.

Something dropped to the floor beside him. He felt it. Her belt. Her tunic landed on his hand. Something else. The guard's belt. He ran his fingers around it, picturing shower time, the guard reaching for the key at his waist in order to unlock Ridge's stun belt. The key, a distinctive one, square, with twin forks, hung between the buckle and the taser holster, among a set of keys. He found the buckle. Ran his fingers further around the belt. The keys. Fingered through them until he felt what he thought was the belt key. Slithered forward so he could insert it into his own belt without dragging the guard's belt towards him with the risk of making a noise. The stun belt would snap as it unlocked but he had to risk it.

He turned the key. His belt snapped open.

The movement in the cot above him stopped abruptly.

He rolled clear of the belt and lay still, listening.

Meru moaned, "Don't stop."

He rises silently.

He's transcended instantly. Can't tell by the lack of color because there is none in the pitch dark. But he feels it.

He slides his hand gently and swiftly over the blanket, as if blessing the bodies beneath it. Feels hair. Meru or the guard? The head rears up. Ridge slides his hand from hair to face. Feels stubble. He throws himself on top of the guard. Wraps the blanket around his head and locks an arm around his neck. The guard pushes himself up on one arm and flails backwards with the other. Ridge pulls the guard's supporting arm from under him and he falls heavily face down. His forehead smacks against something. Meru grunts. Ridge rolls the guard to the floor, bundled in the blanket, and launches himself from the bed. His knee strikes the guard's head, smashing it against the floor with an unforgiving thud. Ridge half rises, ready to knee the guard in the head again. The guard doesn't move.

Ridge stands over the cot and whispers, "Meru."

No response. Maybe stunned by the guard's forehead crashing into hers, maybe fainted from shock.

Someone calls from the dark, "What's going on?"

Ridge says, "Shut the fuck up."

He slides his hand across the cot until it touches Meru. She's naked. He moves his hand to her shoulder and shakes her.

No response again.

He could leave her now. The focus of his transcendence is on his own escape, and on finding and being reunited with Isolde. He doesn't need Meru. She'll slow him down. Isolde is the only one who can keep up with him.

The guard is stirring.

Ridge turns away to head for the door.

Hesitates.

She'll come round at any second. She'll call him back, rage at him for thinking of abandoning her, rouse all the other retrainees, bring guards at the run.

He can't risk it.

He reaches down for her tunic and ties it around his waist. Stuffs her shoes in his pockets. Throws her blanket over his arm. He's aware of the guard fumbling for support on the other side of the bed, trying to haul himself to his feet. Ridge leans over Meru and picks her up in a fireman's lift. She weighs nothing. It's like lifting a rag doll. With one hand steadying her across his shoulder he makes his way through the darkness towards the door.

There are more sounds of movement and whispering from the cots, and someone calls out, "Who's there?"

Ridge says, "Guards on business. Stay where you are unless you want to be tasered."

He doesn't want to answer questions, and he doesn't want anyone else deciding they're going to break out with him, slowing him down. He fumbles for the handle, hoping the guard, in his excitement at the prospect of lying with Meru, has forgotten to lock it on his way in. If not, he'll have to go back, tackle the groggy guard, try and get his keys. He should have thought of it before but too late now. He turns the handle. The door's not locked. He opens it, bracing himself for an alarm.

Nothing.

Steps outside. There's just enough light to see across the compound. With Meru still over his shoulder, he runs to the fence and lays her down.

He can leave her now if he's quick. He'll be over the fence and into the woods before she comes round.

A siren wails.

Footsteps approaching at a run.

A flashlight beam sweeps across the compound.

A shout from the darkness. "Who's there?"

"Guard apprehending escapee," Ridge calls. "One guard down in the dormitory. Needs assistance. May be more retrainees attempting escape."

The footsteps veer towards the dormitory. Ridge throws Meru's shoes and tunic to one side. Folds the blanket, making it as thick as possible, and flings it over the fence. Stands on tiptoe, feeling for a grip between the talons of the barbed wire at the top. Prepares to swing himself up and over.

She stirs and murmurs, "Ridge?"

Her voice is muffled, coming from the other side of Colorland. He still has time. She's slowing him down already. Escape without her will be a snip. He'll be over the fence and into the woods in seconds. With her, with having to somehow get her over the fence, it will take at least twice as long.

He felt her hand brush his leg.

She said, "There you are."

She could feel him.

He reached down and touched her, to be sure. Yes—he could feel her, too.

He was no longer in Colorland.

He couldn't leave her, not now. His conscience wouldn't let him. He wondered what brought him back.

She murmured, "What happened?"

"The guard's head hit you, or you fainted. Are you all right?"

"Yes."

"Did he ..?"

"No."

"Can you stand?"

"Yes."

"I'm going to lift you so you can sit on the fence, on the blanket. Don't jump down. I don't know what you'll land on."

He swung her up. He felt around on the ground for her shoes and tunic and threw them over.

Lights appeared. Guards coming at a run from the Control Unit at the end of the compound.

He felt along the fence until he came to a post. Backed up and ran at it. Grabbed it and swung himself up, getting one foot on top of the fence. He walked himself up the post hand over hand until he could roll over the fence. He felt barbs ripping the thin cloth of his tunic and tearing at his skin. He felt something grind and splinter under his feet as he landed. He reached down carefully. Broken glass, strewn along the outside of the fence where anyone climbing over would land.

He stood under where she perched. He could just make her out, a pale shape caught by the faint light from the sliver of moon. He said, "Jump— but don't land. Hang on to me."

"Where are you?"

"Right under you."

Her hands landed on his shoulders and slithered around his neck. She wrapped her legs around his waist. He stepped away from the fence, still holding her, until he felt grass under his feet. He set her down. She clung to him for a few seconds, breathing heavily.

He whispered, "Wait."

The lights were nearer, sweeping across the compound as they approached. He ran back for her shoes and tunic and pulled the blanket from the fence. Floodlights came on all around the compound and in all the dormitories.

They slipped into the shelter of the woods.

10

Wenden gazed through the trees in the wrong direction. He was supposed to be keeping a lookout in case a patrol came along this remote stretch of dirt road in the Hinterlands. Instead he was watching Isolde.

Their leaky boat had carried them out past a jagged rock with a light mounted on it that marked the channel into the harbor, and had come ashore on a sandy beach in the widening bay beyond the harbor, just before the swell of the open sea. They could make out the lights of the city centre in the distance. Wet and cold, they slept in woods at the top of the beach. In the two weeks since then, they'd wandered the Hinterlands, sleeping in abandoned houses and barns, eating the leaves of dandelion and wintercress, and the tubers of arrowhead when the food they'd brought from the warehouse ran out. They found wild apples from the previous year, soft and wrinkled but edible. They searched empty houses for food, found cans of meat, vegetables and fruit and smashed them open by holding a sharp stone against the can and bludgeoning it with a heavy rock. Isolde discovered a box of matches in one of the houses and they made fires for cooking in the evening. Wenden made a fishing line from a bramble stem and using a worm as bait caught trout and rudd. They skewered the fish on sticks and roasted them. It was mid-July but the nights were cool and they slept huddled together for warmth. Wenden could feel his clothes hanging looser on him and was flattered one night when Isolde commented as she snuggled against him, "You're getting quite svelte."

They'd seen a few patrols as they searched for a road gang that would lead them to the Hinterlands Education Centre. Some of them seemed to travel with purpose, as if heading for a destination, probably the Centre or the city, because there was nowhere else to go. Others drove slowly, pausing to scan the road ahead and the land each side, as if searching for something—or someone.

Twice they'd seen walkers in the distance and had hidden until they passed, afraid they might be informers, or predators like the gang they'd fought off in the industrial park. Both times, when the walkers came near, they'd looked like fugitives, like themselves, but still they didn't want to risk contact.

Today they'd been walking since dawn, first through scrubby hardwood forest on a high plateau, then descending into a valley where the road followed the course of the wide, fast flowing Black River through meadows and fields of abandoned farms. They'd stopped to lunch on last year's apples in an overgrown orchard, after which they'd decided to bathe and wash their clothes. Wenden had cautioned that they were close to the road—usually they chose well hidden ponds and streams—but Isolde said they could take turns keeping watch from the shelter of the orchard. Wenden positioned himself so that he had a good view of the road from where it rose over a low hill in one direction to where it turned to skirt an outcrop of rock in the other. His eyes roved between the road and Isolde, lingering on her as she made her way through the orchard. When she reached the river bank and he could still see her through the trees and she threw her clothes aside he drew in a sharp breath, felt he was in some kind of paradise, his senses filled with sun and breeze and rushing water and the lissom girl who was bound to his best friend by ties beyond childhood friendship, beyond boyfriend and girlfriend, ties he didn't understand.

He didn't hear or see the jeep until it stopped beside the orchard and one of the two guards in the patrol, a man, ordered, "Stand in the clear and identify yourself."

The other guard, a woman, still in the jeep, was looking from Wenden to photos on a tablet. She called, "I thought so. He's wanted." She climbed from the jeep, taser in hand, and said, "Where's the girl?"

"We split up," said Wenden. "I don't know where she is."

As he spoke, a furious splashing sounded from the river.

The woman guard said, "Smart arse," and fired her taser. Waves of astonishing, debilitating pain shot through Wenden. He felt as if his body was exploding and imploding at the same time, his limbs first flung outwards as if in celebration and then curling inwards, foetus like. The male guard strode past him, heading for the river. Wenden tried to move to stop him, tried to shout a warning to Isolde, but couldn't move or speak. He closed his eyes, cursing the infatuation that had betrayed him, made him betray the trust Isolde had placed in him to watch over her.

Far out in the river, Isolde swims in slow circles.

Water and sky and trees are grey in Colorland. So, too, are the guards, who are putting themselves in the way of her search for Ridge. She is Rage, her anger focused on the woman who has just shot her faithful friend, and the man striding through the orchard, his footsteps like thunder, thinking he is going to apprehend her. She knew, when she splashed, that it would be the man who would come. She'd seen him watching her before his partner spoke.

He reaches the river bank.

She waves.

He calls, "Come on in, little miss. You're in trouble."

She says primly, "But I don't have any clothes on."

He grins. "Too bad."

She smiles and says playfully, "Why don't you come in and get me?"

His grin is wide and foolish. "There's nothing I'd like more, miss, but I can't swim."

She thinks—Good.

She swims towards him, rolling in the water to give him a flash of bare thigh. She sees him lick his lips. She comes to the big, flat topped rock she'd grazed her knee on as she swam out. She remembers how the river shelves suddenly, from shallows to over six feet where the current scours the bank. She feels the rock under her. Plants her feet on it, keeping her knees bent. Rises slowly as she walks forwards on the rock, as if reaching the shallows. Water streams down her. She stands at the lip of the rock. The guard's mouth hangs open. She calls, "Can you bring me my tee shirt so I can make myself decent?"

Without taking his eyes from her, the guard picks up the tee shirt lying on the bank beside him and steps into the water.

Isolde breathes, "Thank you," and holds her hand out to take it.

His eyes still fixed on her, he takes another step and disappears under the water, his arms flailing. Isolde swims towards him, takes the tee shirt, now floating, and pushes him further out into the river, past the rock, where the current grabs him.

She finds a big stone in the shallows, steps onto the river bank, and calls, "Help!"

The other guard runs through the orchard.

Isolde points to where the current is carrying the man away and says, "I think he's drowning."

"Get in and rescue him," the woman says. "I'm ordering you."

"The current's too strong."

The guard watches her partner's frantic efforts to stay afloat. Isolde steps behind her and smacks the rock against her head. She falls. Isolde takes her taser. The guard rolls over and starts to sit. Isolde kicks her in the face. She steps back and levels the taser at her. The other guard has fetched up in shallows downriver. He gets unsteadily to his feet, takes two steps towards the bank, and retreats when he immediately finds himself in deeper water.

His partner, glaring up at Isolde, snarls, "I recognize you. You and your friend back there."

"That's good," says Isolde. "So you can tell me where my other friend is, the one you'll have seen linked to us in your list of fugitives."

"I'm not telling you anything."

Isolde sticks the barrel of the taser between the guard's legs. "You will—or we'll find out what kind of orgasm a thousand volts gives you."

Wenden staggers through the orchard and says, "Sorry, Is."

The stranded guard calls, "Will someone help me, please?"

The woman guard snaps, "Your friend's at the Hinterlands Centre, where he belongs, where you belong, too, you and all the other useless, disrespectful kids whose parents never taught them the meaning of authority."

Isolde demands, "Where's the Centre?"

"I don't know. We patrol out of the city. The Centre's nothing to do with us."

Isolde nudges her with the barrel of the taser. "I said—where is it? Or do you want a thousand volts between your legs?"

Wenden mutters, "Whoa, Is."

The guard says, "All I know is it's somewhere north of here, around fifty miles, deep in some woods. You won't find it even if you get close to it, and you certainly won't get anywhere near it. Now let me up, you little bitch."

"In a moment," says Isolde. "First—strip."

"You're joking."

"Do it—or I fire."

The guard strips slowly.

Isolde orders, "Now lie on your stomach."

"Pervert."

Isolde gestures with the taser and the guard obeys. Isolde kicks the guard's clothes in the river and they float away in the current. She tells Wenden, "Get a rock and drop it on her head if she moves."

Wenden finds a rock the size of a football and stands over the guard. Isolde marches along the river bank until she is opposite the man. She aims the taser at him and says, "Strip."

"You can't talk to me like that, young lady."

"Strip—or I'll fire and let you float downstream unconscious."

The guard slowly undresses until he stands in his underpants, clutching his clothes. Isolde orders, "Take them off."

He turns his back and obeys.

"Throw everything in the river."

His clothes float away.

Isolde returns to the woman and asks, "Can you swim?"

"Some."

"Join your friend, then."

Isolde covers the woman with the taser until she stands in the shallows beside her partner, then throws the weapon in the river, retrieves the rest of her own clothes, and gets dressed.

Wenden is eyeing her nervously. He mutters cautiously, "Is?"

She blinks.

He repeats, "Is, are you okay?"

She blinked again. "Sure. Are you?"

"Kind of shaky, bit of a headache, but … yeah, I think so."

"Better get moving, then."

They walked back towards the road.

"Let's take the jeep," Wenden suggested. "I'll drive."

He broke into a trot but stopped after a few paces. He felt top heavy, his head like cement. Isolde overtook him and reached the driver's seat first. She grinned. "I'll let you have a turn. Maybe." She started the engine.

"Which way is north?" Wenden asked.

Isolde pointed to a compass on the dashboard.

"How long d'you think it'll be before someone back in the city realizes something's up, or another patrol discovers our friends back there?" Wenden asked.

Isolde shrugged.

A voice issued from the radio. "Patrol 93. Where are you?"

A few seconds later it came again. "Patrol 93. Repeat. Where are you?"

Isolde floored the accelerator. Fifteen minutes later they came to a crossroads. With a glance at the compass she swung left.

Wenden watched her from the corner of his eye as she drove. He'd always been in awe of her, often wondered how she and Ridge tolerated his company, felt a clod beside their vitality and ease of action, their brilliance, Ridge's insouciant cool, Isolde's staggering allure. Now he felt an even wider gulf between his friends and himself as Isolde, as well as Ridge, discovered this new power. They seemed to belong in another world, one he couldn't reach or even understand. He wished he could transcend to Colorland with them.

She was aware of Wenden watching her and demanded, "What?"

"You're not still in Colorland, are you?"

"Nah."

"But you were back there at the river—right?"

She nodded.

"What's it like?"

"It's a rush like I can't describe. Guess you have to get there to know." She grinned. "Can't wait to do it again."

"Kind of grows on you, does it?"

"Like Ridge said."

"Can anyone learn to do it—to transcend?"

"Anyone who has the confidence and the concentration."

He asked timidly, "Even me?"

"Why not? Seems some people are just born to it …"

"That'd be you. Ol' Ridge, too."

"… And some get driven to do it because of what happens to them, even if it's not in their nature."

"You mean someone like me."

"Who knows?"

"Did Ridge teach you?"

"No. But he was always talking about Colorland, and I wanted to transcend, and suddenly, when I—we—really needed it, back at the warehouse, and when that guy came at me with the steel pipe, it just happened."

"It was like you were possessed."

"It was like the regular me disappeared and nothing was left except who I really am, and that was driving me so strongly I had the confidence and the … the … single-mindedness to do stuff I could never normally do."

"Like kicking the crap out of that man, and sending the guard at the warehouse over the railings, and threatening to taser that woman guard."

"I wouldn't have tasered her."

"Not even when you were in Colorland?"

"Nah."

"Why not?"

Isolde grinned. "Don't know how to fire a taser. There's all sorts of switches and stuff on them."

Wenden laughed, then said seriously, "And when you're in Colorland, you're Rage."

"Right."

"Rage at what?"

Isolde shrugged.

"The guards, and what's happened to the city?" he persisted.

"More than that. It's from way back." She fell silent, concentrating on driving, then suddenly burst out with, "Men!"

"Men?"

"All I've got from them for as long as I can remember is … is leering and … and groping. And that uncle, called himself an uncle. I thought Dad was going to kill him …"

Her voice tailed off. She shrugged again, biting her lip.

She'd never said anything about this to Wenden before. He didn't know what to say. He wondered what the so called uncle had done. Thrust it from his mind. He didn't want to contemplate it. No wonder she was angry. He felt himself blush, remembering all his daydreams of Isolde, his secret glimpses of her occasional careless décolletage, and his conscience and honesty forced him to confess, "Guess I'm guilty, too. Sorry."

She reached across and put her hand on his, where it rested on his knee. "I know you think of me. But you'd never dream of doing anything more than look."

"I might dream about you," he said sheepishly.

She smiled. "That's a compliment."

"Who's Ridge, when he's in Colorland?"

"He's Ruthless."

"Where does that come from?"

"I'd guess from his dad."

"I never met him."

"He was a drifter. Didn't believe in organized society, just wanted to live without bothering anyone, and without anyone bothering him. Of course the government can't stand anyone living like that, and he was always getting harassed by officials and bureaucrats, 'til he got so he didn't care what he did to live the way he wanted. I guess it sort of rubbed off on Ridge. He's like his dad, doesn't respect—doesn't even know—any kind of rules of how you're supposed to behave."

"And Sadie is Vendetta, Liz Revenge," said Wenden. "Wonder where that comes from."

"Prob'ly from the way they were treated in the city's Clean up the Streets campaign. Remember how the council sent the street women for retraining, then took their homes? Guess they have plenty to want revenge for."

"If I got to Colorland—wonder who I'd be."

Isolde took her eyes from the road for a second to look at him steadily. "Do you really want to know?"

"Why not?"

"Maybe you wouldn't like who you really are, what drives you. Do you think I want to be driven by rage? Think I'm proud of it?"

"But it comes in handy, doesn't it? And I was useless back there. I didn't know what to do. Just sort of froze. 'Spose that means I'm a coward."

"It just means it's not in your nature to harm people. That's hardly a bad thing."

"But if it hadn't been for you, the guards would have taken us in. I don't feel I'm much use to you—or to Ridge, when he's around."

"Don't put yourself down. Ridge and me—we need you."

"Nah."

"Yes. You're like a balance for him, making him think twice—sometimes—before doing something really stupid. It's like he sees himself through your eyes and that stops him." She looked at him again and added, "And do you really think I'd be wandering the Hinterlands if I didn't have you with me?"

They drove on in silence, through empty, undulating countryside of meadow and bog.

The radio crackled into life again. "Patrol 93. Where are you? What's going on?"

A few seconds later: "Red code. All available patrols to Black River Road."

"Time to ditch the jeep," said Wenden.

"Too late," said Isolde. She pointed to the road ahead. A mile away a jeep like the one they'd stolen appeared briefly at the peak of one of the rolling hills.

"Better turn around," said Wenden. "Try and outrun them, eh?"

He was thrown back in his seat as Isolde gunned the jeep forwards, wheels churning mud and gravel. She set a course down the middle of the narrow road, her knuckles white with the strength of her grip on the wheel. Her eyes flickered rapidly for a moment, then fixed on the road.

He said uncertainly, "Is? You're doing it again—right? What do you want me to do?"

She doesn't answer. They're still gathering speed. They shoot over the brow of another low hill and roar into the dip before the road rises again. At the same time the approaching jeep appears two peaks ahead of them. As Isolde comes over the top of the next hill, the other jeep crests the one ahead. Their stolen jeep picks up speed on its descent. Isolde pulls into the left lane, directly in front of the approaching vehicle.

Wenden muttered, "Jesus, Is."

She was going to get them killed. He put his hand on her shoulder, to shake her, to bring her to her senses. But she wasn't there. He sensed a kind of resistance, but felt nothing. He moved his hand to her arm. Nothing.

The approaching patrol—she can see two guards—veers to the other side of the road. She pulls across so she still faces them. The other driver brakes hard and stops broadside, blocking the road. Isolde aims straight for the patrol jeep. At the last second the driver guns his vehicle forward. It shoots across the ditch beside the road and lands in a pond, sending the guards flying from it. Glancing back as she hurtles on, Isolde sees them swimming for shore.

Wenden saw her eyes flutter. He said quietly, "Are you back, Is?"

She blinked again. "Yup. Wow. Better not do that again for a while. Better try and get the high out of my system."

"You were scaring me. I went to shake you to make you slow down. But I couldn't feel you."

Isolde frowned. "I didn't even know you touched me."

"So you couldn't feel me either."

"Guess not. Ridge said something about not being able to feel when he was in Colorland—remember?"

She slowed at the top of yet another low hill, staring ahead at a dark, jagged mass that stretched across the horizon.

"Is that cloud?" Wenden asked.

Isolde shook her head. "I think it's the forest the Centre's hidden in."

They drove on.

"We better get rid of the jeep," said Wenden. "There'll be patrols swarming all over the place if we're near the Centre, and after we—you—forced that jeep back there off the road."

Isolde braked suddenly and backed up. They were at the brow of a hill. They climbed out and slithered on their stomachs to the summit so they could peer ahead through the long pampas grass that grew at the side of the road. At the foot of the hill before them twelve figures dressed in red were tramping from a narrow lane onto the main road. Two pulled carts. They wore thick belts and carried shovels and were followed by two guards.

"'Spose one of them is Ridge?" said Wenden.

"It's too far to see."

"So what's the plan?"

"Haven't got one. I thought we'd find him first, then decide what to do, either break into the Centre and get him out, or get him free from a road gang somehow." She looked at the dark band of trees on the horizon. "You follow the retrainees. The way that woman guard spoke even if we got to the woods we still wouldn't be able to find the Centre. I'll hide the jeep, maybe somewhere up that lane they're coming from. Then either I'll catch you up, or if you get to the Centre, you backtrack and meet me on this road. Then we'll get Ridge free somehow, make our way back here, pick up the jeep, take off, and—bingo!"

A third figure, clearly not one of the gang but not a guard either, emerged from the lane and looked sharply in their direction. They flattened themselves in the grass.

"Did he see us?" Wenden murmured.

"No way," said Isolde.

"He was looking right at us like he could."

They raised their heads cautiously. The newcomer, tall, wearing a black trench coat over a dark suit, and a black stocking cap, scanned right and left of them. Then he turned away slowly and followed the gang. As he turned, his jacket swung open, revealing a cudgel hanging at his waist.

They lay flat until the retrainees and their guards disappeared over the next hill. Then they coasted down to the intersection in the jeep.

"I'll catch you up, or I'll see you on the road," Isolde reminded Wenden.

They hugged, and Wenden set off at a cautious jog. He slowed as he approached the top of the hill, and slithered the last few yards on his stomach, peering ahead. The road meandered through a barren, desert like landscape interspersed with outcrops of rock that extended as far as he could see. The road gang was already disappearing around the first bend.

Wenden looked back. Isolde was standing beside the jeep. She blew him a kiss. He waved and jogged over the hill.

11

As soon as they were hidden by the trees, Ridge turned and followed the fence until they were behind the Control Unit at the end of the compound.

Meru complained, "Why don't we just get away through the woods?"

"Because that's what they'll expect us to do," Ridge explained. "They'll be waiting for us wherever we come out on the road. Besides, we don't know these woods and we can't risk getting lost. We'll have to follow the access road out when things quieten down."

As he spoke, three jeeps drove away from the Control Unit, crossed the compound, and headed out on the access road. The first sped away, while the others cruised slowly, spotlights directed into the trees on each side of the road. A squad of guards walked slowly behind, sweeping the forest with powerful flashlights.

Ridge and Meru stayed awake through the night and the next day as the search continued. They scooped and slurped brackish water from the forest floor, but had nothing to eat. No road gangs left the compound. The cuts and scratches Ridge received as he vaulted over the strand of barbed wire were already closing, all but one, a deep slash on his thigh, which was inflamed and still oozed blood.

As dusk came on, Ridge built a shelter deep in the woods behind Control, evergreen boughs above, ferns and bracken below. That night they wrapped themselves in the blanket and lay together for warmth, but Ridge was too watchful to sleep more than a few minutes at a time, and spent most of the night listening to the constant coming and going of patrols. He couldn't believe how easily and peacefully Meru slept. He was used to Isolde, who slept with clenched fists, grinding her teeth and sometimes shouting incoherently in her sleep.

On the third night jeeps patrolled the access road constantly, but no foot patrols ventured out, and in the morning the road gangs resumed work.

That night there was no activity, and they made their way to the access road and followed it out of the woods, keeping in the shelter of the trees. They headed south, Ridge trying to recall his journey from Bayport. His only plan was to return to the city, find Isolde and Wenden, and let them know he was okay. After that, he didn't know, just that he'd have to stay on the run. Meru said she had an aunt in the city she could go to.

They walked all day, keeping careful watch for patrols. In the evening, they sat by a shallow, stagnant pond and Ridge bathed the cut on his thigh with wet leaves.

Meru watched for a while before commenting, "That's not going to do any good. It needs cleaning out properly, not with dirty leaves and stagnant water."

"Do you think I haven't been looking for clean water?"

"I know something that'll do instead."

"Like what?"

"Pee."

"I thought of that. But it's kind of difficult to pee on your own thigh."

"I didn't mean for you to do it."

"You're not saying ..."

"Women's pee is better, anyway."

"You're kidding—right?"

"Take your pants off and lie down."

He hesitated and she said, "Either do it, or just wait for the infection to get worse and spread through your leg and turn to gangrene and ..."

Ridge muttered, "Okay," and lay on his side.

He slipped his pants down.

Meru did the same. Ridge looked away.

She straddled his thigh. "Ready?"

He nodded.

Positioning herself carefully over the wound, she peed as forcefully as she could into it. Ridge felt her warm urine flushing through his wound and running over his thigh. She climbed off his leg and examined the cut.

"I think it's clean. Best not bandage it unless we have to. We'll have to watch it for a day or two, just in case."

He muttered, "Thanks," and added, "How d'you know this stuff, anyway?"

"I'm a member of Junior Red Cross. Used to be, anyway. They probably threw me out when I got sent for retraining."

"So what did you do, to get sent here?"

"Social services put me in care and I ran away."

He didn't think kids like her got put in care, and wondered what had happened to her parents for social services to get involved, but he didn't say anything.

"How about you?" she said.

Ridge shrugged. "Fooling around and stuff."

"Were your folks mad at you?"

"They don't know."

"How come?"

"'Cos they're not around to know."

They slept in the woods and walked for another day. Ridge's thigh at last seemed to be healing. They drank from springs and ponds, and ate dandelion leaves, wintercress, choke cherries and old apples. They both had diarrhea. It was six days since their last proper meal, and Ridge worried that Meru was wasting away. There seemed to be less of her every night when they wrapped themselves in the blanket.

During their second day of walking she asked, "Can we rest for a while?"

He was going to tell her he knew she'd slow him down but reminded himself how young she was, and offered, "I'll piggyback you." He kneeled and she climbed on his back and put her arms around his neck and tucked her legs around his waist. She seemed to weigh nothing.

Isolde never would have admitted to him that she was tired, but that was Isolde.

The next evening, after walking all day, they came upon an abandoned farmhouse, the door hanging open. They went in to forage for food but found it stripped of everything. They were about to give up when Ridge discovered a tin at the back of the cupboard under the kitchen sink. He opened it and discovered six boxes of matches.

"I could maybe get us a partridge or a rabbit to cook if I had my sling-shot," he muttered.

"Make one," Meru suggested.

"Don't have any elastic, or material for a cradle," said Ridge.

Meru slipped out of her tunic and handed her underwear to him. "Now you got both. Go make a slingshot."

He snapped a bough from an old apple tree in the yard and broke it to form a Y shape. He pulled the elastic from Meru's underwear and tied it between the prongs of his sling. He folded the material to form a cradle. He pulled the elastic back, testing its strength. He thought it would do.

While Meru waited in the farmhouse he walked around the yard picking up stones, then lay at the edge of a field. Within minutes a small partridge appeared. He fired and it fell. He ran to it and wrung its neck, ripped the feathers from it, and took it back to Meru. She was asleep on the kitchen floor, wrapped in the blanket. He made a fire in the yard, making sure it was hidden from the road, stuck the partridge on a stick, and roasted it. He woke her and they ate sitting on the kitchen floor, ripping the meat from the carcass with their fingers. It was earthy and tough but they didn't mind.

In the morning Ridge found a dilapidated bicycle and a pump in a pile of rusting equipment in a corner of the farmyard. He inflated the tires and to his surprise they stayed firm. He rode the bicycle around the farmyard while Meru whooped and clapped. She sat on the handlebars and he rode around again. He rode standing on the pedals and she sat behind him, her arms wrapped around him.

"Can we ride it the rest of the way?" she asked.

"It's risky, because if we meet a patrol it'll take us longer to hide, but if we don't get to the city soon we'll starve, anyway," he decided.

They rode, sometimes taking turns, one jogging alongside, sometimes sharing the bicycle. As they approached the outskirts of the city, they passed a house where washing flapped on a line. They stopped a quarter mile further on, hid the bicycle by the road, and returned on foot. They watched the house for an hour and saw no sign of life. They each helped themselves to an outfit from the line, Ridge jeans and a sweater, Meru a light flimsy dress. They hid their red uniforms in a ditch.

They slept by the road near one of the city's resettlement areas, and then waited for the morning rush to get underway before joining the cars and bicycles and mopeds heading into Bayport, again taking turns riding and jogging, all the time hoping the patrols wouldn't spot them in the crowded streets.

As they changed places Ridge said, "We'll go to my place first, get some food, rest for a bit. Then we'll go to your aunt's."

They turned into one of the sprawling subdivisions that lined the busy road. Meru rode on the handlebars. Ridge hoped they looked like two teenagers fooling around. He thought they should be safe unless some busybody reported them for not being in school. When they came to the end of the development, and the paved road became a muddy trail winding into a boggy wasteland of alders and scrub and stunted spruce, he kept going until the trail petered out.

"Where are we?" Meru asked, jumping from the handlebars.

"On the way to my place."

"You live in a swamp?"

"Sort of. My ma's uncle built the cabin years ago, on the river bank, with a bunch of other weekend places, nice ones. Then the power commission built a dam way up the river, and that changed its course, and left acres of marshland between the new channel and the cabins. So people abandoned them. Ma's uncle left his place to her, and we moved in. The guards will likely be watching it, but not this side where it's all swamp and alders. This is my secret way home." He hid the bike beside the trail and said, "Follow me."

After struggling through the undergrowth and splashing through bogs for fifteen minutes they joined a deer trail, and another fifteen minutes later came to a clearing with an overgrown garden, a wood pile, a tire rim half filled with ashes, and a low cabin with a veranda. A rocking chair stood on one side of the door, an old car seat on the other. Ridge opened the door and paused at the smell of damp and mold.

"Don't you lock the house?" Meru asked.

He grinned. "Nothing worth taking."

The room they entered was furnished with a worn couch in front of a small, ancient television, a card table with two metal, fold-up chairs tucked under it, a woodstove with a pile of logs beside it, and in one corner a cooking stove, refrigerator, and sink. Ridge tracked the smell to rotting potatoes and carrots in a vegetable bin and threw them out.

"How come you're allowed to live by yourself?" Meru asked. "Why don't social services take you in?"

"Because they don't know Ma's gone," said Ridge.

He pointed to three doors at one end of the cabin. "Ma's room is at the front, mine at the back, and the washroom in between."

He looked out of the front window to where a rutted and heaved cement driveway was barely visible under the grass and alders growing through the cracks and encroaching from each side.

He told Meru, "I'm going to see what sort of watch they're keeping on the house. Then we'll find something to eat."

He slipped out of the back door. He stopped on the veranda and lifted the lid of the box where he kept a supply of dry logs for the stove. He pushed the logs aside and found a slingshot and a supply of stones at the bottom of the box. It was one of a half dozen he had hidden in and around the cabin. He'd fashioned them after the one his father gave him. He peered around the side of the cabin. Listened. Distant hum of the city. A racket of crows somewhere behind the cabin, probably on the bank of the river a quarter mile away. He ducked into the bushes and moved cautiously alongside the driveway until he could see the road. A jeep was parked across the end of the drive, two guards lounging against it.

He returned to the cabin and checked the food supply. They each had a can of stew, followed by a can of peaches. After their meal, he checked on the guards again and found them sitting in the jeep. One seemed to be asleep. He stayed until another jeep, with two new guards, arrived. They all conferred for a few minutes without a glance towards the cabin. Ridge waited until the first jeep left, and the guards in the second made themselves comfortable in their vehicle—he thought they were playing cards—before making his way back through the undergrowth.

He found Meru asleep on the couch. He'd planned to give her his room, and to sleep on the couch himself, knowing that if the guards ventured up the driveway he'd wake in time to rouse her and escape out the back. He shook her gently. She didn't stir. He fetched a blanket from his mother's room and tucked it around her. He sat by the front window, keeping watch, until it was dark. When he could no longer fight off sleep, he took the empty cans, tied them to a length of string he found under the sink, and strung them across the driveway where anyone approaching the cabin in the dark would set them banging together. He fetched another blanket to put over Meru and went to his own bed. He woke in the night and found her draped across him.

In the morning they ate stale cereal and some cheese Ridge found at the back of the refrigerator. He tucked his slingshot and a supply of stones in his back pocket, hidden under his sweater, and they made their way through the boggy wilderness to where they'd left the bicycle the day before. They rode through the subdivision and abandoned it when they reached the busy road leading into the city. They walked among the morning traffic and pedestrians until they came to an apartment block near the centre.

Meru found her aunt's name and pressed the buzzer beside it.

A voice said, "Who's there?"

"It's Meru."

"Meru! I thought … Aren't you supposed to be … You'd better come up."

The door sprang open.

Meru turned to Ridge. "Thank you."

"What for?"

"For breaking me out."

"It was your plan."

"But you made it work, got me safely home."

"What will you do now?"

"Stay with my aunt for a while. See if she knows where my parents are. What about you?"

"Find my friends. Then … I don't know."

She hugged him. Kissed him on the corner of his mouth.

He said, "I'll see you around."

She entered the building, turned and waved through the glass door as it locked behind her.

It was just after 8:30. Isolde would be on her way to school.

He hurried across town to Bayport Regional High and hid in the doorway of a nearby store while he looked for Isolde among the throngs of students arriving.

How foreign and juvenile and easy the world of school seemed. Maybe it would have been better, easier, if he'd served his time at the Centre and returned to spending his days with Isolde and Wenden, fooling around at school, hanging out in the malls, playing soccer, arguing about music with Isolde, teasing Wenden about his crush on her. Maybe that would have been the mature, responsible, sensible thing to do. But he had to make some protest about the way he'd been treated, couldn't simply accept the injustice.

As he watched the students arriving, he recognized some of his former classmates. There was Larsen, who wouldn't have his homework done, and Thomas, who'd spend the day boasting of his exploits on the basketball court, and Jay, who'd leer at Isolde all day, the way he always did when Ridge wasn't around. Most of them wore a Teens4Progress armband although it wasn't compulsory. Next thing it'll be a uniform, Ridge thought. Did they really believe the shit Glut and his cronies were putting out? Or were they just going along with it because that was the easy thing to do?

The crowd of students was thinning. He peered up and down the street. Still no sign of Isolde.

What would he do when he found her? Did he expect her to join him, be a fugitive, risk him leading her into trouble, maybe danger? Wouldn't it be better if he didn't see her, just got away from the city while he could, found somewhere to stay beyond its jurisdiction, maybe joined his mother? But Isolde would never forgive him. He couldn't do it, anyway. It was inconceivable to be without her.

He waited until 9:30. She was careless of time, but not that careless. She must be goofing off school, which meant she was probably at her father's home in the trailer park, or next door at Mrs. Arnold's, where she was supposed to stay while her father was banished. Wenden hadn't gone past, either. He was pathologically incapable of doing something wrong, like arriving late for school, unless he was with Ridge or Isolde, which meant he was goofing off with her, or home sick.

He walked through backstreets to the trailer park, wary of patrols all the time. With the morning rush over the streets were quiet. The trailer park consisted of one road that went in a wide loop, plots for the trailers radiating from it like the spokes of a wheel. The centre of the loop had been planted with grass, shrubs and trees to form a little park, with playground equipment and picnic tables. Isolde lived at the top of the loop. Ridge wondered if patrols were keeping her home under surveillance because of her father's banishment but it seemed unlikely. As far as the city was concerned the trailer was empty.

The park was as quiet as it usually was during the day when most of the inhabitants were at work and only a few retirees and shift workers remained. Ridge found the key in its usual place behind the trailer, under a rock between the little vegetable garden and the log pile. He let himself in and looked around. It was like a model home, no dishes in the sink, no books and newspapers and magazines lying around, no dirty washing in the laundry room. Isolde's bed was undisturbed, her pillow and sheets neatly made up, no clothes strewn over it and across the floor. He paused to look at a photo of her father on the bedside table. He looked like her, same heart shaped face, same chestnut hair, same almond eyes. There was no photo of her mother because neither Isolde nor her father knew who she was. Isolde said that was the way it was when you were an in vitro baby.

He crossed to the neighbor. Mrs. Arnold opened the door before he could knock. She was a small, stocky woman with thinning grey hair.

She greeted him with, "What are you doing here?"

"Looking for Isolde."

"They sent you for retraining."

"I was released early."

Mrs. Arnold looked up and down the road nervously. "No. You ran away. They're looking for you, and for Isolde."

"Why are they looking for Isolde?"

"Her and Wenden, for causing a disturbance and assaulting a patrol."

"What? When?"

"The same time you were sent away. The guards have been here I don't know how many times. They said I had to call and let them know right away if Isolde or her friends came here. They said it was my civic duty and I'd be punished if I didn't."

"So you called them already."

"Sorry, dear. I had no choice. I saw you next door and …"

She broke off at the sound of sirens. Ridge ran back to Isolde's trailer and crawled under it. The sirens grew louder.

Mrs. Arnold slammed her door as a jeep pulled up. Two men climbed out, both tall and broad. They wore long black trench coats over dark suits, with white shirts and striped ties, and black stocking caps. They carried cudgels at the waist. The nose of one seemed to fill his face, leaving barely enough room for tiny round eyes above and thin lipped mouth below. The other had protruding ears, while his eyes and mouth were set close together in the middle of his face. They stood beside the jeep, talking as they looked back at the road into the park.

Ridge slithers nearer on his stomach, watching and listening. The men are in color. Transcenders. The first he's seen, apart from Leigh Dirk. He stares at them, reading them. One is Olfaction, the other Listener. A car arrives, no siren. Leigh Dirk steps out. She's in color, too. He still doesn't know what Ephebiphobia means, still can't read her, but remembers how she reduced him to a whimpering infant. She knocks at Mrs. Arnold's door and says, "You called to say the fugitive, Ridge, is here."

"He's a good boy. He always …"

"Was he accompanied by the girl, Isolde?"

"No. I haven't seen her for days."

"And the boy, Wenden?"

"Him neither."

"Where is Ridge?"

"He took off."

"When?"

"A minute or two ago. I don't know where he went."

"You realize the consequences of withholding information."

"Yes, ma'am."

Leigh Dirk nods to the two men. "Agents Olface, Lister—find him."

Ridge squirms towards the back of the trailer as fast as he can, watching the Transcenders as they unclip their nightsticks and turn in a slow circle, Olface/Olfaction's wide nose in the air, wrinkling, nostrils flaring, Lister/Listener with his head cocked.

Olface says, "He's close."

Lister adds, "Noise—under the trailer. Maybe an animal. Maybe …"

Ridge freezes.

They move along the trailer, peering under it. Ridge fits a stone into his slingshot. He scoots clear of the trailer and stands as they come around the back. Olface is in the lead, his cudgel raised above his head. Ridge fires at his face. The Transcender stops, swearing and clutching his nose. Lister keeps coming. Ridge turns and runs towards the woodpile. Just before he reaches it he falls to his hands and knees and tucks his head. Lister trips over him and crashes face first into the pile of logs. Ridge heads for the woods behind the trailer. Just before he reaches the shelter of the trees, he glances back. Leigh Dirk is standing at the corner of the trailer, watching him as she speaks into a radio. A patrol, four guards, has arrived. Still talking into her radio, she points the guards towards the back of the trailer. Ridge plunges into the forest. It rises steeply, wet and slippery with dead leaves, pine needles and mud underfoot. He comes up against a wall of rock that extends as far as he can see in each direction. He stops with his back to it. He hears heavy feet tramping through the woods towards him.

Then Leigh Dirk calls, "Agents Olface, Lister, wait. Agent Watch has sighted the boy, Wenden. He's near the Hinterlands Centre. That means the girl will be somewhere nearby. I need you to help find her. Agent Miso is waiting for us."

12

As Wenden jogged down the hill he heard Isolde start the jeep. He paused to listen until the sound of the engine grew faint and disappeared. At the foot of the hill he peered around the rocks beside the road. The guards and retrainees were a half mile ahead, about to disappear as the road wound around another mass of rock.

He missed Isolde already. She and Ridge were his only friends. It had started when his parents moved to the city and he found himself in a new school, insecure and timid, a target for a bunch of older kids who made fun of his tall, bulky awkwardness. He met their teasing with smiling attempts at ingratiation, until one day, suddenly, Ridge and Isolde were beside him, Isolde raging at them before Ridge moved in. For reasons Wenden never understood, Ridge became his protector. Although he was slight and not tall, there was something about him the older kids feared, something to do with his reputation for being always close to the edge, so that, if provoked, his retaliation might easily slip beyond the bounds of convention. Who else did Wenden need, as long as Ridge and Isolde were around?

But now he was separated from them, and he hadn't felt so alone for years.

He looked around the rocks again. The gang was out of sight. He followed, keeping close to the side of the road, all the time noting places to hide in case people or vehicles came along.

He tried to plan what he would do when the gang reached the woods. Should he follow all the way to the Centre, risk being seen, with patrols coming and going? How dense were the woods, anyway? Too thick to dive into if a patrol came along? Would Isolde be satisfied if he followed the gang just as far as the woods? But the guard at the river said they'd never find the Centre even if they got that far. He'd have to follow all the way, risk being caught and sent for retraining, and spending his days in a road gang like the one he was following now, never seeing Ridge or Isolde for months. He didn't think he'd survive. It was different for Ridge. He could handle stuff like that, Isolde, too. But Wenden knew he didn't have their courage and fortitude. He wished again he had the power to transcend, like his friends.

He followed the gang for an hour. The rocky landscape gave way to marshland that stretched away on both sides of the road, interrupted by occasional clumps of straggly trees. The only sound was the cawing of a flock of crows fussing in the tops of a stand of spruce ahead of him. He was on a straight road that ended at the wide swathe of woods that extended across his field of vision like a wall in the distance.

He was hanging far back from the gang, afraid of being spotted in the stark, open landscape. He stopped. A vehicle was emerging from the forest. He turned, looking for somewhere to hide, and saw a solitary figure in the distance behind him, walking in the middle of the road. He turned back. The vehicle—he could see now it was a patrol jeep—was passing the road gang. Wenden pushed into a low tangle of alders and sumac beside the road. The jeep drove past. Two crows detached themselves from the main flock and wheeled above him, squawking. The jeep stopped beside the lone figure. Peering from his hiding place, Wenden recognized the walker as the guard in the trench coat and dark suit and black stocking cap he and Isolde had seen with the gang. The jeep turned around and drove behind the guard as he continued his slow march. He stopped, scanning the landscape ahead, and pointed directly to where Wenden crouched in the trees. Wenden moved further from the road and flattened himself among the long stems of burdock and cowparsnip. The lone guard resumed his steady walk, the jeep still behind. He stopped again and pointed straight at Wenden. He was at least two hundred yards away. How could he see him? Wenden eyed the group of spruce trees. He thought he could make it safely there before the jeep or the guard caught up with him. He took off, splashing through the marsh. The crows erupted in the tops of the trees. The jeep picked up speed, overtook the lone guard, and stopped beside the stand of spruce. Two guards climbed out and stood in the road. Wenden flattened himself against a tree. He peered around it. The crows had settled down. The spruce were thick between his hiding place and the road. He willed himself into stillness, sure he was hidden. The lone guard stopped and pointed the other guards directly towards Wenden. The copse wasn't big, but offered plenty of places to hide. Enough, he thought, for him to keep moving and hidden and frustrate their search until they grew tired of it, or until it grew dark and he could make his getaway. He moved sideways and threw himself down, flattening himself among wild rhododendron. Peered out. The lone guard's arm and pointing finger had moved with him. The two guards were entering the trees, checking back all the time and following the directions of their colleague. Wenden retreated further into the woods, moving to his right. The lone guard's arm swung with him. It was impossible to hide. What would Ridge do? Transcend, of course. It was time for him to do the same. Wenden closed his eyes in concentration, willing himself to be confident, to believe he could elude capture, continue to follow Ridge, lead Isolde to him, not let them down.

Who would he be in Colorland?

He opened his eyes.

Ridge and Isolde said everything was grey when you transcended, but the only grey now was the sky. The rhododendron was green, its flowers dull purple. The spruce needles were green, the spruce cones brown, and the marsh mud was black, like the uniforms of the two guards approaching through the trees. Wenden decided if he couldn't hide, he could at least run. Self-respect demanded something more than capitulation. He waited until the guards were almost on him before leaping up and barreling between them. He raced for the road. The guard in the dark suit was still there, nightstick in hand, no longer pointing. He had protruding eyes, a tiny nose that seemed little more than two hairy openings in the middle of his face, and ears that seemed to recede into the side of his head. Wenden tried to run past him.

He came round in the jeep. He was lying on the back seat. His forehead felt wet. He touched it. Sticky, too. He looked at his fingers. Blood. The two guards were in front. He wondered where the third one, the one in the suit, had got to. He sat up and looked around. The dense woods were only a few hundred yards ahead.

The guard in the passenger seat turned and threatened, "I'll taser you if you try anything."

Wenden looked at the road behind and the other added, "If you're wondering why our colleague isn't with us, it's because he's staying out here to look for your girlfriend. And don't think he won't find her."

The jeep slowed as it entered the woods. The driver negotiated a series of intersections, sometimes turning, other times going straight through. Wenden tried to remember the route, but gave up after the first few turns. The jeep slowed as it passed the road gang Wenden was supposed to be following. He scrutinized the faces of the retrainees. Ridge wasn't among them. Maybe he wasn't even here, or he'd been transferred. Maybe the whole quest had been futile from the start.

The jeep entered a fenced compound, passed three interconnected low buildings, and stopped at a fourth, smaller and separate.

The driver gestured at the door and told Wenden, "Inside."

Three men, all in trench coats and dark suits like the lone guard, lounged nearby. Two had bruised and bloodied faces. They watched him silently as he climbed from the jeep.

He opened the door. The room was bare except for a desk behind which a broad shouldered woman with short red hair sat, facing him. She wore a pale green trouser suit and looked as if she should be on her way to a home and school meeting, not sitting in a fenced compound in the middle of the woods. Two guards stood behind her. She smiled at Wenden. Rose and paced around him. He tensed, couldn't help cringing, expecting her to assault him.

She laughed and said, "You have been watching too much TV." She resumed her place behind the desk. "I am Leigh Dirk, Chief of Security for the City of Bayport. Are you a Transcender, like your friends?"

He shook his head.

"No. I did not think so. You are too unimaginative, too much a clod and a follower, are you not? Loyal, devoted and … not too bright. I wonder what they see in you." She looked him over. "You do not look like a delinquent. You look like a nice boy who obeys his parents, does his homework, goes to school and does not get in trouble unless he is led into it by his undesirable companions. A boy too weak to get in trouble by himself and too weak not to go along with the juvenile escapades of his friends. By the way, your friend, Ridge, is Ruthless, in name and action, in Colorland. Did you know that?"

Wenden nodded.

"And Isolde is Rage. Talking of whom, where is your girlfriend?"

"She's not my girlfriend."

"But you would like her to be, would you not? It is what you fantasize about, although you know a girl like her is way beyond your expectations. She is in all your wet dreams, is she not? And you like it when someone describes her as your girlfriend, because she is as close to a girlfriend as someone like you is likely to get, you with all the charm and charisma of a dishcloth. Do you think your friendship with Ridge would save you from his Ruthlessness if he discovered the sordid extent of your fantasies about Isolde?"

Wenden sometimes wondered the same thing. It was like Leigh Dirk could read his mind.

She went on, "Maybe you should be wary of both of them. Do you think they would not turn their Ruthlessness and Rage on you if you got in their way?" She leaned forward, her voice suddenly as grating as fingernails on a chalkboard. "Where is she?"

"Don't know."

"You are lying. You will do her a favor by telling me before I send my Agents out to find her. Agent Olface can detect the smell of human flesh from a mile away when he transcends, and he tells me the smell of a young girl is the easiest to detect, while Agent Lister will hear her if she as much as breathes anywhere near him, and Agent Watch will see her ... But of course you have already experienced Agent Watch's transcendent abilities. Then there is Agent Miso. In particular you might want to avoid him finding her. When he transcends he is Misogyny. Do you know what a misogynist is?"

Wenden remembered a language arts class on word origins. "Someone who—er—hates women."

"Well done! Maybe you are not as stupid as you look. Agent Miso hates women, and he hates young girls especially. What do you think will happen to Isolde if I am not there to, shall we say, rein him in when he finds her?" She stared at him, her eyes like lasers. "Where is she?"

What would be best? Tell Leigh Dirk where Isolde was, or risk the Transcenders tracking her down, hurting her? What would Isolde want him to do? What would Ridge expect?

He muttered, "I told you. I don't know."

She shook her head. "You stupid boy."

She fixed her eyes on him and suddenly he was back in grade two, Mr. White the teacher, lank hair and smelling of sweat and cigarettes. Wenden was in front of the class, had to spell night on the board. Wrote nit. The class erupting with laughter. Mr. White commenting, "We all know you have them but do you have to write about them, too?" More laughter. He didn't understand. Just that he was the object of derision and scorn. The class ended, but not the humiliation.

He hung his head, ashamed. He wanted to cry.

Leigh Dirk looked down at a paper on the desk and said abruptly, "You are wanted for causing a disturbance in the city, failing to obey guards of the International Security Executive who were acting on behalf of the city, assaulting the same guards, and assisting in the theft of a car owned by the city." She looked up. "I am not going to bother to ask you if you have anything to say for yourself. I will simply deliver the standard sentence of six months retraining. You may as well do it out here in the Hinterlands Centre, since you are already here."

One of the guards cleared his throat. "Excuse me, ma'am, but the boy's parents are Party members and guards, and are close to Mayor Glut."

"I know them. Their son's behavior is exactly what they expect of him. They will appreciate our efforts to discipline the boy. Take him out."

"Where shall we put him, ma'am?" the other guard asked.

"He can take the place of his friend, Ridge. He can have his cot, and his place on the road gang."

Wenden had managed to keep his face blank, with his eyes fixed on the wall behind Leigh Dirk as he tried not to betray his fear and dismay, but at the mention of Ridge he dropped his eyes to her.

She smiled again. "Yes. Your friend, Ridge, was here. You and the girl were on the right track. But you are too late. He has gone. He took off two nights ago, which means when he is arrested again his sentence will be doubled. And he soon will be arrested, if he has not been already, because even as I speak he is trapped against a rock face behind the girl's house in Bayport and is surrounded by my guards."

Wenden fought the wave of despair and futility that washed over him. Not only had he failed to find Ridge, and got himself arrested, but now Ridge was going to be at the Centre for a year, and Isolde was going to be arrested, too, and there was nothing he could do to warn her. What a total mess he'd made of everything.

"Take Retrainee #010857 out," Leigh Dirk told the guards.

There was a knock at the door and a guard appeared. "Excuse me, ma'am. We've just heard from Agent Watch. He has the girl in sight. Do you want him to arrest her?"

"Tell him to wait, and tell Agent Miso and the others to get out there."

"Ma'am."

Leigh Dirk smiled at Wenden as she added to the guard, "And tell Agent Miso he is to be the first to apprehend her."

13

Four guards moving in, one each side of him, two in front. He looks behind at the sheer rock face. He's already tried to find a way around it, twice has tried to climb it, twice has fallen. No point in trying again. He's trapped near the remnants of a cabin. The forest floor is strewn with slabs of rotting wood, rusty nails, pieces of material, curtains, bedding.

One of the guards calls, "Do yourself a favor, boy. Give yourself up. That's better than making us arrest you, maybe hurt you, isn't it? One of your friends is already at the Hinterlands Centre, and your girlfriend's about to join him. The three of you can do your six months at the Centre together. The time will soon pass, and you'll have one another for company."

Ridge doesn't answer. Through the trees he can see the guards climbing the steep slope towards him. No Transcenders among them. He can't use his sling because the trees are too thick for him to get a line on the guards. He picks up a length of wood. A weapon? It crumbles in his hand. He throws it away. It would be useless against the guards' tasers, anyway. He eyes another piece of wood, a wide board, maybe a floor board. One end is slightly raised where it lay against the rock face. Two rusty nails protrude from it, one each side.

He calls to the guards, "Please don't hurt me."

At the same time he grabs a scrap of material and tears a strip from it. He tests its strength.

The guard who called before says, "We don't want to hurt you, boy. That's why we're asking you to give yourself up."

Ridge folds the scrap of material in two for strength and ties it to the nails so that it stretches across the board. He thrusts his toe under it. Exerts pressure. Thinks it will hold. Surveys the trees, the spaces between them, the best route through them. Eyes the forest floor, the dead leaves, the pine needles, the mud. Should be slippery enough.

He calls, "Do you want me to come down to you?"

The guard calls, "Stay where you are. We promise not to hurt you." He calls to his colleagues, "Hear that, guys? Turn off tasers."

Ridge moves the board so the front overhangs the steepest part of the slope. He shifts his weight on the board. Braces his other foot behind it, against the rock.

The guards move in, still one each side, two in front. The lead guard is only six feet away, the second another six feet behind. The other two are concentrating on keeping their footing on the steep slope. The lead guard looks at Ridge's feet and frowns.

Ridge pushes off with his back foot. The board slides forwards. The lead guard jumps aside, slips and falls. The next stands directly in Ridge's path, holding his hand up like a traffic cop. He manages, "Stop, or I'll ..." before the board slams into his shins. He stumbles. Ridge pushes him aside and is off, slaloming through the trees. He has a fleeting glimpse of the other guards as he sails between them. The board comes to rest at the log pile. Ridge jumps from his makeshift snowboard. He hears the guards slithering through the trees behind him. Looks back as one falls and cracks his head against a rock and another slips and crashes into a tree. Two keep coming. One stumbles the last few yards down the slope and his momentum carries him into the woodpile. The other slithers to a stop, arms held wide for balance. He looks up as Ridge hurls the board at him like a frisbee. It whirls into his neck. He splutters and falls, gagging. Ridge runs to the road. No sign of Leigh Dirk and the Transcenders.

Mrs. Arnold is backing out of her driveway. Ridge jumps in her car.

"I'm going shopping, dear," she said. "Can I give you a ride somewhere?"

She dropped Ridge in the subdivision where the trail to his mother's cabin started. He'd thought of asking her to drive him out of the city but was afraid of landing her in trouble and anyway he needed supplies.

He was going to be on the road again, out to the Hinterlands, to free Isolde.

He'd been on the trail for only a few minutes when he saw two guards ahead of him. One was stuck in oozing mud like quicksand, the other trying to pull him out. Ridge stole through the undergrowth until he was close to them, then ran up behind them and pushed the rescuer in the mud with his partner. He ran on.

Meru was in the cabin. She cowered as he opened the door.

He said, "What's going on?"

"My aunt reported me. She said it was for my own good and the guards were already on their way. So I ran back here. I don't think they followed me. Did they?"

Ridge nodded.

She bit her lip. "Sorry."

He said, "They'd have been after me, anyway. I had a bit of a run in with them, too."

He grabbed a backpack and stuffed it with food, warm clothes, a blanket, matches in a waterproof container, money from his mother's emergency stash in the tin over the sink. He was sure she'd understand. Through the front window he saw a patrol coming up the driveway. He glanced out the back window and saw the guards he'd left in the mud approaching through the trees. He lifted the rug that lay in front of the couch, revealing a trapdoor. He raised it, explaining, "Ma's uncle used to store stuff in the crawl space under the cabin. Mum and me turned it into a drainage ditch. Follow me. Keep flat."

He felt the flutter in his eyes that signaled he was about to transcend but fought off the urge. It was tempting to cross over again, but he wanted to try and scour the exhilarating memory of his last transcendence from his mind before doing it again. He didn't want to get hooked on the adrenalin thrill of it, get stuck in Colorland without Isolde. Anyway, maybe it was just as well he didn't cross over just now. At least he wouldn't be tempted to leave Meru behind.

They lowered themselves into the hole. Ridge closed the trapdoor behind them, first adjusting the rug so it would cover it as it closed. They squirmed to where the floor ended and the ditch went under the veranda.

They heard an order from the front of the cabin. "The girl, Meru! Show yourself!"

The guards from the marsh stepped onto the veranda. One shouted, "The boy's in there, too."

Ridge and Meru slithered on, Ridge dragging his backpack behind him. They made it under the veranda and started across the yard, hidden by the long, thick grass that overhung the ditch.

The cabin door opened. An eruption of voices. "Not inside ... Not out front ... Form a line and make a wide sweep through the yard and down to the river."

It was slow progress slithering along the narrow trough past rocks and roots and a dead porcupine. They heard the guards behind them tramping through the yard and into the tangle of growth, alders and redroot, panic grass and sedge, bayberry and manna-grass, which lay between the cabin and the river. They reached the exposed section of bank. The guards were getting closer. Ridge pushed the backpack into the river, slipped in after it, and turned to support Meru as she slid in after him, head first. He noted the incoming tide and the stiff breeze blowing upriver. Both would be in their favour. Staying hidden in the shelter of the bank, they swam upriver as the guards poured from the trees.

14

It was like school, but worse. The boring lectures. The handouts to be studied. The fill-in-the-blank tests. The physical exercises, as useless and mindless as phys. ed. He didn't mind the uniform, although red wasn't his favorite color. He'd have preferred something less conspicuous, didn't feel red was in keeping with his personality, but it was loose and comfortable, except for the belt, and it felt good to have a clean set of clothes. He didn't mind being called #010857. He'd been called plenty of worse names. The food was okay and there was lots of it.

Wenden didn't go out the first two days. Instead he was assigned odd jobs at the Centre, cleaning washrooms and showers, sweeping the dormitories, preparing food. On the third day, after the morning lectures and worksheets and exercises, he was marched to the Control Unit where Leigh Dirk told the guard accompanying him, "Send him out on the road."

The guard protested, "But the girl is still on the loose."

"Exactly," said Leigh Dirk. She looked at Wenden and smiled. "You can be the bait for your friend. And we are not going to have any trouble from you, are we?"

Wenden sought for a retort to deflect the humiliation of being considered so submissive and unthreatening but came up with nothing.

She patted his cheek. "Of course you are not."

For a week he went out on the road, and to his surprise found he didn't mind it. The work wasn't too arduous, and he'd always liked walking in the countryside, and the guards who accompanied his gang were friendly and considerate. All in all, he thought he could tolerate living at the Centre for six months, except that Isolde haunted him. She always had, but this was different. He saw her everywhere, her face peering through the pampas grass beside the road, her slender silhouette among the trees on a hillside, her lithe figure disappearing across a field. Sometimes he thought she was real, daydreamed she was watching over him, but knew, if she was real, she would be searching not for him but for Ridge, still believing he was at the Centre. He wished he could get a message to her to let her know Ridge had escaped, was on the run like her. At the same time a guilty part of him was glad she didn't know. If she knew Ridge had escaped, and she found him, would they take off together, abandoning Wenden? He knew their bond superseded their friendship with him. They were rock and lichen, burnover and fireweed, Ken and Barbie.

Every morning he watched the Transcenders leave the compound in search of her at the same time as the road gangs set out. At first he feared for her, but after a few days decided she'd found a way of eluding them, although he couldn't imagine how.

On the Monday of his third week at the Centre, it was his turn to haul the cauldron of hot blacktop. It had rained heavily overnight, and as the gangs set out, a guard hurried from the Control Unit and told the lead guard of Wenden's gang, "There's a washout on the main road to the city, ten miles out. Take gang 6 and fix it. All traffic has been ordered to halt for the day."

The gangs set off through the forest. The Transcenders were standing at the end of the access road. Agent Olface had his nose in the air, Agent Lister his head cocked.

Olface stopped Wenden's gang and said sharply to the lead guard, "I thought all traffic was stopped."

"Correct, sir."

"But something's moving. I can smell it." He sniffed the air again. "One of ours. A patrol jeep."

Lister added, "And I hear it."

Agent Miso sauntered up to Wenden. He loomed over him. He had a long face and a drooping moustache and bad teeth. "You and the girl stole a jeep. What did you do with it?"

Wenden shrugged. "Abandoned it when it ran out of gas."

"You're lying," Miso scoffed. He looked back at the other Transcenders. "The girl's using it. That's how she's getting away from us. That's how she got away from you, Watch, when you had her in sight weeks ago."

"She ran so fast …"

"… Back to the stolen jeep and took off in it. By the time we arrived you and Lister and Olface couldn't detect it because of all the other jeeps out there looking for her."

"And I still couldn't detect it before now because of all the traffic moving in and out of the Centre," Olface added.

"So the girl drives here in the jeep, hides it, comes looking for her friends, then uses it to take off when we get close to her," said Watch.

"But not today," said Miso.

"We still have to find her," Watch pointed out.

"We have to find the jeep," Lister corrected him. "Then we just wait for her."

Olface raised his nose in the air. "The jeep is south west. About fifteen miles."

The lead guard said, "That's near where this gang is headed."

Olface said triumphantly, "She's parked somewhere on the other side of the washout, and she'll be heading through the woods towards the Centre right now. We'll pretend we're guards with this gang, in case she's watching, and when we get out there I'll lead you to the stolen jeep. We'll surround it and wait for her." He looked at Miso. "Then you can move in."

A three hour march took the gang to the washout, where a small, fast flowing stream had overflowed with the downpour and forced a passage across the road. As the retrainees set about filling the crevice, retrieving the road base of rocks from the ditch where the stream had deposited them, and collecting more rocks from the roadside on each side of the washout, Olface and Lister continued on foot. They returned an hour later. Wenden was changing the propane tank. The other retrainees were filling the washout. The guards were talking with Miso and Watch.

Olface called, "The jeep's where I thought it would be, tucked in a woods road, five miles ahead. The girl's been there within an hour or two. She's probably snooping around the Centre now. That doesn't matter. We'll hide in the woods and wait."

Miso told the lead guard, "Inform Leigh Dirk. Then accompany us and liaise with her."

"But the gang, sir ..."

"... Will be in the capable hands of your colleague, who has the monitor for the retrainees' stun belts, as well as his taser." He looked at the rear guard. "Right?"

"Yes, sir."

The Transcenders and the lead guard crossed the half repaired washout and moved off down the road. The gang resumed work.

The rear guard said, "Don't knock yourselves out, boys. We've got all day."

Wenden adjusted the flame.

What could he do? He was going to let Isolde down again. Let her walk into a trap. Images flooded his mind. Isolde surrounded. Held by the Transcenders. Approached by an angry Agent Miso. Wenden daydreamed of what he would do, how he would rescue her, if he had the nerve and the confidence. If he was like Ridge.

The afternoon wore on. The gang finished filling the hole in the road and lined up at the cauldron with their shovels, ready to scoop out the hot blacktop and throw it over the gravel. Wenden tipped the cauldron, which hung in an iron cradle, so the retrainees could scoop out the steaming black guck.

When the road was sealed the guard ordered the gang to form up for the march back to the Centre.

Wenden, at the end of the line, bent over the propane tank.

The guard sauntered over, his hands in his pockets. "What's the problem?"

"The collar's jammed. I can't shut it off."

"Let's have a look."

The guard laid his taser and the belt monitor beside him on the road and kneeled by the propane tank. As he worked at it he asked, "Are you worrying about your friend?"

Wenden nodded and asked mildly, "Why don't you let me go and help her?"

The guard looked up. "Sorry, my friend. I'd like to, but you know I can't."

His refusal was all it took. It was something to do with the way the resignation and hopelessness of it mirrored Wenden's own shameful helplessness. Suddenly the anger that had been smouldering since Leigh Dirk's contemptuous dismissal of him flared, tipping him into action. He felt a fluttering sensation in his eyes. Color drained from the guard, and the retrainees, and the landscape, and the cauldron. Sounds, wind in the trees, birdsong, chock chock of a retrainee's shovel tapping the road, chatter of a squirrel, receded.

He blinked twice.

The guard, still looking up at him, said, "Are you okay?"

So this is Colorland.

And this is who he really is. He should have known, of course. It's a relief to discover the power and authority and confidence and daring, all the things he lacked on the other side, have been there all the time, if latent. It's heady, like his first drink of alcohol. He understands what Ridge and Isolde mean when they say you can get hooked on going to Colorland.

The guard, taser and belt monitor laid aside, is still looking up at Wenden, who tips the hanging cauldron. Hot blacktop pours over the guard's face. He gasps. Screams. His hands fly to his face. Wenden takes his keys. He knows which one unlocks the stun belts. Like Ridge, he's noticed it when his belt is unlocked at shower time. He releases his stun belt and wraps it around the guard, who is thrashing on the ground. He takes the belt monitor. He's seen the guards use it, knows its controls. Turns the dial to General

Administration and presses the firing button. He can't afford to have the retrainees running around the countryside alerting the Centre that something's up. They buckle and fall one after the other like a collapsing house of cards as the current surges through them. The guard twitches and groans. Wenden takes his radio. Surveys the scene. Nods, satisfied.

As color and sound seep back into the world, he sets off jogging in the direction taken by the Transcenders in their mission to trap Isolde.

He is Devotion.

He stopped, appalled. Looked back and surveyed his work. Bodies sprawled, contorted, twitching, flailing. He had to incapacitate the guard, but did he really have to pour hot blacktop in his face? Was it really necessary to stun the retrainees? A distant voice in his head said yes, he couldn't risk them pestering him, wanting to accompany him, slowing him down. He remembered Isolde asking if he really wanted to know who he was, and what he was capable of. He thought of all the times Ridge had defended him, the bloody noses, black eyes, cut lips inflicted on Wenden's behalf. Wenden had always been grateful, while ashamed of his own cowardice and placidity and willingness to appease and endure, but had never considered what it cost Ridge. Had his friend felt the kind of remorse and guilt Wenden felt now, every time he'd defended him?

The retrainees were regaining strength and control, some sitting up. The guard had pulled himself to his knees but still held his hands to his face. Wenden turned and jogged away as fast as he could. After five minutes he was gasping for breath. He slowed and settled into alternate running and walking, one hundred paces each. He had the guard's radio in his hand, listening as he travelled. Mostly queries about the road washouts from traffic wanting to head out to the Centre, and routine checking in by patrols.

Then: "Control to road gang 6."

Wenden's gang.

No response, of course.

The message again. This time Wenden recognized Leigh Dirk's voice: "Control to road gang 6."

No response again.

Then Leigh Dirk: "Patrol 15. Proceed immediately to the old city road, ten miles out. Locate gang 6 working there. Approach with caution. There may be a problem."

Wenden increased his pace. He estimated he'd travelled at least five miles. He stopped, listening. Turned the radio low. Listened again. No sound except the breeze in the trees and the chatter of a squirrel and … something more. Distant voices. One familiar. He felt his eyes flutter as he concentrated on the sound.

Color drains from the landscape. His hearing is more acute, tuned as it is for that one particular voice.

"You don't scare me."

For Isolde to say, You don't scare me, something, or someone, is seriously scaring her.

He trots cautiously on, suddenly finding a second wind. He rounds a corner and sees a woods road on his left. Turns into it. Rounds two bends, walking slowly, peering ahead.

Freezes. Ducks behind a juniper bush.

The stolen jeep is parked facing into the woods, Isolde standing at the front, her back to Wenden.

White skin of her neck, faded blue of her torn jeans, tan jacket, chestnut hair, dull silver of the butterfly ring on her finger.

She's with him—in Colorland.

Agent Miso and his comrades surround her, their nightsticks in hand. Miso stands in front of her, more than a head and shoulders taller. Olface and Watch are on each side of the jeep, Lister at the back. The guard from the road gang stands to one side.

Olface orders her, "Get in the back seat. Miso will ride beside you and make sure you behave. You'll have to hope he behaves himself, too."

They all laugh.

Wenden, listening, remembers Leigh Dirk saying—Agent Miso hates women, and hates young girls especially. He resists the urge to rush in.

Miso says, "I'm sure the young lady will cooperate."

He stretches his hand toward Isolde, to pat her cheek. She bats his hand away. He slaps her, sending her reeling sideways, clutching at the jeep for support.

Wenden moves silently into the cover of the trees, still watching. He comes to a small pond. Leigh Dirk's voice sounds over the radio Wenden took from the rear guard. He turns it to maximum volume. Leigh Dirk's voice crackles through the forest.

"Where are you, Patrol 15?"

Wenden places the radio at the edge of the pond. He selects a strong sapling which is growing bent low, pulls it back as far as he can, and sits among a growth of young pines, holding it. He can see through the trees to the jeep.

Watch and the others are looking at one another, frowning.

Leigh Dirk, her voice more urgent: "Patrol 15. What's going on?"

"Patrol 15, Ms. Dirk. Still seeking road gang 6. We're ... Whoa ... Found them. They're in a mess. Guard and retrainees sitting around."

The lead guard calls from beside the jeep, "Who's there? Identify yourself."

Watch tells him, "Take a look."

The guard makes his way slowly through the trees towards Wenden. He comes to the edge of the pond and sees the radio.

Leigh Dirk's voice sounds from it. "Patrol 15. Update, please."

The guard calls, "Someone's left a radio here."

He bends to pick it up. Wenden releases the sapling. It springs back, slamming into the guard. He cries out as he pitches into the pond.

The radio blares, "Patrol 15 here. We found one guard down, face a mess, badly burned. All retrainees accounted for except one. Fallen guard indicated direction escapee took. We're in pursuit."

The Transcenders turn to look in the direction of the guard's cry. The moment they look away, Isolde whirls around, leaps onto the hood of the jeep, scrambles over it into the front seat, starts the engine. Miso leaps on the hood. Watch gets one foot in the passenger side. Olface reaches in the jeep and grabs Isolde's arm. She rams the gear into reverse and floors the accelerator. Lister jumps clear as the jeep lurches backwards. Miso is thrown off.

Watch is spun around and sent sprawling across the dirt road. Olface is dragged along for a few yards, hanging on to Isolde's arm, before he releases her.

The jeep disappears around the first bend in the woods road, still in reverse.

Leigh Dirk's voice sounds from the radio in the woods: "Status report, Patrol 15."

"Stolen patrol jeep ahead, ma'am. Came from woods road at speed, in reverse, headed north. We're in pursuit."

Olface, listening, snarls, "Lister and me will check this out. You two get after the girl."

Wenden watches as Miso and Watch set off at a run down the woods road, while Olface and Lister start towards where he lies hidden.

Olface stops, scanning the woods, his nose lifted, and calls, "Good afternoon, #010857. Who would have thought you had the nerve and initiative to pull off a stunt like that? I wonder how Leigh Dirk will express her disappointment in you when we take you in."

15

The water was about six inches below the level of the bank. The houses and factories they had looked up at as they started swimming had given way to open sky and trees that overhung the river. Ridge estimated they had been in the water for at least three, maybe four, hours. More and more often Meru was having to stop and rest, clinging to clumps of grass that hung from the bank. It was getting dark and they were swimming against the current because the incoming tide didn't reach this far upriver.

He grabbed a tussock of grass with one hand and Meru with the other. She was shivering. Her lips were puckered and her olive skin had turned blotchy white. She'd wanted to stop over an hour ago but Ridge, fearing guards would be watching the river and patrolling the banks, had insisted they get clear of both the city and the outskirts. Four times before they reached a stretch of shallows that prevented vessels going further upriver they'd had to hide in reeds as patrol boats nosed slowly past.

"I'm going to haul myself up and look over the bank," said Ridge. "Hold on so you don't start drifting downstream."

He pulled himself up slowly until he could see over the bank. Trees lined both sides of the river, meadows beyond. He threw the backpack onto the bank, water streaming from it. He climbed after it and pulled Meru up. She sank down in the grass. He stood and looked around. No sign of people, no buildings in sight. He knelt beside her. She was shivering violently.

He pulled her to him, trying to stop her shivering, and said, "You have to rub yourself down thoroughly."

"Why?"

"Red bloom algae grows in this river and some people react to it. Rubbing yourself down helps prevent it."

"What about you?"

"I'm immune. Is and me have been swimming in the river since we were kids and have never got it."

"What shall I rub myself down with? Everything we have is wet."

"Use your clothes. Doesn't matter that they're wet. Just rub hard. Then roll in the grass to dry off as best you can."

"I'm cold."

"I'll get a fire going. We'll spend the night here."

While Meru stripped and rubbed herself down he hung everything from the backpack in the trees. Then he gathered windfall branches for kindling and found the matches in their watertight container. He started a fire and went in search of larger boughs. When he returned, Meru sat huddled close to the flames, her arms wrapped around her knees. She was still shivering. He hung her clothes beside his in a tree. He built the fire up and went in search of evergreen boughs to use in place of a blanket. He banked the fire as high as he dared and they lay close to it. He pulled the boughs over them and she wrapped her arms and limbs around him. She felt as small and frail and brittle as a child.

She murmured, "Will Isolde mind us being like this?"

"It's the only way we're going to survive. She'd understand."

"But us spending the night like this, and her being your girlfriend."

"Isolde's not my girlfriend."

"What is she then?"

"She's … Isolde."

They lay in silence for a while.

Then Meru asked, "What shall we do in the morning?"

"We'll set off for the Hinterlands Centre. I think I remember the way."

"What d'you want to go back there for?"

"Is and Wenden are somewhere out there. I heard Leigh Dirk tell the guards who were coming after me."

She giggled. "Seems strange, us getting out of there, and then heading straight back."

"You don't have to come."

"I want to," she said quickly. "Where else would I go, anyway?"

He realized she had stopped shivering, and said, "You're getting warm at last. Try and sleep."

As soon as Ridge woke he knew the river fever had invaded Meru. She was sprawled across him and he could feel her shivering at the same time as her body was slick with sweat. He eased himself from under her and fed kindling to the embers of the fire. He didn't know how close they were to a road and worried the smoke would be visible to a passing patrol, but she needed warmth, and the blanket and her clothes dry. He dressed—his clothes were still damp but they'd have to do—and gathered more windfall to stoke the fire. He held the blanket over it until it steamed. He knelt beside her. She was breathing in shuddering gasps and her hair was as wet as when she climbed from the river the night before. He pulled the boughs aside and laid the blanket over her.

She opened her eyes.

He said, "It's still damp but it's better than nothing." He pulled the boughs over the blanket.

"I got the river fever, didn't I?" she said.

He nodded.

"What will it do to me?"

"Usually people get welts, and a sore throat and itchy eyes, and a fever, and maybe vomiting and diarrhea, could be both, depends how much water you took in."

He didn't say that sometimes the fever paralyzed arms and legs.

"How long will it last?"

"About 24 hours, but you won't feel like travelling for at least another day after that."

"You better get going, then. I said I wouldn't slow you down."

"I'm not leaving you."

"You are."

"I couldn't, even if I wanted to."

"You could—if you got yourself in that head space you were in when we broke out of the Centre, when you got like you were possessed."

"Still couldn't."

"Wrong. You nearly left me when we were by the fence in the compound, but I came round and you snapped out of it just in time to stop yourself—remember?"

He remembered.

She smiled. "I could tell what was going on in your head."

"I'm not leaving you here," he insisted.

"Think of Isolde—in trouble ..."

"No."

"... In danger, guards closing in on her ..."

"I'm not listening."

"She'd put up a fight, wouldn't she? So they'd taser her, or grab her, throw her down, hold her down ..."

Ridge's eyes fluttered.

Meru is grey. Color drains from the grass around her and from the trees and the river. His consciousness narrows to one goal, the rescue of Isolde, and no longer can he let Meru slow him down. He should have left her in the dormitory, or at the fence in the compound. He should have left her when she led the guards to the cabin. If it hadn't been for her, he would have been clear of the city without having to swim up the river and waste a night and half a morning fussing over her because she got the river fever. She'd have an unpleasant couple of days but she'd get over it.

Just before he's completely crossed over into Colorland, he leans close and says, "I'm sorry."

Her voice comes from a distance, muffled. "No need. You don't owe me anything. I owe you. You got me out of the Centre, and you rescued me from the city when I had no-one else to go to. And ... and I've loved being with you."

He grabs his pack and sets off across the field.

He is Ruthless.

Later that day, a fugitive from the city, like Ridge and Meru, flagged down a passing patrol and said, "I saw a fire last night, smoke this morning. I'll tell you where if you reduce my sentence."

16

Isolde had been on the run for six weeks, surviving on early hazelnuts and choke cherries, wild apples and gooseberries and elderberry. She begged from the occasional lonely farm house, hoping the occupants wouldn't betray her to the guards. She found corn growing wild, stole carrots and potatoes from rare fields still under cultivation and ate them raw. She slept wrapped in the quilt from the warehouse hideout, pulling ferns and grass and boughs over her when she was in the open. She was glad the nights were warm. She thought it was July.

She spent her days running across marsh and field and fighting her way through woods. Every time she thought she'd lost her pursuers they turned up again. She'd had time to read the Transcenders when they ambushed her, knew they had the power to track her through smell and sight and sound. She was exhausted from the constant flight and from all the times she'd had to transcend in order to escape. She knew she was at the limit of the energy and concentration she needed to cross over, was more and more tempted to give in to the temptation of staying in Colorland.

She'd driven as far and as fast as she could away from the ambush in the woods. If the jeep that had appeared in the distance behind her as she shot from the woods road hadn't stopped to wait for Agents Miso and Watch she never would have got away. Ten miles down the road the stolen jeep had begun to splutter. She slowed and jumped out, leaving it to continue on its way until it ran completely out of gas or ran itself off the road. Either way, she hoped it would lead her pursuers at least a short distance from where she was starting out on foot. She'd struck out across the fields, with no plan other than first to escape, and then to return and resume her search for Ridge.

She'd spent the night beside a muddy river, the banks of which were slick with grey clay. There was a thick stand of fir between her hiding place and the road which she'd thought would give her time to escape across the river if—when—they caught up with her again. During the night, a fox had disturbed her as it made its way along the bank, dragging a trap behind it. She'd pinioned the trap with a branch with the intention of freeing the fox, but then had staked the trap instead, leaving the fox captive.

She'd woken before dawn to the sound of jeeps, three, she thought, moving slowly along the road. She heard them slow and stop, and a few seconds later Agent Olface's voice. "She's close. Follow me."

She heard her pursuers making their way into the trees. She stood over the trap and urinated on the fox. Then she freed it. It bolted along the bank.

A few seconds later she heard Olface again. "I smell her. She's making a run for it. Heading east."

She heard them moving away and thought she'd bought a few minutes of safety. She was about to cross the river when she heard, "Through here. I see her."

Agent Watch.

He, with Olface and Lister, had followed her every move since the ambush, leading the guards relentlessly after her. She was familiar now with the enhanced abilities they had when they transcended, and how they used them. Watch would have detected her because for him the color of her clothes and skin was like a beacon in the uniform green of the trees. She stepped from the grassy bank into the wet clay and writhed in it, covering her body and her clothes with it, careful to obscure the shine of the butterfly ring, which daily felt looser on her finger. Then she reached for a patch of dry clay and scratched a handful, as fine as dust, into her palm. She lay still as Watch reached the river at the head of a troop of guards. He stood, peering around. She was grey on grey, tucked in close to the bank, almost under it. He opened his eyes wide as he scanned the river and the river bank for her. She rose and threw the clay dust in his face. He groaned, pawing at his eyes. As the guards clustered around him, she slid through the clay and started swimming. She was nearly across the river before they turned their attention from their stricken leader to her. She scrambled out on the other side and ran into the cover of the trees. She'd thought, with Olface diverted and Watch temporarily blinded, and the river preventing pursuit by the jeeps, she could get clear of them, but Lister and Miso had been close behind.

Lister plunged into the river after her, while Miso told the guards, "There's a ford half a mile up the road. Get the jeeps and cross there. The rest of you—follow me." And he plunged into the river, too.

She ran across one field. Glanced back. They were climbing from the river. She crossed another field. They were still coming, gaining on her. She made it half way across the next field before collapsing, exhausted, unable to transcend, unable to flee any further. She didn't know how she could escape them and she was too tired to try any more. She knew they were close behind her, knew she couldn't do anything about it.

She closed her eyes.

She felt herself being lifted. She assumed it was one of her pursuers and was surprised but grateful he was holding her so gently. Probably she should struggle but she was too tired.

She heard, "Put your hands around my neck and hold on."

A woman's voice, deep and husky, slow and halting, as if carefully considering every word before uttering it. She didn't know if she'd fallen asleep or had passed out. She wondered whether she was dreaming. She obeyed, and felt herself being carried at speed over fields and streams and marshes, heard the rhythmic fall of her captor's feet like horses' hooves but with a rhythm of two beats instead of four.

Da-dop. Da-dop. Da-dop.

She fell asleep, or passed out, again, wondering who, or what, was carrying her so effortlessly and so fast.

When she came round, she found herself looking into soft brown eyes. She was lying on a bed of straw in what seemed to be a cave. The woman leaning over her had a wide nose, thick lips, and a long face that ended in a broad, square chin.

Isolde struggled to rise but the woman pushed her gently down by the shoulders, saying, "You are safe. We are in one of my hideouts. Your pursuers are far behind and will not find us here. Rest now. We have a long way to travel."

When Isolde woke again—she thought it was early morning—the woman was sitting beside her and told her, "Chew on this. It is wild asparagus. It will feed your thirst and your hunger. There are dried poppy leaves under your bed that will help you sleep." She supported Isolde with an arm round her shoulders while she ate. Isolde could feel the muscle of her arm through the rough serge of her brown tunic.

As Isolde felt her eyes closing and her mind shutting down, she murmured, "Who are you?"

"I am Speed," the woman said.

17

Fifty miles east, Wenden stumbled from the overgrown gravel pit in which he'd spent the night. He didn't know where he was. The dirt road he'd been travelling on for two days stretched in both directions as far as he could see.

He'd escaped from Olface and Lister by stepping into the open with his hands up, trying to look contrite, still in Colorland, as they approached.

"Sensible boy," said Agent Olface.

"Yes, sir," said Wenden.

He'd thrown himself between them, turned, and hurled himself, shoulder first, into Lister's back. The Transcender staggered into Olface, clutching at him for support. Meanwhile the guard was still struggling from the pond where the sapling had pitched him. As Olface and Lister collided with him, tipping them all into the water, Wenden blundered after Miso and Watch, his only thought to keep Isolde safe. But by the time he reached the end of the woods road, neither she nor the Transcenders were in sight, and only a lingering swirl of dust over the road indicated the direction in which they'd gone.

He'd run half a mile in that direction when he heard a jeep somewhere behind him. He'd just passed a cattle barn beside the road. He ran back to it and jumped in the partly filled manure alley. He heard the jeep pull up. He ran through the muck and buried himself in a pile of manure at the end of the barn, grabbing a length of cow parsnip growing beside it and using its hollow stem to breathe through. He heard footsteps approaching through the barn. Heard Lister say, "I don't see him," and Olface snarl, "But he was here. His smell is still in the air." After a few minutes the footsteps retreated, but Wenden stayed there for another hour. When he emerged, there was no sign of them, and he set off after Isolde, stopping only to immerse himself fully clothed in the first pond he encountered.

Since then he'd seen no-one as he wandered the Hinterlands, looking for her.

He wasn't gregarious by nature, counting only Isolde and Ridge as his friends, but he found his alone-ness unnerving. He talked and sang to himself as he wandered. Fancied himself by turn a drifting vagabond, destined to roam the back roads for the rest of his life, a medieval explorer, roaming the edges of the known world, a hermit crab scuttling across nameless undersea plains, an auk drifting over distant, lonely seas.

He grew excited when he encountered animals, feeling a kind of companionship with them. He kept a tally of the larger ones, one bear, three moose, one distant caribou, countless deer, a herd of wild horses, one lynx. He felt a special kinship with the lynx, knowing it to be solitary by nature.

He thought he'd never see Isolde or Ridge again, pictured himself friendless when life returned to normal, saw himself spending weekends in bed, sitting self-consciously alone in cafés, grocery shopping on Saturday nights, ultimately an old man sitting alone in a mall sipping cold coffee and pretending to read a forgotten newspaper.

Every night wherever he settled down he imagined himself in front of the television at home, his father dozing beside him, although inwardly he still railed at his parents for their rejection of him.

He dreamed of Isolde bathing in the river and woke guilty and wet.

Waking, he sorted his days into hourly segments, although he had no means of telling the hours—walk for an hour, search for water and food for an hour, rest for an hour, repeat, hour after hour, day after day.

At the end of six weeks—he thought it was six weeks—he gave up hope of catching up with Isolde, and began to retrace his steps, heading back towards the Hinterlands Centre. It was the only place he could think of where she might go, to continue her search for Ridge, when—if—she was safe from pursuit.

18

Isolde woke to the sound of approaching footsteps.

Da-dop. Da-dop. Da-dop.

Her memory of the previous evening and that morning was hazy. All she remembered was lying in the cave, and Speed bringing her food, and telling her she would sleep.

Speed appeared at the mouth of the cave.

Isolde tried to rise but her limbs wouldn't respond. She said, "I feel drugged."

"You are," said Speed. "I fed you a sedative of crushed black beech mushrooms. It was the only way of getting you to relax so that you could start to recuperate. The effects will last another two or three hours, but we should get going now."

"I thought we were safe here."

"We are, as long as we stay in the cave. But you will not regain your health and strength living in a dank and dark cell."

She slid her arms under Isolde and lifted her effortlessly.

Isolde murmured, "Where are you taking me?"

"To my home, another two days journey eastward."

"What are you doing so far from home?"

"Every year I travel in a wide circle around my home looking for different strains of root crops and herbs and fruit to add to the ones I grow."

Isolde felt herself falling asleep again as Speed carried her outside.

The next time she woke the sun was high and they were sitting in meadows that seemed to stretch around them forever.

"Where are we?" Isolde asked.

"The eastern prairies," said Speed.

"How did I get here?"

"I carried you."

"You *carried* me? What are you—some sort of Olympic athlete?"

"I was never actually in the Olympics, but I trained for them, as a runner."

"How come I never heard of you, or saw you on TV?"

"It was a secret programme. A group of us, all elite in our sports, were injected with hormones to turn us into super athletes."

"Isn't that illegal?"

"That is why it was secret. We were kept at an isolated research and training camp until an animal rights group broke in one night and freed us, thinking we were animals being experimented on, which I suppose we were. Everyone except me was quickly recaptured. I managed to get away and ever since I have been hiding out in the place where we are going."

"What were you injected with?"

"Hormones of animals that matched our special abilities. I was a long distance runner, so they injected me with the hormones of a horse, in the hope it would increase my strength and endurance and speed. It was successful, but the side effects were too obvious for us to compete."

"What side effects?"

"The way I speak."

"It just sounds careful, like maybe you're foreign."

"I am not foreign, but speech—human speech—became like a foreign language. And also—look at me. The hormones made me ugly. My appearance frightens people, so they laugh at me."

"I'd never laugh at you."

"But people less sensitive than you do laugh, especially men."

19

Ridge pulled the guard's uniform from his pack and changed into it.

He was in the woods beside the approach road to the Hinterlands Centre. He'd found two uniforms on his journey there after leaving Meru. They were washed up on the banks of the Black River. He had no idea how they got there and they were in poor shape but he'd managed to piece them together to make one outfit which he'd stuffed in his pack, thinking it might be useful.

It had taken him three weeks to reach the Centre. He thought he'd remember the way after the long drive there from the City when he was first sentenced, but it had taken him a long time to orientate himself from the place where he and Meru had climbed from the river, and even when he found the way, he'd had to detour constantly to avoid all the patrols and traffic that moved between Bayport and the Centre.

He thought often of Meru, wondered where she was. He thought she'd recover from the river fever, but where would she go, and how would she survive, alone in the Hinterlands? He'd left her with no advice on finding food and shelter, no plan of where she might go. He'd simply abandoned her. He remembered her frail body shivering under the pathetic coverings, her frightened eyes looking up at him, even as she urged him to leave. He told himself he'd done it only because he transcended, would have been incapable of abandoning her otherwise, and anyway she'd told him to leave her, had promised from the start not to slow him down, but it didn't help.

He'd spent another three weeks hiding in the woods around the compound and looking in vain for Isolde and Wenden in the road gangs as they passed him, before deciding the only way to find them was by getting into the Centre. He knew the layout of the compound. He had a plan to get in and didn't think getting out would be a problem. He'd done it before and could do it again, especially with Isolde and Wenden alongside him.

In his guard's uniform, he made his way cautiously through the trees to the access road. The gates of the compound were about two miles away, less than a half hour walk if he could remember the way on the narrow, twisting dirt roads, and through the maze of intersections. The gates were usually open during the day because all the retrainees were out with the road gangs, most of the guards with them. Once he was inside, he'd find somewhere to hide until the gangs, and Isolde and Wenden, returned.

He stepped into the road and marched as confidently as he could towards the Centre.

He'd gone only a few hundred yards when he heard movement in the woods behind him, then footsteps on the road, and a shout, "Guard! Wait!"

He kept going.

Another shout, "Guard, I asked you to wait."

He walked on, faster, hoping his uniform and confident manner would forestall the challenge. If they didn't, he'd stop and deal with his pursuer. He felt himself tense, felt his eyes flutter, knew he was about to transcend, anticipated the high of the adrenalin surge that would lift him above the ordinary. He risked a glance behind without slowing his pace. A young man, tall, raggedy and dirty, following him, waving. Ridge looked again. There was something familiar about the young man's heavy build and the rolling motion of his walk.

His pursuer called, "Excuse me, Guard."

Something familiar about the voice, too. Ridge stopped and turned slowly.

The young man started, "Would you please arrest me, Guard, because I'm guilty of ..." He stopped, his mouth open. "Well fuck."

Ridge muttered, "Jesus Christ," as the hefty figure flung his arms around him.

"Not Jesus Christ," said Wenden. "Just me."

Ridge, staggering backwards with the force of Wenden's embrace, said, "Where did you come from?"

"I don't know."

"What d'you mean—you don't know?"

"I don't know where I've been for the last few weeks, so I don't know where I've come from."

They scuttled into the trees at the sound of an approaching vehicle and watched as a patrol jeep went past.

Ridge looked around. Said sharply, "Where's Is?"

Wenden hung his head.

"I thought she was with you," Ridge went on. "I thought you were looking after her."

"I was. But we got separated while we were looking for you, and I got arrested and put in the Centre, and she must have been hanging around, still looking for you, as well as me, because one day four guards, special ones, nasty, too, called Miso and Olface and Watch and Lister ..."

"I know them."

"... Well they had her trapped, near where I was working with one of the road gangs, but she got away."

"How d'you know she got away?"

"I was there. I ran away from the road gang."

"To help her."

"Well—yeah."

"How d'you get away?"

Wenden shrugged. "Tipped hot blacktop on the guard. Electrocuted him with his belt. Ran off."

Ridge looked curiously at his friend. "I didn't think you had it in you."

"Me neither."

Wenden didn't say he'd electrocuted the retrainees as well as the guard. It wasn't an action he was proud of. He thought again of Isolde's warning: *Maybe you wouldn't like who you really are.*

Ridge was still looking at him. "You transcended, didn't you? You'd have to, to do something like that. So you finally made it to Colorland. Who are you?"

Wenden mumbled, "Devotion."

"Devotion to what—or who?"

Wenden felt his face coloring and said quickly, "How should I know?"

Ridge stared at him for a few seconds before going on, "So why are you trying to get yourself arrested now?"

"I tried to follow Is after she got away from Agent Miso and the others but I lost her. I guessed she'd come back here sooner or later, looking for you, but I can't find her, so I thought I'd get in the Centre, thinking maybe they'd caught up with her and she was back there. I wanted to make sure she was okay, then maybe find a way to get her out, but I'm not sure she's even in there."

"I've been watching the road gangs for days, looking for the both of you. Haven't seen Is. Thought I'd do better by getting inside, too."

"I thought you were in there already."

"I was. I escaped."

"How?"

"Long story." Ridge thought guiltily of Meru, alone in the Hinterlands. "I'll tell you later." He pretended to recoil from his friend. "Jesus, you smell."

"You're pretty ripe yourself."

Wenden looked Ridge up and down. "Nice outfit. How d'you get it?"

"Found it on the bank of the Black River."

Wenden laughed.

Ridge said, "What?"

"I'll tell you later."

"You've lost a shitload of weight," said Ridge. "What did you live on while you were wandering around the Hinterlands?"

"Nuts, berries, a few roots. Stuff Mr. Betts told us about in that Outdoor Pursuits course." He grinned. "Who ever would have thought we'd be grateful for something we learned in school?" Wenden thought of his days wandering alone. "I thought I'd never see you or Is again."

Ridge said, "Well now you've found me, let's break in the Centre, find Is."

"Wait up. I had another idea. Couldn't do it by myself, but now you're here, it might work. Before we look for Is in the Centre, where she might or might not be, let's look for Miso and his pals, maybe let them lead us to her. They'll still be looking for her, if she's not inside."

"But if we found them, how we gonna follow them?"

"We could steal a jeep."

"Yeah—right."

"Is and me did. Well—Is did."

Ridge grinned. "How'd she manage that?"

"Went crazy. Threatened the guards who were after us, made them strip, took their jeep, drove off like a maniac. Wouldn't let me drive, either."

"How come the guards left their jeep in the first place?"

"Told you—they were coming after us."

"That's what we need to do, then. Find a vehicle, somehow get the driver out, and steal it. But not a jeep, or anything belonging to the Centre. We don't want the guards to know something's going on. And we have to take it on its way from the Centre, not going to it, so if they're expecting it there, they don't start asking questions."

"How do we get the driver out, even if we manage to stop something?"

Ridge was silent for a few moments, thinking. Then he said, "Do you remember something else old Betts told us—about drinking the juice from dock leaves if you can't find water?"

Wenden laughed. "Yeah—you can drink it, but it'll make you want to pee—urgently—about five minutes later."

"Right," said Ridge thoughtfully.

20

"I have to get back," said Isolde.

"But you are happy here, are you not?"

"I'm very happy here."

"But you want to return to danger and, perhaps, loss, and unhappiness."

"Ridge will be looking for me, Wenden, too."

"This Ridge. He is special to you?"

Isolde shrugged. "He's ... Ridge."

Speed nodded sadly. "I am surprised it has taken you so long to decide. When shall we leave?"

"You don't have to come with me."

"I know that, but I will. I want to."

"You don't have to put yourself in danger for the sake of me and my friends."

"We are friends, too, are we not?"

"Of course."

"Then I will come, out of friendship. In any case, I cannot stand to see bullying and injustice. Also, it would take you two weeks to return to where I found you."

"And if you come with me?"

"Two days, maybe three."

They were on the veranda of the dilapidated farmhouse that was Speed's home. It was built with vertical boards, weather stained and grey. They were watching the sun go down across the rolling grassland that stretched away on all sides as far as Isolde could see. Speed had told Isolde how she stumbled across the ranch during her flight from the secret training facility and had watched it for a month before moving in, confident it was abandoned. She said she thought the land had once been used to rear and train horses.

"Appropriate, is it not?" she'd said bitterly.

Six weeks had passed since Speed carried Isolde there. Isolde had spent two weeks recovering from her days on the run, another two regaining her full strength, and another two training with Speed. They ate a vegetarian diet, everything grown, harvested and stored by Speed, potatoes, turnips, corn, peas, and carrots, supplemented by apples and berries Speed found growing wild.

Isolde had never seen so much sky. She spent hours watching the shifting patterns of clouds, weather systems approaching, sometimes passing in the distance, so that while she sat in sunshine she might watch a cloudburst across the plain.

Every morning Speed disappeared for two hours while she made a circuit of the borders of the ranch, making sure there was no sign of intrusion. She said no-one could approach the house without being visible for at least an hour as they travelled across the plain. While she was gone, Isolde sat on the veranda, watching for her return, listening for the footsteps that had become familiar.

Da-dop. Da-dop.

21

"Truck's coming," Wenden called. "Can't see what it is, but definitely not one of the Centre's vehicles."

"It'll have to do," said Ridge.

They were on a lonely stretch of road between the Hinterlands Education Centre and the city. Wenden was half way up a tree, watching the road. Ridge, in his guard's uniform, stepped out in front of the truck as confidently as he could and held up his hand. Wenden climbed down from the tree but stayed hidden.

The truck slowed and stopped.

Ridge motioned for the driver to open his window. "Have to ask you to wait a few minutes, sir, by order of the Mayor and Chief of Security. The Centre's conducting training exercises on the road ahead. We'll have it open shortly."

"What are you—some kind of junior guard?" the driver scoffed. "You look like you should be in kindergarten."

Ridge drew himself up and said sternly, "I am a cadet guard but I have the same authority as a full guard and I hope it won't be necessary for me to report you for showing disrespect towards an agent of the city."

"No, sir," said the driver. "Sorry."

Ridge offered him a bottle of water, saying, "The Mayor and Chief of Security would like to offer refreshment to compensate for the inconvenience."

He and Wenden had spent most of the previous day searching for dock plants. When they at last found a clump they'd spent an hour squeezing the juice from the succulent, fleshy leaves by rolling them between their hands over a curved length of birch bark. Then they'd poured the juice into a plastic water bottle they'd found discarded by the road, before filling the rest of the bottle with water from a spring.

"'S all right," said the driver.

"The Mayor and Leigh Dirk insist," said Ridge firmly. "I'm sure they would be very disappointed to hear of a driver scorning their generosity."

The driver grunted and took the bottle. With Ridge watching, he opened it and took a long swig.

"Just another five minutes and we'll have you on your way, sir," said Ridge.

He paced backwards and forwards across the road in front of the truck for five minutes, hoping nothing else came along.

The driver climbed from his cab.

"What's up?" said Ridge.

"I gotta go," said the driver. "Can't wait."

Ridge smiled. "There are plenty of trees. I'll watch your truck for you."

As soon as the driver disappeared behind a tree Ridge leapt in the cab while Wenden ran from his hiding place and jumped in the passenger side. Ridge started the truck and crashed it into first gear. It rumbled forward. The driver ran from the trees, waving his arms.

"It's not exactly a speedy vehicle," Ridge grumbled when they were safely away. "What have we got—a delivery truck?"

"Didn't you see?" said Wenden.

"I was too busy trying to convince the driver I was a real guard."

"It's the poop truck," said Wenden. "We're driving a month's worth of shit from the Centre's septic tank."

22

On the second day of their journey—Isolde alternately running beside Speed, holding her hand, half pulled along by her, and riding on her back, as she was now—Speed slowed and said, "Someone is on the road ahead. A young woman, just a girl, I think."

Isolde slipped from Speed's back and they advanced towards the slight figure, who was walking slowly, her back to them. She stopped and turned at their approach.

"Who are you?" Isolde asked.

"I'm Meru. Are you Isolde?"

"How do you know?"

"I was with Ridge. He talked about you. We travelled together. I was doing six months at the Centre and he helped me escape and get to the city. Then he helped me escape again, out of the city, when I found I had nowhere to go and the guards came after me."

"Where is he now?"

"He left me in the Hinterlands so he could go looking for you and someone called Wenden."

"Ridge wouldn't leave you on your own in the Hinterlands," said Isolde.

"He didn't want to," said Meru. "I told him to go."

Isolde thought—he would transcend in order to leave her, in order to find me.

"How long have you been wandering alone?" Speed asked Meru.

"I don't know. I've lost track of time. Weeks, I suppose."

Isolde looked Meru up and down, her grey gabardine coat, her pale blue slacks, her clean hair. "You've taken good care of yourself, and of your clothes."

She thought of her own emaciated state, and her clothes in rags, when Speed rescued her.

Meru shrugged. "I've been lucky. Found good places to sleep, and wash ..."

"What is your plan?" asked Speed.

Meru shrugged again. "I don't have one, except not to get arrested again, maybe find someone to travel with, but I don't know where to go."

"You can travel with us," Speed offered, with a glance at Isolde.

"Where are you going?"

"To find Ridge, of course," said Isolde.

23

Ridge cawed like a crow. It was the signal that a jeep was approaching.

Wenden started the poop truck. He was parked among the trees at the side of the woods road where weeks earlier the Transcenders had ambushed Isolde. Ridge was at the end of the road, watching for passing traffic.

Wenden opened the window and stuck his head out, listening. Silence meant another false alarm. A second caw meant the Transcenders were in the jeep, a third that they'd passed the woods road and to set off in pursuit. Three caws in quick succession meant they were turning into the woods road and to hide and hope they didn't find the stolen truck.

A few days before, Ridge and Wenden had set out after the Transcenders in what had turned out to be a wasted and dangerous mission. They'd followed them for a few miles until they stopped where the retrainees in a road gang had got into a fight among themselves. It had been too late for Ridge and Wenden to stop and reverse without looking suspicious so Wenden kept his head down while Ridge grabbed a pair of sunglasses he'd found in the truck and they cruised past the scene, hoping they wouldn't be recognized and the truck wasn't on a list of stolen vehicles.

"We can't do that too many times," Ridge had commented afterwards. "We're not exactly inconspicuous."

Wenden waited until he was sure enough time had gone by for the jeep to have passed without another signal from Ridge. He climbed from the truck, taking from behind the seat a long steel rod. He'd found it attached to the rear of the truck. He thought it was for gauging the depth of waste in septic tanks. He walked around the truck twirling and swinging it. He held it in front of him, in both hands, as if fending off imaginary assailants. He held it at one end and swung it at imaginary legs and heads. He thought it would make a useful weapon. He fancied himself a medieval knight, wielding the poop dipstick like a staff.

Ridge signaled again. His caw seemed louder, more urgent, than last time. Wenden climbed back in the truck. Listened.

Another caw.

The signal that the Transcenders were approaching. He started the engine. Listened.

A third caw.

He gunned the truck from its hiding place in the trees and headed down the woods road, slowing only for Ridge to jump in.

24

Isolde, Speed and Meru spent the night in a tiny church, just half a dozen pews and an altar. The main doors were missing, the stone lintel of a side door had collapsed, jamming it shut, and part of the roof had fallen in. For supper, Speed passed around some of the food she had brought from the ranch and they drank from a big iron bucket that someone had placed near the altar to catch the rain that dripped through the hole in the roof. Then they took turns staying awake to keep watch. Meru took the last shift and was still sleeping, curled up on the threadbare rug in front of the altar, when Speed and Isolde were ready to move out.

"Shall we wake her, get moving?" Isolde asked.

"She has had a rough time, wandering alone, and we are not in a hurry to get anywhere," said Speed. "Let us give her a few more minutes."

"It's too easy to get trapped in here if a patrol comes along," Isolde muttered.

The church was at a crossroads in an abandoned settlement. A squat building stood on the opposite corner, a fading sign, P. Hooper, Conveniences & Groceries, above the smashed display window. A few houses, doors hanging open and glassless windows like accusing eyes, were scattered along each of the roads leading from the junction.

Speed cocked her head. "Vehicles are approaching."

Isolde heard them a few seconds later. She peered from the opening where the main doors had been. Pulled back and flattened herself against the wall. "Jeeps. Two of them. Slowing down." She peered out again. "They've stopped."

"Do we have time to run?" said Speed.

"We might make it if there were just the two of us," said Isolde. She glanced down the aisle. "But not with her, especially having to wake her first."

"We can not leave her," said Speed.

"I know."

Speed shrugged. "So we fight, if we have to. Remember what I taught you. Charge. Butt. Kick. Bite. Stamp."

Isolde thought back to afternoons at the ranch, Speed her instructor in ways of defense and attack, charging, head butting, kicking, biting, trampling.

She risked another glance through the door. "Four guards, plus the ones who were after me when you rescued me."

"Maybe they are just checking out empty buildings," said Speed. "Maybe we could wake Meru, hide somewhere in here, and ..."

A voice from outside interrupted her. "The girl, Isolde, and her companions, the building is surrounded. You will be arrested. Do not attempt to resist. Repeat—do not attempt to resist."

"How do they know you are here?" Speed asked.

"Dunno," Isolde muttered.

"How do they know anyone is hiding here?" Speed went on.

Isolde shrugged.

Speed was looking carefully at her. "Your eyes ... Are you all right?"

"I'm transcending," Isolde explained.

Color is draining from Speed, and from the church, and from the four guards who are climbing from the second jeep. The guards hold tasers ready to fire. The Transcenders, their dark suits and black stocking caps intense against the surrounding grey, follow them, swinging their nightsticks as if warming up with baseball bats.

"What do you mean, transcending?" Speed asks.

"It's something I do sometimes in a tight spot. Ridge, too. It seems to give us the power to do what normally we'd only think of doing. Thing is—when I transcend, I do stuff I'm not always proud of."

She thinks of how she threw the guard over the fire escape at the warehouse, and made the two guards at the Black River strip before leaving them stranded and humiliated.

"You do what you have to do to survive," says Speed.

"Just don't want you to think too badly of me," says Isolde.

"I would never think badly of you," Speed promises.

Isolde glances outside again. "Two guards approaching. I can't see the others."

Speed moves beside her. "Cover the side door in case they try to get in that way. I will take care of these two."

She turns her back and puts her hands up as the guards enter.

"This is going to be easy," one of them says.

Speed kicks backwards with her right foot, then with her left. Isolde hears two sharp cracks. The guards fall, howling, their kneecaps smashed. Speed delivers two more kicks, one each to their undamaged knees. Two more cracks. They cry out again before passing out.

As Isolde reaches the side door, it crashes inwards. Agent Miso fills the opening. He steps into the church, Olface, Watch and Lister close behind. The other two guards follow.

Agent Miso says, "I've been looking forward to arresting you. I hope you resist, so we have to use force."

Speed leaps nearly the length of the church, clearing the half dozen pews and crashing into Watch and Olface and Lister, sending them reeling. As she turns to face the guards, they fire simultaneously. She falls. Half rises. Both taser her again and she lies still.

Isolde, facing Miso, spins and kicks backwards, catching him on the side of his leg. There's no crack—she's not as brutal or accurate as Speed—but he staggers sideways. Watch, Lister and Olface are up, advancing on her. Miso recovers his balance. Isolde tries another kick but he seizes her foot. She hops backwards. He twists her foot and she falls onto her stomach. He straddles her. Presses and grinds the side of her face into the stone floor with one huge hand, pinions her wrists behind her with the other.

Watch, Lister and Olface stand over her.

Isolde, her head pinned against the stone floor, sees feet in the porch of the church. She manages to raise her eyes a fraction to look up.

Ridge.

Stopping to arm his slingshot.

And—she can't believe it—behind him, Wenden, in Colorland, like Ridge. The thought flies through her mind: Where and when did her gentle friend learn to transcend? He's holding an iron bar. He steps back and disappears, while Ridge saunters through the door like a gunslinger in a western movie.

The Transcenders stare at him. He fires. Agent Watch drops, covering his right eye. Ridge fires again and Agent Lister staggers sideways clutching his ear. Another stone and Agent Olface tumbles backwards, blood spurting from his nose. Before Ridge can fire again Agent Miso grabs the iron rain bucket and holds it like a shield.

He growls, "Put your toy down—unless you want to get yourself tasered while I make a mess of your friend's face."

He pulls Isolde up by the hair and pushes her down and grinds her face into the floor again.

The two guards aim their tasers at Ridge.

Wenden steps through the side door. He holds his staff in the middle. He says, "Excuse me, boys," and as the guards turn, twirls like an overweight ballet dancer. One end of the staff smashes into the first guard's face and the other end catches the second guard across the back of his neck. As one staggers forwards and the other backwards, Wenden sticks the bar between their legs, spins again, and whisks their feet from under them. He lays his staff against their necks, and jumps on it.

Miso snarls, "You children don't learn, do you?" He raises his nightstick over Isolde's head.

Wenden calculates effortlessly and astonishingly. Miso will swing his nightstick at 30 mph with a force of 500 psi, which means Wenden will have to move his hands at a speed of 25 mph in order to create a speed of 30 mph at the other end of the staff, which will bring it into contact with Miso's nightstick six inches above Isolde's head with a countervailing force of 750 psi, enough to knock it from Miso's hands and send it skittering at least six feet across the floor.

The thought flashes absurdly through Wenden's mind—If only I could have done stuff like this in math class.

Agent Miso, holding his shield with one hand, brings his nightstick down. At the same time Wenden slips the iron staff through his hands so that he holds it by the end.

He swings it and knocks Miso's nightstick from his hands just before it smashes into Isolde's head. It clatters across the stone floor. Ridge strides forward. He kicks Miso in the face, knocking him off Isolde. The Transcender scuttles backwards, past where Lister, Olface and Watch still lie. Ridge continues his advance until Miso's back is against the altar. Ridge steps back and arms his slingshot. The stone lands between Miso's eyes. He lowers his head into his hands and Wenden smashes his staff against the back of his neck. He collapses sideways and lies still.

Meru peers sleepily over the front pew and says, "What's going on?"

25

They decided to sleep in the truck.

Speed was in the back seat, slipping in and out of consciousness. Ridge sat in the passenger seat, Isolde on his lap, her hand with the butterfly ring resting in his, while with a damp cloth he bathed the cuts and bruises on her forehead and cheekbone and chin left by Miso's grinding of her face against the floor. Wenden and Meru shared the driver's seat, Wenden leaning against the door, Meru leaning against him, watching Ridge.

They'd fled the church immediately after Ridge and Wenden had floored Agent Miso. Meru had helped Isolde to the truck while Wenden and Ridge carried Speed out, unconscious. Wenden had driven as fast as the poop truck would go, turning at every possible corner in an effort to make it difficult for the Transcenders to follow, until they found themselves on a series of narrow dirt roads that seemed to go nowhere, and Wenden had warned, "We're getting low on gas. Better find somewhere to hide the truck."

They came to a tumbledown barn. Ridge and Meru wrenched the doors open. It was empty, except for a pile of rusting tools on one side. Wenden reversed in. They used foliage to sweep their tracks and the scrape marks where the barn doors had opened. They left the doors an inch ajar so they could peer out.

They shared the last of the food Speed had brought from the ranch. Isolde, exploring the pile of tools, picked up a rusting, two pronged pitchfork to use as a weapon. They spent the evening huddled in the cab, sharing stories of what had happened since they'd last seen one another, and how they all came to be at the church. Speed told her story, and Isolde related how Speed had rescued her when she was exhausted by her long flight from the Transcenders, and had taken her to the ranch to recover, and how they'd come upon Meru, wandering alone in the Hinterlands. Wenden and

Ridge described how they'd stolen the poop truck in order to follow Miso and the others. Isolde hugged Wenden when he revealed that it was he who had distracted the Transcenders at the ambush on the woods road, and allowed her to escape.

They decided that in the morning they'd set off for the safety of Speed's home, driving until the truck ran out of gas and then going the rest of the way on foot. Speed promised they could stay there while they planned what to do.

They took turns staying awake on watch through the night, except Speed, who fell asleep early, although she seemed to be recovering from her quadruple tasering. Meru offered to take the last watch, after Wenden.

When they changed over, just before he drifted off to sleep, she slipped from the cab.

"Where you going?" he murmured drowsily.

"Gotta pee," she whispered.

When he woke again, he thought he was dreaming. Agent Miso, a bloody hole in his forehead, was staring at him through the window of the truck. Wenden blinked and looked again. The face was gone. Meru was asleep, leaning against him. Ridge and Isolde were sprawled together on the other side of the cab, Isolde with her head on Ridge's shoulder. Speed slept in the rear seat. Wenden remembered Meru was supposed to be on watch. Should he wake her? He looked at her sleeping, elfin face. She seemed very young to be separated from her parents, and to have been wandering alone in the Hinterlands. Best to let her sleep. She needed it more than him. Anyway, it didn't seem worth waking her now that he was awake and could keep watch, and with dawn light seeping through the crack they'd left between the barn doors. The space seemed wider than before. The wind must have picked up in the night and blown them apart. He had to pee. He'd try and slip out without waking the others. He opened the driver's side door as quietly as he could and eased away from Meru, who sighed in her sleep. He climbed out and felt his arms seized. He was dragged to the rear of the truck, where the Transcenders stood, the hole in Agent Miso's forehead weeping blood and pus, Agent Lister's ear red and swollen, blood caked below Agent Olface's nose, Agent Watch's right eye inflamed and half closed. Four guards stood with them in addition to the two who had grabbed Wenden.

Miso pushed Wenden against the back of the truck and whispered, "Don't make a sound or I'll have your friends tasered while they sleep."

Two guards trained their tasers on Wenden while Miso and the others sidled along the side of the truck. A few seconds later they were back, Miso dragging Meru with one hand clamped over her mouth and the other pinning her wrists behind her. He leaned close and whispered the same message he'd given Wenden. She looked at Wenden, her eyes wide and staring. Watch and Olface, with four guards, slunk along the other side of the truck and reappeared holding Ridge, Isolde and Speed.

Wenden, leaning against the truck, felt something digging into his back. He put his hands behind him. A lever. Beside it a hose. He pictured the rear of the truck. He thought back to the idle time he'd spent waiting in the woods while Ridge watched for the Transcenders. Half the time he'd played with the iron staff, the other half he'd explored the truck and its various attachments. He'd climbed the ladder and found an inspection cap on top of the tank. He'd opened it and discovered the tank was nearly full. He'd examined the lever and the hose and the big red on/off button beside them. He'd turned the lever and pressed the button to see what would happen.

Miso's voice cut into his thoughts. "You, fat boy. Put your hands where I can see them."

Wenden says, "Sorry, sir," and brings his hands forwards, hauling the lever upwards and leaning his elbow against the on/off button as he does so. One thousand gallons of clotted, festering faeces and rancid urine start to gush from the hose and pour across the floor towards the Transcenders and the guards. They reel back against the wall of the barn, gagging. Olface covers his nose and flees outside. Watch follows, pawing at his watering eyes as the ammoniac stink of concentrated urine reaches him. Wenden detaches the hose and directs the torrent of sewage at Miso, Lister and the guards, pinning them against the wall.

He passes the hose to Ridge and says, "Keep them there while I start the truck."

Miso takes a step towards Ridge, holding his hands up to shield his face. Isolde grabs the rusty pitchfork from where she left it leaning against the wall the night before and advances on him, holding it pointed upwards at his face. She slots the twin tines of the fork around his neck, pinning him against the wall. One of the guards raises his taser. Speed turns and lashes backwards with her foot, knocking the weapon from his hands. She kicks again, his chest this time. Air bursts from him and he collapses. Lister takes a step forward, nightstick raised. Speed spins and kicks his feet from under him, sending him sprawling in the sewage. Meru hasn't moved, stands with mouth and eyes wide. Speed takes her arm and hustles her to the passenger door, lifts her and throws her into the back seat. Ridge climbs the ladder, hooks his arms through the rungs, still hosing the Transcenders and the guards, and tells Isolde, "Go." She withdraws the fork from around Miso's neck and stabs upwards, catching him under the chin and whipping his head back against the wall. She runs after Speed and Meru, sits in the passenger seat with the door open, the fork still in her hands.

She shouts to Wenden, "Drive!"

He hesitates. "Ridge ..."

"On the back. Drive!"

Wenden floors the accelerator. The truck lurches forwards and smashes through the barn doors. Watch and Olface stand outside, nightsticks in hand. Watch rushes at Isolde, stick raised. Her door has swung inwards with the momentum of the truck. She kicks it open and it slams into him. He staggers back, recovers, and runs at her again as Wenden slows to turn into the road. She stands on the step of the cab, Speed holding her around the waist, and jabs the fork at his eyes. He swings his nightstick to fend it off. It lands between the tines. Isolde twists the fork, wrenching the nightstick from his hands and sending it spinning aside. He runs to retrieve it. Ridge, riding shotgun on the ladder, plays the hose over the Transcenders and guards as they try to pursue. Olface has jumped on the driver's side step and has reached through the open window. He puts one hand around Wenden's neck and squeezes while he tries to open the door with the other. His battered face fills the window. The truck swerves wildly from side to side as Wenden struggles against the choking grip.

Speed pulls Isolde into the cab and says, "Support me."

Isolde slams the door and braces herself against it as Speed leans against her. Half lying across the front seat, she brings her knees up and lashes out with both feet. They miss Wenden by a fraction of an inch and smash into the Transcender's face. He flies six feet from the step, lands on his back, and slides another six feet through the dirt.

Wenden regains control of the truck and guns it out onto the road. Two jeeps are parked one hundred yards ahead. He crashes into the first, sending it into the ditch. He glances in the mirror, wondering if he has time to do the same to the other, but Ridge shouts, "Keep moving." As the truck picks up speed, Ridge turns the torrent of sludge from the guards to the jeep and fills it with the last of the sewage.

A mile along the road, Wenden slowed while Ridge jumped down, ran forward, and swung himself up into the cab beside Isolde.

"Everyone okay?" he asked, looking around as Wenden accelerated.

Isolde, Wenden and Speed nodded.

He looked back at Meru. Her eyes were still wide and staring. "You?"

She nodded.

Isolde warned, "We better find a good place to hide and stay out of trouble for a few days."

"I thought we had a safe place last night," Wenden muttered.

"Me, too," said Ridge. "How did they find us?"

They'd been on the road for half an hour when the truck faltered, picked up speed, faltered again, and started to cough and buck. Wenden steered it to the side of the road before it finally wheezed to a stop.

"Out of gas," he said. "We got further than I thought we would."

They climbed out and looked around. They were on a dirt road in high country that looked down on the familiar landscape of bog and woods.

They listened.

All they could hear was wind in the pampas grass.

Wenden looked at Ridge, his eyebrows raised. "What now?"

Ridge shrugged. "No sign of Miso and the others, but we thought we'd lost them yesterday. Let's ditch the truck and keep moving."

They collected their packs from the cab. Wenden took his iron staff and Isolde her pitchfork. Then they stood behind the truck, feet braced in the dirt road.

Ridge said, "Ready?"

Wenden patted the truck. "Thanks for the ride."

They leaned their shoulders against it and heaved. It rolled slowly over the grass beside the road, picked up speed as it started down the hill, and smashed through the first few trees it encountered before coming to rest.

"'Spose we should try and hide it?" Isolde wondered.

Ridge shook his head. "It'd take too long. Let's keep going, get clear of here, in case they're on our tail."

They didn't know their exact location, but Speed thought if they kept heading east sooner or later they'd come to the plains, from where she could lead them to the safety of the ranch. They set out, taking turns to bring up the rear and watch the road behind for signs of pursuit.

At noon they stopped at an overgrown blueberry field to glean a few cups of early berries, while Speed ranged further afield and returned with apples and gooseberries she found growing wild. They shared what they'd gathered.

As they continued their trek, Meru sighed, "Maybe we'll come to a farm, or a settlement, where we can beg some real food."

She'd been dragging her feet and occasionally stumbling throughout the morning. Speed had offered to carry her on her back but Meru said it wouldn't seem right when all the others were walking.

"But you are the youngest," Speed pointed out.

Still Meru shook her head.

"If you can hang in for a couple more days, I think I can run to the ranch and bring supplies back for everyone," Speed told her.

Three times they came to places where the road split, and despite the need to head east, each time had taken the smaller road, heedless of direction, being careful not to leave any tracks. Late in the day, as the road took them down from the high country, it started to rain. They came to another blueberry field and stopped to scavenge. Isolde, in the corner of the field furthest from the road, waved her companions to her and pointed into the woods that bordered the field on three sides. A trailer stood in the trees, almost hidden from the road. They approached it warily. A porcupine waddled from beneath it and scuttled into the woods. A fox watched them from the other side of the field.

"It was probably used when the blueberries were still being harvested," said Isolde.

They explored the trailer. It was small, and leaned to one side, but seemed dry. It consisted of a dining area, one bedroom, a bathroom, and a kitchenette with a burner attached to a propane tank outside.

Isolde, checking out the bathroom, sighed, "No running water."

"We can still use it," said Ridge. "Just can't flush, but who cares? At least we can go in the dry."

Wenden, investigating the kitchenette, found a can of peaches, rusting at the seams, and said, "Supper!"

"When's the best by date?" Isolde asked.

Wenden inspected the can. "Five years ago. Practically fresh."

He ransacked the single draw and found a can opener. The peaches seemed okay. He turned one of the burners on and a faint hissing sound came from it.

"I don't believe it," he murmured, shutting it off quickly. "Wish we had something to cook."

"Give me an hour or so," said Speed and was gone before they could stop her.

She returned, soaking wet, a half hour later, with three potatoes and two beets she'd found in a field five miles ahead.

They dined on boiled potatoes and beets with peaches for dessert. They passed the can around twice, taking one slice each time. When the can reached Meru for the third time there was one slice left. She refused it but they insisted.

All the time they watched the road across the field, ready to flee into the woods if they were discovered.

They took turns using the bathroom, except Meru, who said she felt too self-conscious using it in such close proximity to the others, and went outside. She'd been quiet and withdrawn all evening, and had fallen asleep while Speed was away. Wenden, watching her, remembered how he'd found her asleep that morning when she should have been on watch, and was glad he'd let her rest then.

While she was outside, Speed said, "She can not walk much further. She is exhausted. I will carry her tomorrow. I will insist."

They stayed awake one at a time through the night, on watch, in the same order as the night before.

At four in the morning, Wenden shook Meru gently and said, "Your watch—but I can do it for you if you like."

He'd spent a long time before waking her, looking down at her slight form as she slept on the floor. She looked too young and vulnerable to be on the road with them, hunted.

She insisted, "I'll be okay."

He took her place on the floor and drifted into sleep.

26

Roar of an engine.

Clanking metal.

Wenden half woke.

A thunk at one end of the trailer.

He sat up.

Speed and Isolde were already at the windows. Ridge had his shoulder to the door.

"They're towing us," said Isolde.

Wenden jumped up. Through the window he glimpsed Agent Miso directing a jeep, driven by Agent Lister. Agents Watch and Olface stood nearby, watching. Miso waved Lister forward and the trailer lurched wildly and started to move. Wenden joined Ridge at the door.

"It won't budge," said Ridge.

"They have put some kind of metallic band around the trailer," said Speed, peering from the window. "We are trapped."

The jeep started across the field, the trailer bouncing and lurching behind it, Miso, Olface and Watch walking beside it.

"I can get us out of here," said Ridge. "Speed can kick a hole in the front of the trailer, I'll take out Lister with the sling shot, we uncouple the trailer, that'll be your job, Wen, while I keep the others busy avoiding stones from the slingshot, Is and Speed you toss Lister out the jeep and one of you drive, and bingo we'll be out of here and on the road and ..."

"No!" said Isolde.

"Why not?"

"Because you can't do it without transcending."

"Why shouldn't I transcend?"

"Because you're getting hooked on it. You can't wait to do it again. I can tell, the way you're behaving, antsy all the time, and the way you're talking, like you're lit up. You've got to give it a rest for a few days, get it out of your system. Otherwise you're going to be trapped there."

"Isn't that better than getting arrested again?"

She saw his eyes flicker and begged, "Please, Ridge, don't do it. I couldn't bear to lose you."

He gestured helplessly.

Wenden asked suddenly, "Where's Meru? She was on watch. She took over from me."

Speed pointed to the jeep. "They have her already. She must be terrified."

As they looked, Miso signaled Lister to stop. He and Watch climbed in the back and sat with Meru between them, while Olface climbed in the front.

The strange procession bounced over the field.

It was evening by the time they reached the Centre. The jeep moved slowly through the returning gangs on the access road. As soon as they stopped inside the compound, guards surrounded the trailer. Two of them removed the metallic band. A jeep drove up from Control, Leigh Dirk in the back, looking out of place among the uniformed guards in her pale green trouser suit.

She marched to the trailer and barked, "Out! The boy, Ridge, first."

The retrainees were dawdling, watching.

A guard said, "Hurry along."

Leigh Dirk said, "Let them watch. It will be educational."

Ridge opened the door and stepped from the trailer. He saw Meru being led away by Agent Miso and demanded, "Where's he taking her?"

Leigh Dirk didn't move but the stinging slap across the back of his legs nearly felled him.

"Her welfare is no concern of yours. We will take care of her."

"If you hurt her, I'll ..."

Another slap.

"You will do nothing, except answer for your misdeeds, starting with the fact that you left the Centre without permission."

Slap.

The back of his legs burned.

"And you took Meru with you."

Slap.

He staggered but managed to stay on his feet.

A guard threw a uniform and belt on the ground in front of Ridge.

Leigh Dirk ordered, "Strip!"

Ridge looked from her to the watching guards and retrainees. "No—not in front of everyone."

Slap.

His legs buckled and he fell to his knees.

She hissed, "You will do as I tell you. And do not even think of transcending. I can do it faster and better than you, and in any case you will probably distress your friends by stranding yourself in Colorland." She moved close and prowled around him as she went on, her voice almost a whisper, "Your disobedience and defiance are growing tiresome. You see yourself as some kind of revolutionary challenging the conventions and laws of our society, whereas in reality your pitiful defiance is no more than an excuse for you to swagger in the adoration of a hormonally unbalanced trollop whom you imagine sees you as her gallant protector but to whom in reality you are little more than a convenient dildo, and to wallow in the admiration of a pitiful boy who would admire anyone with an iota of the personality and intellect he so sorely lacks himself. Now—strip!"

She nodded at the uniform on the ground.

Ridge stripped and donned the red uniform.

"And the belt," said Leigh Dirk.

He buckled on the belt.

Leigh Dirk nodded to another guard, who came forward with the belt monitor.

"Give him a jolt," she ordered. "It may encourage him and his friends to be properly subservient to authority."

Ridge buckled and slumped to his knees in front of Leigh Dirk again as one thousand volts shot through him.

He tried to rise but she said, "Stay down there." She looked up at the trailer. "Next—the girl, Isolde."

Isolde stepped out.

Leigh Dirk traced with her finger the abrasions on Isolde's forehead and cheek and chin, murmuring, "Your rebellion is leaving its mark." She took Isolde's hand and held it as she examined the butterfly ring. "I watched your delinquent friend steal this for you. It obviously means a lot to you, for you to have kept it so carefully through all your travels."

Isolde nodded warily.

"Unfortunately jewelry is not allowed at the Centre," Leigh Dirk went on. She slipped the ring from Isolde's finger and hurled it over the compound fence into the surrounding woods. Isolde watched the arc of its flight. Heard a plop and a gurgle. Looked back at Leigh Dirk, who smiled and said, "I think it landed in a bog."

The guard threw a uniform and belt down in front of Isolde.

Leigh Dirk said, "I know what you are thinking—that I resent your youth and beauty, and that is why I treat you like this. You are wrong. I pity you them. You think they will last for ever but they are ephemeral. You revel in them and flaunt them now, but soon you will lament them as they disintegrate into flagging energy, broken veins, and lusterless hair. The ripe firmness you are so proud of will turn everywhere to sag. You will stoop. Your skin will dry up and wrinkle. You will smell of seeping urine."

Isolde felt her body shrivel and stoop, her shoulders slump. Suddenly she had too much skin. Flab hung from her arms and under her eyes. She looked from Leigh Dirk to the guards and retrainees. The guards stared at her. Some of the retrainees looked away.

"Strip," said Leigh Dirk.

Isolde undressed and put on the red uniform and the control belt.

Leigh Dirk said, "On your knees. Head down."

Isolde knelt beside Ridge.

"The fat boy, Wenden," Leigh Dirk called.

Wenden stood before her.

She caught and held his eyes, and suddenly his mind was filled with the image of his sixth grade music teacher, lank-haired, malodorous Mrs. Marsh, whose class he had led, to the tune of Eine Kleine Nachtmusik, in the singing of, "Mis-sis Marsh, She likes it up the arse." He remembered her tears, her flight from the classroom, the rumors of mental breakdown, of her never working again. He'd always wanted to apologize, had always longed for her to denigrate him, to absolve him of his burning guilt.

Before Leigh Dirk could speak, he mumbled, "Sorry."

"No wonder your parents disowned you," Leigh Dirk spat. "You are an overweight blob with all the personality of a turnip, whose only identity derives from hanging out with a pair of juvenile delinquents whom you mistakenly think possess a kind of lustre that might reflect on you and brighten your dowdy nonentity, and whose inexplicable toleration of your presence you mistake for friendship. It is time you grew up and recognized your so called friends for what they really are. One is a petty crook and a borderline psychopath, the other a juvenile nymphomaniac who secretly laughs at your crippling infatuation for her and who, despite the lurid, wet fantasies of her you nightly entertain, would vomit at the mere thought of a seedy blimp like you lying with her."

Wenden, his mind still filled with Mrs. Marsh, hung his head and repeated, "Sorry."

"And you are another who left us without permission."

"Sorry." His head hung lower.

"… And who injured a guard, not to mention his fellow retrainees, in the process of leaving."

"I'm sorry." He wept.

"You are pathetic. Strip."

He blubbered as he undressed. He knelt beside Isolde.

"Next," Leigh Dirk barked.

Speed appeared at the door.

Leigh Dirk looked her up and down. "Who are you?"

"I am Speed."

"You are also stupid, for getting yourself involved with this sad crew. Strip."

She stared as Speed undressed. The guards and retrainees, too.

Her long face. Her hugely muscled legs. The backwards slant of her shank, the forward thrust of her immense haunches. Her flat chest, no breasts at all.

"I should have said—What are you?" Leigh Dirk scoffed.

The guards laughed.

"I am Speed."

"Are you human?"

"What else would I be?"

"A freak."

More laughter.

"On your knees, freak."

Leigh Dirk stepped back. "You smell—all of you. You will shower, eat, and report to me." She turned to her Transcenders, who had been watching from their jeep. "Assign two guards to each of them. Have the prodigals brought to me in the Control Unit after supper so that I can make clear to them their status here at the Centre and what the future holds for them. Meanwhile burn the trailer."

They were marched, each escorted by two guards, to the showers, where they were allowed hot water and twice the normal time. Ridge had to admit it felt good to wash away the grime that seemed to have permeated his skin during his weeks on the road, despite his bathing whenever he could in rivers and ponds. He thought of Meru as the water sluiced over him, of their first contact through the drain in the floor, of the escape plan they made that way. He thought of her in her cot, her pitiful body, the guard pawing at her. He wondered where she was now. Had Leigh Dirk turned her over to Agent Miso? He shut his mind to the thought of what she might be going through, swore he would avenge her.

After the shower they were escorted to the canteen. The retrainees had eaten and it was empty. They were allowed to help themselves to as much as they wanted from what was left in the food bins behind the counter—a thick stew, apple pie—and were directed to separate tables by the guards. It was the first proper meal they'd had for days. When they'd finished they were marched outside and past the dormitories to the Control Unit at the end of the compound. The guards lined them up and stood behind them.

Leigh Dirk swept in and sat behind her desk. "I hope you feel better after your shower and your supper. You certainly look and smell better. Those of you who have visited us before will remember that we treat our retrainees well as long as we are satisfied that they accept responsibility for their misdeeds and of the necessity for remedial training. Our desire is that they repay their debt to society and return to the community as responsible citizens aware of the need for conformity and submission to authority. If retrainees fail to undertake this transformation, they are required to remain here until they reform. Which brings me to you. I have decided your behavior—the wrong you have done to the city, to its reputation and its citizens, and the injuries its guards have sustained in their efforts to help you—requires two years each of retraining, starting tomorrow. You will be assigned numbers by which you will be addressed and by which you will refer to yourselves. This is your only identity. You are nameless henceforth. Finally, I will remind you that the rule for retrainees is total silence at all times. This is your last chance to speak. Do you have any questions?"

Ridge said, "Meru ..."

"I have told you repeatedly. Meru is no concern of yours."

"If anything happens to her ..."

Tingling with the lure of Colorland, he took two steps towards Leigh Dirk, intending to tip her desk and trap her under it, tell the guards to throw down their tasers, find Meru, go over the fence like before, his friends with him. But Leigh Dirk had already flowered into color as she, too, transcended. He felt Mrs. Harpic's steel ruler lash the back of his legs. They gave way and he fell backwards between the guards.

"You stupid children have no idea who you are dealing with," Leigh Dirk snarled. "I am Ephebiphobia."

"You hate young people," Isolde murmured, staring up at her, reading her.

Ephebiphobia strode forward and stood over Ridge, still sprawled on the floor. "How dare you transcend, thinking you can threaten me? I was transcending before you were born." She looked from Ridge to Isolde to Wenden. "I have seen more arrogant, disrespectful young people like you than I care to remember. I spent twenty years in the Education Ministry before I decided reason and education and tolerance were useless in the face of their relentless questioning and undermining of my wisdom and authority. I transferred to the Ministry of Security because repression and retraining are the only way of dealing with them—and with you."

She came out of her transcendence, sat behind her desk and said quietly, "Guards, take them out."

27

For six weeks they followed the monotonous routine of the Centre, attending classes, going out with the road gangs, collapsing exhausted at the end of the day. They were model retrainees and no longer had guards assigned especially to them. All the time they felt their strength returning with regular meals and uninterrupted sleep in the relative comfort of the dormitories. They never spoke, but watched one another constantly. They saw no sign of Meru, not at meals, or in the gangs, or in the classroom.

One morning in the seventh week they filed into class for a lecture on The Importance of Individual Responsibility in a Modern Society. The guard with the belt monitor sat in a corner of the room, his eyes constantly roving over the retrainees. The instructor slung his taser over his shoulder as he recited his talk in a bored monotone, pacing at the front of the room between a tall bookshelf loaded with text books and a white board. Ridge had heard the lecture during his previous sentence and daydreamed through it, although he was careful to maintain a show of paying attention.

Half way through the lecture Leigh Dirk strode in and announced, "Good morning, retrainees. You have a visitor today, who will serve as an example to you of the effectiveness of the city's retraining programme, and whom I suggest you use as a model for your own successful reintegration into society."

She swept her arm towards the door.

Meru walked in.

She wore a short green dress of shiny material, slit at the side. Her body seemed fuller, her face no longer pallid and drawn. Her black hair was sleek and smooth.

She didn't look at her former companions.

Ridge stared at her.

Isolde mouthed, "Bitch."

Wenden shook his head in puzzlement.

Speed thought—Poor girl. You have some explaining to do.

Leigh Dirk went on, "I have a meeting to attend, otherwise I would stay and listen." To Meru she added, "I will see you later, my dear."

She nodded to the instructor and left.

Meru stood before the class and started, "I am a retrainee who is privileged also to be an ambassador for the Centre's education programme. I know you think I am siding with the city authorities in return for favors, or a shorter term, but you are wrong, and I need you to understand that." At last she looked at her old companions of the road as she repeated slowly, "I need you to understand."

She paused. Wenden, watching her carefully, thought she was going to cry, but she went on, "I am still a retrainee, still one of you. I am not against you. I am for you, just as Leigh Dirk and Mayor Glut are for you. They, like me, want you to successfully complete your retraining and return to the caring fold of the city as lifelong contributors to the public good in the best way you can. I have learned, in classes like this one, that while sometimes the city may punish, it is only because it has to play the part of a stern but loving parent who wants the best for a wayward child."

Wenden saw Ridge shift in his seat, saw a familiar flutter in his eyes. The guard holding the belt monitor was watching him, too. Wenden willed his friend to control his anger, not to react, not to get himself jolted into submission by the belt.

Not to judge Meru too quickly, too severely.

But ...

Had she really sided with Leigh Dirk?

If so—how long had she been working for her? Was she acting all that time she was with them on the road, not really a fugitive, but an informer? Surely not. Surely she was acting now and this was all part of a clever plan of escape for them all.

Meru concluded, "I hope your stay at the Centre is a true learning experience, and I wish you a successful return to our city community." She turned to the instructor. "Let's dismiss the class early, so the students get an extra ten minutes break."

The instructor nodded and told the class, "You may dismiss."

As the retrainees made their way out, Meru added, indicating her former friends, "I'd like to speak further to these four students. I think they still need some convincing of the city's concern for them."

The instructor said, "You four—wait!"

Meru told him, "Thank you for letting me speak to the class and for helping me become an ambassador for your work."

She shook his hand. She crossed the room and offered her hand to the guard with the belt monitor. As he half rose from his seat to take it, he held the belt monitor awkwardly with his other hand. Speed, seeing the guard without a hand free to fire the monitor, jumped across the room and kicked it from his hand. She kicked again, this time landing her foot on his chest. He flew into the wall, his head slamming against it. He slithered to the floor.

As soon as Speed moved, Ridge seized the instructor in a bear hug, pinning his arms and his taser against his sides. Isolde said, "Push him." Ridge suddenly released the instructor and shoved him in the chest. As the instructor staggered backwards, raising his taser to fire at Ridge, Isolde tripped him and he fired harmlessly at the ceiling. She jumped out of the way as Wenden heaved the heavy bookshelf from the wall, sending it crashing down onto the instructor, books raining around him. He tried to push the bookshelf off his chest but Ridge stacked four chairs together and piled them on top. Isolde did the same. The instructor, legs and arms pinned, squirming helplessly, shouted, "Guard down! Help!" Isolde took the cloth used for cleaning the whiteboard and stuffed it in his mouth, muffling his voice. The other guard was stirring. He pulled himself up until he was half sitting against the wall and lifted his head. Speed kicked him under the chin, slamming his head against the wall again, and he was still.

Ridge made for the door. Meru got there first. She turned to face her former companions.

Ridge spat, "You fucking bitch."

"I'll explain later," she said.

"You betrayed us."

"No!"

"Get out of my way."

Wenden caught a tremor in Ridge's eyes and said, "Don't transcend."

He was afraid of what his friend might do if he was Ruthless and Meru stood in his way.

Isolde put her hand on Ridge's arm. "Wen's right. Save it."

Meru said, "I can get you out of here."

"You got us in here," Ridge snarled. "We'll get ourselves out."

"They made me help them. They're holding my mom here."

"Your mother?" said Wenden. "What did your mother do to get sent here?"

"Don't have time to tell you now. Leigh Dirk promised she'd let me see her, and reduce her sentence, in return for giving you up."

"So what's changed your mind?" Ridge asked.

"Seeing you here." Isolde looked sharply at her and she added quickly, "I mean—all of you."

"Why should we trust you?" Isolde scoffed.

"Got a better idea?"

Speed said, "Go on."

"We have ten minutes before classes finish and we're discovered. In the meantime no-one will be around. The retrainees who were here are in the canteen. All the others are in class. The guards are in the classrooms or off duty. I'll lead the way to the Control Unit where they're holding Mom and I'll ask the guard if I can visit her."

"Won't Leigh Dirk be there?"

"You heard her. She's in a meeting. The guard will be alone. He won't have a belt monitor. I'll distract him so you can slip in and take care of him."

"How will you distract him?"

Meru smiled. "He likes me."

Ridge thought of the guard who had liked her so much he broke every rule in the book in order to come to her cot. He wondered what had happened to him.

"There's always a jeep parked beside Control," Meru went on. "We get Mom, pile in, and drive out of the compound."

"But the gates ..." said Wenden.

"... Are open through the morning for maintenance work. I heard Leigh Dirk say."

"What makes you think the guard will let you see your mom?" Ridge demanded.

"I told you—he likes me. And they trust me here."

"We don't," said Ridge. "And you better remember that." He looked at his friends and back at Meru. Nodded. "Okay."

They followed her through the dormitories. The drone of instructors' voices came from the classrooms. The sound reminded Wenden of walking with Ridge and Isolde through the empty hallways at Bayport High after hiding in the washroom at the end of recess and then sneaking outside instead of going to class. It seemed a hundred years ago.

Meru stopped at the end of the last dormitory. She opened the door and looked out. The others clustered behind her. The Control Unit was fifty yards away at the end of the compound. Wenden nudged Isolde and pointed at a pile of debris and ashes beside it. His iron staff and her pitchfork lay in the remains of their burned trailer, as well as the length of metallic fabric the guards had wrapped around it to trap them. A spool containing more of the fabric lay beside the fence.

Meru said, "Give me thirty seconds, then come in and take care of the guard."

She walked briskly across the compound, knocked, and went in.

The guard sat at his post on one side of the room. He smiled at Meru. On the other side of the room, Leigh Dirk stood beside her desk, leafing through a pile of papers.

Meru stuttered, "Ms. Dirk, I ... I thought you were at a meeting."

She thought—five seconds.

"It was a short one," said Leigh Dirk. She looked keenly at Meru. "Are you all right? Did seeing your friends upset you?"

"No."

Ten seconds.

"You came to see your mother, did you not?"

"Yes. But it's okay."

Fifteen seconds.

"I sent her to the Intensive Therapy Unit at the Bayport Centre."

Meru stared at Leigh Dirk. "But you promised Mom and me could go to the city together and she'd be under house arrest and have a bit of freedom."

Twenty seconds.

"I changed my mind."

"You used me to get my friends arrested."

Leigh Dirk laughed. "Boo-hoo. Just like you used your friends to get favours for your mother."

Twenty-five seconds.

"I have to go."

"Do not walk out on me because you are mad, my dear. It is how the world is. Do you think just because you are a teenager you are too special and precious to be part of it? Suck it up, as you young people like to say."

Thirty seconds.

Meru turned to go.

The door burst open.

Ridge pulled up as he met Meru in the doorway. Isolde and Wenden, unable to stop, collided with him.

Leigh Dirk laughed. "Now the whole kindergarten is here. What fun. I only wish I could say I was surprised. I guessed you were up to something, Meru, and could not be trusted despite all I have done for you. I suspected you would need some kind of punishment, as a reminder that you are subject to my authority. That is why I did not merely send your mother back to the city."

"What d'you mean?"

"I also told her there had been an accident, that you were trying to escape again and had to be tasered and reacted so badly to it that you passed away. It happens sometimes. She was quite upset. I think she was fond of you. I told her we were very sorry."

Meru stared at Leigh Dirk. "I have to see her, tell her …"

"You should have thought of that before you decided to throw in your lot with your delinquent friends and their strange companion." Leigh Dirk frowned. "Where is your equine friend?"

Isolde looked behind her. Where was Speed?

The guard was standing with his taser levelled at them.

Leigh Dirk told him, "I will deal with these children. Call Agent Miso. Tell him to assign a guard unit to find the retrainee Speed, and then to come here with my other Agents. They can take care of the children when I have finished with them." She pointed to a bench at the side of the room and rasped, "Sit!"

They hesitated.

Suddenly Leigh Dirk seemed to fill the room, to tower over them. She roared, "Sit—when I tell you!"

They did as they were told.

"Hands in your laps!"

They obeyed again. They had no choice.

Isolde found her head full of her grade seven teacher, mild Mr. Daggett, his flabby chin, his round shoulders, who was tormented by email, text, hidden voices, facebook entries, calling him Daggett the Faggot, driving him at last to conduct his classes and himself with a malevolent fury that seemed always to be on the verge of spilling into violence, the memory of which stayed with her and frightened her. Now it seemed as if he was staring at her through Leigh Dirk's eyes. She sneaked a glance at Ridge and Wenden, sitting each side of her. They also sat mesmerized.

"You will not transcend," Leigh Dirk snapped. "Do you understand?"

They chanted, "Yes."

"Yes—what?"

"Yes, Ms. Dirk."

She growled, "Think of all the adults in your life, parents and teachers and coaches, whom you have teased mercilessly, made fun of, provoked, mimicked, ignored, disobeyed, behind whose backs you have pulled faces and passed notes, whose lives you made so miserable they could not sleep at night, and every morning dreaded having to face you again."

Ridge winced at the sting of Mrs. Harpic's steel ruler on the back of his legs. Isolde shrunk from Mr. Daggett's savage wrath. Wenden cringed, helpless before the sad, accusing stare of Mrs. Marsh.

"I am all those you are thinking of," Leigh Dirk went on quietly. "All those you hurt and especially those you feared, the sting of whose sarcasm hurt you like physical pain, the threat of whose unchecked violence kept you awake at night. I am all those who could wither you into docility and immobility with just a look. All the power they held over you, and all the power those whom you humiliated wished for, is accumulated in me. That is why I am Ephebiphobia, and why I like to take revenge, on behalf of all of them."

She stared at them, her eyes seeming to bore into their memory. "I can tell what you are thinking. I hope you remember the pain and damage you caused, the irretrievable loss of self-respect, the permanent destruction of self-confidence."

They looked down, ashamed.

Agent Miso appeared at the door, Agents Watch, Lister and Olface close behind.

Leigh Dirk barked, "Take the primary class away. Put them in detention, separate rooms, for the rest of the day. They will go without lunch and supper. Tomorrow assign two guards to each of them again, to stay with them at all times." She sat on the bench beside Meru and put her arm around her as she added, "Meru has decided she no longer wishes to work with us. Would you please remind her of the consequences of that choice, both in personal terms of her being, shall we say, available for your enter- tainment and that of your colleagues, as well as in terms of how her mother will be treated during her stay at the Intensive Therapy Unit?"

Meru sat like a deer caught in a flashlight beam, staring.

Miso strode to her and with a laugh plucked her from her seat and threw her over his shoulder. He turned to the other Agents. "I'll take care of this little darling. You take the others."

He sauntered out.

Watch, Lister and Olface glanced at one another and back at the friends, who still sat in docile silence.

"He gets all the fun," said Watch.

He flew across the room, crashed over the desk, and landed against the back wall. Speed, in the doorway, hair flying, feet flashing, kicked twice more. Olface and Lister followed Watch, taking the guard with them.

Leigh Dirk roared, "Sit down, Speed!"

Speed ignored her. She fell on her back, drew both feet back, lashed out at the desk. It flew across the room and slammed into Leigh Dirk, hurling her backwards.

Speed turned to the others. "What is the matter with you?"

They half rose.

Leigh Dirk roared, "You will stay where you are!"

They sat.

Speed put one foot against the desk, pinning Leigh Dirk against the wall. At the same time she picked up Ridge and threw him through the door. She took Wenden under her arm, Isolde over her shoulder. She booted the desk again. Leigh Dirk flopped over it. Speed ran outside, carrying Wenden and Isolde. Miso was disappearing into the dormitory with Meru still over his shoulder. Ridge was picking himself up.

He muttered, "Where did you come from?"

"I jumped up on the roof as soon as I realized things had gone wrong."

Speed deposited Isolde and Wenden and said, "Pull yourselves together while I go after Meru."

She ran towards the dormitory.

Isolde called, "Wait."

She collected her pitchfork from the pile of debris and ran after Speed.

Wenden stood blinking, trying to shake off the debilitating, transcendent form of Leigh Dirk. He stumbled through the remains of the trailer and picked up his iron staff. Through the window of the Control Unit he saw Leigh Dirk and the Transcenders standing, gathering themselves.

He puts the staff aside and shouts to Ridge. Together they heave the trailer's screen door from the ashes and drag it to the door of the Control Unit. Wenden holds it there as Ridge takes the end of the metallic fabric from the spool and runs around the Control Unit with it. Wenden jumps aside as Ridge flies past and completes a second circuit. As they tie the cable, Leigh Dirk opens the door and is confronted by the screen door. She growls and leans against it. Watch joins her. The door bulges but holds.

The boys run to the jeep, parked, as Meru promised, beside the Control Unit. No key.

Ridge mutters, "Shit. Now what?"

A siren wails.

"Leigh Dirk's calling out the cavalry," says Wenden.

"It means lock down," says Ridge. "The girls will be trapped inside."

171

The compound gates clang shut.

The makeshift door of the Control Unit bulges repeatedly as Leigh Dirk and the Transcenders throw themselves against it.

"I am ordering you to open this door, children," Leigh Dirk shouts.

Wenden and Ridge ignore her.

By the time Isolde follows Speed into the dormitory, she is in Colorland.

Half way down the room, Miso straddles Meru on a bed, his coat thrown aside, his belt unbuckled, her dress around her waist, her thin legs kicking helplessly. He looks round at Isolde and Speed. Stands, flowering into color, and picks up his cudgel from beside the bed. Meru half rises. He swats her down with the back of his hand. He stalks into the aisle between the beds. He looms over Isolde. Dwarfs even Speed. She lowers herself for Isolde to climb on her shoulders. Behind Miso, Meru stands unsteadily on the bed and totters towards him. He backhands her again without taking his eyes from Speed and Isolde. She crashes back against the headboard of the bed, blood spurting from her nose.

The siren wails through the dormitory and outside. The doors lock with a metallic snap.

Speed runs at Miso. Isolde holds her pitchfork under her arm like a lance. She aims it at his neck but he draws himself up as he swings his cudgel back and it lands on his chest. She thinks she feels the tines penetrate. He gasps. As Speed's momentum carries them past he lunges with his cudgel, catching Isolde on the side of her head. She feels the wounds left from the encounter at the church burst open and spurt blood. She slips sideways but Speed's hands come up and right her. They turn. Isolde adjusts her pitchfork. Speed paws the ground as she prepares to charge again. Miso turns to face them. Meru crawls forwards on the bed, one eye red and closing, blood dripping from her nose, a trail of red the length of the bed behind her. She reaches both hands towards Miso's arms, as if to try and pinion them while Speed charges. He sees her and swings his elbow around at her face. She flattens herself on the bed to avoid him, her hands still reaching for his arms. They miss and instead land, clutching for support, at his waist, dragging his still unbuckled pants down.

Miso backs away. His pants falling to his ankles trip him and he falls. Speed advances. Isolde stands on her shoulders like a circus acrobat. She launches herself and lands with both heels on Miso's chest. Air explodes from him.

The door at the other end of the dormitory crashes open and guards rush in.

Speed picks up Meru and tucks her under her arm. They run to the door that opens to the compound. Speed turns and kicks backwards. The lock splinters and the door bursts open, almost hitting Ridge and Wenden as they try and wrestle it open from the other side. Wenden and Isolde jam their weapons against the door to hold it shut against the guards rushing through the dormitory, while Ridge and Speed, Meru still under her arm, run to the compound fence. Ridge pulls a plastic panel from the remains of the fire. It's bent in the middle, maybe a corner section from the old trailer. He slings it up and over the fence so it covers the barbed wire at the top like a saddle. He throws the burnt metallic fabric after it. He's about to move away but stops, staring into the ashes. He stoops. Grins. Picks up his slingshot, unscathed by the fire although covered with soot.

A squad of guards is running towards them from the other end of the compound. The door of the Control Unit bulges as Leigh Dirk and the Agents and the guard take turns throwing themselves against it.

Speed calls to Ridge, "Make me a back."

Ridge leans over with his hands on his knees. Speed backs up, still holding Meru. She races towards Ridge, leaps, touches him lightly with one foot—he hardly feels her— and lands on top of the fence, straddling it on the plastic. She lowers Meru to the ground on the other side. Lowers her hand to Ridge and hauls him to the top of the fence, where he sits on the plastic, facing her.

He shouts across the compound, "Is! Wen! Run!"

The squad of guards running up the compound is nearing the end of the dormitory. They slow as they prepare to fire their tasers at Wenden and Isolde. Pick up speed again, now holding their tasers at the ready. Wenden and Isolde pull their weapons abruptly from against the door and jump clear, timing it between the repeated rhythmic heaves of the guards inside. With the obstruction suddenly removed the door flies open at the next heave and the guards crash though, falling over one another and colliding with the squad as it rounds the corner. Isolde dodges past them and races across the compound. She plants her pitchfork and pole vaults over the fence, flying between Speed and Ridge. Wenden catches the pitchfork as it falls behind her and throws it after her with his staff. He stands by the fence with his hands up. The guards start firing as Speed and Ridge haul him over the fence and jump down behind him. They run into the trees to shelter from the tasers as the sheet of plastic tumbles after them.

The guards turn and run for the gate. At the same time more guards start the jeeps parked there.

Ridge calls, "Speed, tie the gates."

He throws her the end of the metallic fabric. She streaks towards the gates with it, overtaking the guards on the other side of the fence before they're even aware of her. Ridge and Wenden chase after her, carrying the plastic, while Isolde helps Meru, still groggy from Miso's attack, further into the forest. The guards fire on Ridge and Wenden but they hold the plastic like a shield as they move along the fence. They shelter Speed with it as she lashes the gates together. They huddle close together and walk backwards down the road, away from the compound, still sheltering behind the plastic sheet. They hear the zing of taser darts hitting it. Isolde and Meru run from the trees and join them. The guards struggle to open the gates but the fabric holds. A jeep backs up and rams the gates. Still the fabric holds.

When they are beyond the range of the tasers, they throw aside the shield and stand in the road watching the guards trapped in their own compound.

28

They joined hands and skipped down the access road, away from the Centre, Speed in the middle pulling them along.

Isolde hung back, peering into the trees.

Ridge said, "It landed in a bog. We'll never find it. There's no time to look, anyway."

Isolde sighed. "I know."

As soon as they were clear of the access road and out of the dense woods surrounding the Centre, Ridge said, "We're acting like we're safe, but we've got a long way to go, plenty of chances for them to pick us up, and they'll be coming after us from the city as well as from the Centre."

"At least we ate well while we were inside," said Wenden. "So we're good for a day or two on the road."

"It'll take longer than that to get to Bayport," said Isolde.

"Why are you going to the city?" Meru asked.

"To find your ma, of course," said Ridge. "You want her out of the Centre so she can join your dad, don't you? Anyway, we can't leave her thinking you're dead."

"But I can go alone," said Meru.

"You won't make it," said Ridge. "We're coming, too, even if you don't deserve our help."

Meru stopped walking. "I said—You don't have to."

"We know we don't *have* to," said Wenden. "But we *want* to."

"You don't have to come, Speed," said Isolde. "You don't have to risk getting arrested when Bayport isn't even your home."

"I am not leaving you now," said Speed. "You have become a sort of family. I have never had a family since I was taken for training when I was little more than a child. Now I have one, I am not giving it up."

They left the main road that ran between Bayport and the Centre, and cut across fields until they found a grassy trail that headed south. The trail eventually joined a meandering dirt road. As the sun started to go down they came to an abandoned cottage, set by itself on the lonely road. They'd seen no sign of pursuit all day, but made sure there was an escape route from the back of the cottage into the woods, just in case. They gathered wood and made a fire in what was left of the living room. The chimney was blocked but the smoke escaped through the broken windows.

Isolde explored upstairs. She came down with a pile of clothes in her arms and said, "We can change out of our uniforms and put these on if we can get rid of the belts."

"I do not think they pose a problem," said Speed.

She directed Isolde to lie on her back, and to keep her head down, and Ridge to use the little bit of slack in Isolde's belt to pull it as high as he could, and kicked the lock apart. She repeated the operation with Ridge and Wenden.

"What about you?" Wenden asked.

She took his staff and jammed it through her belt until it reached the floor. She told Wenden and Ridge to hold the top firmly, then kicked the bottom of the staff. The belt flew open.

When they had changed, Isolde sat with Ridge in a musty armchair. The cuts on her face were still oozing blood. Speed settled in a rocking chair that had only one arm. Meru sat at her feet. One of her eyes was black and almost closed, blood was caked under her nose, both sides of her face were bruised, and the imprint of Miso's hand where he slapped her was still visible. She leaned back against Speed's legs while Speed stroked her hair.

Wenden, on watch at the glassless window, contemplated the scene of quasi domesticity and ached for comfort and normality.

"What got your mother in trouble, Meru?" Isolde asked suddenly.

"And how did you end up at the Centre in the first place, anyway?" Wenden added.

"My mother is Amali Winter," Meru started.

"The councilor who was in the news because she criticized the Mayor and what he was doing to Bayport," said Wenden.

Meru nodded. "Glut accused her of leaking confidential documents to the media and breaking the confidentiality rules of the council. And he was right. She did both those things. It was the only way she knew to warn people of what Glut and his cronies were doing. Then, when she got re-elected, they made up charges of bribery and cheating and had her arrested and sent to the Bayport Education Centre."

"How come she got sent for retraining?" Isolde asked. "Isn't she too old?"

Meru smiled. "Not quite. She had me when she was very young."

"Didn't your dad work for the city?" said Wenden. "And he got arrested, too?"

Meru nodded. "How d'you know?"

"My parents talked politics all the time," Wenden mumbled. "They're big on Glut and his Party."

He felt like apologizing for them.

"My father was chief medical officer," Meru explained. "The Mayor said he broke privacy rules by leaking immunization records. And he did leak them—to show that the council had voted to charge for immunization. It was kept secret, so parents didn't know they had to pay until they took their kids to get their shots. Of course lots of people couldn't afford it, so just didn't get it done. Dad kept on at Glut to change his mind, but he wouldn't listen, told him just to do his job. He kept quiet about it for as long as he could, but he couldn't let it go because with only a third of the kids being immunized he said it was only a matter of time before there was a major outbreak of one of the diseases which had been eradicated for years, like diphtheria, or measles, or whooping cough, or mumps. Dad leaked the immunization records to the media so people knew about it and he was banished for it. Mom and Dad's plan was he'd find somewhere to live outside the city's jurisdiction and send for me. But before he did my mom was arrested, too, and I was taken into care by social services. I wanted to see Mom so I ran away from the home they put me in and was arrested for truancy and breaking social services' rules. They sent me to the Hinterlands Centre because Mom was at the Bayport Centre and they didn't want us in the same place. It was like an extra punishment, no chance of seeing one another."

Ridge grinned. "Your folks are a couple of renegades."

"I wish mine were," Wenden muttered.

"You can't help your folks and what they do," Isolde told him.

"And you can not judge them either," Speed put in. "You never know what sort of pressure your parents are under."

"Like yours were, when they let you be sent for training," Isolde suggested.

Speed nodded.

"So what happened after you escaped from the city with Ridge?" Wenden asked Meru. "You never told us."

She looked at Ridge. "After you left me, the river fever lasted all day. I fell asleep, and the next thing I knew two guards were standing over me. They said a man had flagged them down as they passed on patrol, and told them he'd seen smoke from a fire that morning. They were nice. They wrapped me in a blanket and one of them carried me to their jeep and they took me to the Centre. They called ahead and said they were bringing in a sick girl. They didn't realize I'd escaped from the Centre, but Leigh Dirk recognized me as soon as she saw me. I thought she'd be mad, send me back on the road gangs, but she took me to her suite at the back of the Control Unit, and ran me a bath with some kind of scented oil in it, and let me stay in it for ages. Then I slept in a huge, soft bed for two more days. I only woke up to eat. She had meals sent over from the canteen. I think they were specially prepared because it wasn't the stuff we got when we were retrainees. It was like being in a luxury hotel.

"When I'd recovered she said she had a surprise for me, a special visitor, and Mom walked in. She'd been at the Bayport Centre, like I told you, but Leigh Dirk had her sent out to the Hinterlands and we were allowed an hour together every day.

"Leigh Dirk promised that if I helped her she'd arrange for her to be put under house arrest, which meant she'd have some freedom. I asked how she meant I was to help, and she said—by finding my friends, because they couldn't survive in the Hinterlands and it would be better for them if they were at the Centre, where they'd get regular meals and be cared for while they served their sentence. She said I was to keep it secret from Mom, because she knew she wouldn't go along with it. I said supposing I refused to help and she said then Mom would be sent back to the city and she'd make her a Level 5 Security Risk, which meant I wouldn't be allowed to see her at all, so I agreed … and now I'm ashamed of myself."

"No-one is blaming you," said Speed.

She glanced at Ridge.

He shrugged.

Meru went on, "Every morning the guards drove me out into the Hinterlands and dropped me off somewhere and all day I pretended I was still wandering around until they picked me up in the evening. They said if my friends found me I was to pretend I'd been lost all that time. Leigh Dirk gave me a cell phone and said to just call the number she gave me and that would be the signal I'd met you and she could tell from the call where I was. She said it didn't matter which of you I met because one of you would lead to the other.

"Then one day, there you were, Isolde. You know the rest. I'm the reason they kept finding our hideouts." She added, "Sorry, everyone."

29

In the morning, as they travelled on, they walked beside a broad, shallow lake. They stopped when they came to a faded sign beside the road, Frank's Amusements. The sign pointed up a lane towards a pavilion like building that stood at one end of the lake.

Wenden stared at the sign. "I've been here. My parents used to bring me to the lake when I was a kid. There was a café, and a beach, and you could swim, and there were paddle boats for hire. I remember Frank telling my folks that years ago there was a granite quarry here, and when the mining company pulled out, the quarry turned into a lake. There was a canal between the quarry and the river so they could ship the granite to the city by water." He looked at Ridge. "If the canal's still open, and if it still connects to the river, and if the old paddle boats are still somewhere around …"

They turned into the lane. The door of the pavilion was hanging open. They went inside. There was a counter, little round tables, an ice cream freezer, a big window still intact looking out over the beach and the lake, doors that opened onto a terrace.

"I wonder why it closed, and why no-one comes here any more," said Isolde.

"Probably because it was too far from the city," said Wenden. "It always seemed a long way when I was a kid. Must be at least fifty miles. Also one year the lake got a bad case of red bloom algae—the stuff that did you in, Meru—and lots of people got sick. After that people just stopped coming."

"I can see why," Meru put in.

"Where were the paddle boats kept?" Ridge asked.

"On the beach," said Wenden. He looked through the picture window and added, "They're not there now. Maybe Frank sold them when the business closed."

While the boys explored the pavilion, Isolde, Meru and Speed went outside. When the boys followed to see what they were doing, they found them sprawled in beach chairs, facing the morning sun.

"We found the chairs in the woods," said Isolde. "We had to drag them out. I wonder how they got in the woods, way away from the lake."

"I think I know," said Wenden. "Remember when we had all that rain a few years ago, and the river got really high? The river would have backed up the canal, and the lake would have flooded, and everything on the beach would have washed up in the woods."

"Including the paddle boats?" Ridge asked.

"Can't hurt to take a look," said Wenden.

It took only ten minutes of searching to find half a dozen paddle boats. Three were damaged beyond repair but the others seemed river worthy. Wenden, Ridge and Isolde spent two hours struggling to free them from the limbs of trees they had washed up in and from the vegetation that had grown up around them, while Speed and Meru explored the canal that snaked from the pavilion into the woods. They reported that the river was about two miles away and the canal was clear, except for one place where a tree had fallen across it and another where the bank had caved in.

By the time they had lowered the boats into the narrow canal and made sure they floated and that the pedals worked it was late afternoon. They debated whether to set off right away or to spend the night in the pavilion and start their journey early in the morning.

"If it's over fifty miles to the city, that means two, probably three, days paddling," said Ridge.

Speed shook her head. "We can do it in a day."

"Maybe you can," said Wenden. "But we can't."

"You can if I tow you—with you paddling, too, of course," said Speed. "I found some rope in the woods. We will tie the boats together when we reach the river."

Ridge ripped a shard of rusty metal from the freezer and used it to cut lengths from the rope. He tied them to the front of each paddle boat. Speed threw what was left of the rope in the front of the first boat.

They were hungry and tired after their walk and their struggles to get the boats down to the canal. They searched the pavilion for something to eat but found nothing.

"Looks like we're on starvation diet again," Wenden sighed.

"Maybe not for long," said Ridge. "If Speed can get us near the city tomorrow, we'll rest for a while, and then enter the harbor when it's dark, and make for the downtown wharf where the tour boats operate from. Then surely we can beg or steal something to eat. We could even risk buying something. I've still got a bit of the money I brought from Ma's house."

"What about patrols on the river and in the harbor?" Speed asked.

"We'll have to be on the lookout," said Ridge.

"Better take our weapons, just in case," said Wenden.

He'd walked pilgrim-like with his staff since they left the Centre. Isolde had marched with her pitchfork over her shoulder and Ridge had his slingshot tucked in his back pocket.

"What about you, Meru?" Ridge asked. "Where we're going, what we're likely to face trying to get to your mother, you might want something to at least defend yourself with."

"We could steal a taser from one of the guards," Wenden suggested. "'Cept I don't know how to use one."

"I do," said Meru. "Leigh Dirk taught me. She said I should carry one. It would make me really one of them. She made me taser a guard, for practice." Meru shuddered. "I don't care how they treat us, what they do to us, I never want to do that again. It was like drilling a hole through him and tearing him apart at the same time."

Speed said, "How about a qilumitautit? It is a weapon the Inuit use for hunting birds. It is three weights on three lengths of rope, all tied together."

"How do you know about—er—qilumitautits?" Meru asked.

"My parents taught in the North West Territories for a few years. I went to elementary school there and we learned traditional skills."

"How would I use it?"

"Just throw it. It will be unpredictable because you will not have much time to practice, but the weights will wind around an assailant's arms or legs or throat, and might swing around and strike the body."

Meru nodded. "Okay."

"I will make two for you, because of course you get only one throw and then have to retrieve it," Speed went on. "We have plenty of rope, and we can cut weights from a thick bough, and …"

"No need," said Wenden. "I found just the thing in the woods—the rope and floats Frank used to put around the swimming area in the lake."

He ran into the woods and returned a few minutes later carrying a long rope with plastic weights attached to it. Speed cut the rope into six short lengths, each with a weight at the end. She tied the lengths together in two sets of three. They went outside.

Speed said, "Like this."

Holding a qilumitautit by one weight, she whirled it around over her head and let it fly at the branch of a tree. As the qilumitautit snagged the bough, the weights wrapped the ropes tightly around it and one weight smashed into it.

Meru grinned. She took the second qilumitautit, whirled it around, and flung it at the bough. It missed. She retrieved her weapons and tried again. The first qilumitautit flew uselessly into the trees, but the second caught the bough and two of the weights smacked against it.

"Ouch," Wenden commented.

Meru practiced for an hour. They all applauded every time she hit the bough.

They slept on the floor of the pavilion. Ridge and Isolde lay together, Ridge with his slingshot and a pile of stones close beside him, Isolde with her pitchfork beside her. Speed settled in a corner and Meru huddled to her for warmth, clutching her qilumitautits. Wenden took first watch and stood at the door with a view up the lane to the road, his staff in hand.

At first light they gathered on the bank of the canal, surveying the little flotilla. The front of the first boat was shaped and painted like a mermaid with long golden hair and a tiara. The second was a green and yellow striped serpent, the third a grinning, yellow duck with a smiling face and big green eyes.

"We will tie them in a Y-formation when we reach the river," said Speed. "That will be better for me to tow. And I need about the same weight in each boat, so Isolde and Ridge go in one, Meru and Wenden in the other."

"Meru and me get the duck," said Wenden. "It was always my favorite."

He jumped into the boat and held his hand out to help Meru down, while Ridge and Isolde climbed in the serpent. Speed, alone in the mermaid, led the flotilla.

"Best keep quiet along the canal," Speed advised. "When Meru and I explored yesterday we did not see any sign of life—not human, anyway—but you never know. The water is so low we will be below the level of the banks, which means no-one can see us unless they are close to the canal, but we can not see anyone, either, until we are upon them."

They hadn't gone far when they came to the fallen tree and had to haul the boats one by one out of the water, carry them around the tree, and lower them back into the canal on the other side. They travelled on for a half hour and came to the mud slide that filled the channel. They took off their shoes and socks and kicked water over the mud and shaped it with their feet into a smooth, flat surface which they could slide the boats over. Another half hour of pedaling brought them to the end of the canal. Speed stopped and they climbed out in order to look up and down the river.

"From now on we will be in full view of anyone on either bank," Speed warned. "The only shelter we will get is where the woods come right to the river."

"So we may as well travel right down the middle," said Ridge. "At least that way if there are guards on the bank we'll be out of range of their tasers."

They tied the boats in a Y-formation and pedaled out into the wide river. As soon as they reached the middle, they started travelling fast enough to leave a small wake behind each boat. Speed swayed from side to side with the thrust of her legs on the pedals.

"Take a break any time you want," Isolde called when they'd been travelling for a half hour.

Speed didn't answer, just kept pedaling.

30

It was late afternoon when Ridge woke from a daydream and realized where they were. He'd often played along this stretch of the river when he was a kid. His mother's cabin was only a half mile further, a matter of minutes at the rate Speed was still towing them, and the city not much further beyond that.

Their journey had been uneventful, apart from Speed's astonishing endurance. Even when they passed the old factories and occasional settlements in the outskirts of the city they saw no-one except a man fishing and a couple sitting on the bank with their arms around each other. All three hailed them cheerily and they waved back, hoping that no-one reported the strange flotilla to the guards.

Now Ridge wondered if the guards were keeping the river and road access to his mother's cabin under surveillance, in case he tried to return there. He was about to suggest they find somewhere to hide until nightfall and then sneak past in the dark when Speed called, "Boat ahead!"

They were approaching a long, gentle bend. Looking across the flat marshland that extended on both sides of the river Ridge made out antennae on the approaching boat and guessed it was a patrol. He thought the paddle boats were too low in the water to be seen until it rounded the bend.

He called, "Abandon the boats. Swim to the bank and hide."

He slipped over the side and struck out for shore, Isolde beside him. They hid among the branches of a tree that hung low over the river. Wenden surfaced, gasping, a few yards away, and joined them among the boughs.

"Where's Meru?" Isolde asked.

"She got down by the pedals in the front of the boat. Said there was no way she was ever getting in this river again after she got the fever from it."

"And I suppose she'll expect us to rescue her when the guards spot her," Ridge grumbled.

"Go easy on her," said Isolde. "Getting the river fever is enough to put you off water for life."

There was no sign of Speed.

They watched the boat round the corner. It was low and sleek. It slowed as it came alongside the paddle boats. Two guards, a young man and woman, gazed at the drifting flotilla.

The man said, "Where d'you suppose these came from?"

"Looks like from some amusement park," said the woman. "Let's take them in. If no-one claims them we'll give them to the boys' and girls' club."

She tied the mermaid, the duck, and the serpent to the back of the patrol boat.

"Should we check further up the river?" the man asked.

"Everything seems quiet and dark's coming on," said the woman. "By the time we get back and drop these off it'll be the end of our shift, anyway."

Ridge, Isolde and Wenden watched as the man turned the boat back towards the city. His partner kept her eye on the paddle boats until they fell into place behind, then joined the man at the front, looking back only occasionally.

Speed appeared, holding the end of a long rope that snaked through the water towards the patrol boat. She stopped, paying out the rope and treading water.

"I tied the rope to my paddle boat when I abandoned ship. Hang on to me, or to each other, and we can hitch a ride into the harbor."

"How come they didn't see you?" Isolde asked.

"Because I was under water," said Speed. "Now keep down, under water as much as possible, in case they look back."

As the patrol boat picked up speed, the man switched on a powerful spotlight and shone it on the river ahead, making the surroundings seem even darker. It seemed only minutes before they were churning past the outcrop of rock with the light that marked the channel into the harbor. The boat made for a pair of interconnected sheds not far from the wharf that was the friends' original destination. Speed released the rope and they swam to a breakwater of piled rock that stretched into the harbor beside the sheds. The patrol boat nosed inside, the paddle boats still behind it, and the doors closed.

They waited, wet and shivering, until it was fully dark.

"I hope you're not getting the river fever," Isolde told Speed.

"So much stuff was pumped into me when I was at training camp that I am immune to everything," she said.

They saw no sign of Meru, didn't know whether the guards had discovered her. They made their way cautiously along the breakwater towards the lights on the road beyond the sheds. They heard a whispered, "Hey, you guys." Meru, peering through a crack in the doors of one of the sheds, beckoned them inside.

Speed hugged her. "We were afraid they had found you."

"I was curled up tight and tucked right up the front of the boat. They'd have had to be practically in the boat before they saw me."

"I said to leave the boats," said Ridge.

"So?"

"They might have found you, and then we'd have had to rescue you." He paused before adding, "Again."

She stared at him. Wenden thought she was going to cry, but after a moment she gave a little shrug and said, "Well they didn't find me, did they? And look what I found for us."

She led the way through the sheds and stopped beside the patrol boat that had brought them in. The duck, the serpent and the mermaid bobbed behind it.

"This is a 16 foot Aquacruiser with a 200 HP Davis engine, which means it'll go twenty-five knots if you open it right up," she started.

They all stared at her.

"Dad's a boat maniac," she explained. "We spend lots of time speeding around the harbor and up and down the coast." She added wistfully, "Used to, anyway."

Isolde said, "So you can drive one of these?"

"Easy. Just turn the ignition, shove it into gear, and you're away." She grinned. "And something else." She pointed to a set of keys hanging beside the door that opened onto the harbor. "They left the keys. I've been wondering how we'll get out of the city after we've seen Mom, thinking the paddle boats weren't the ideal getaway transport, even with Speed pulling us. But with this ..." She gestured at the patrol boat. "We'd be out of the harbor and zipping up the river or out on the bay in minutes."

Isolde caught Ridge's eye.

He hesitated before muttering, "Okay."

Meru took the keys and passed them to him.

"It won't be long before they miss them," Wenden observed.

"We'll have to hope they think one of the guards forgot to put them back," said Isolde.

They retrieved their weapons from where they'd left them in the paddle boats. Then Meru, with another grin, pointed them towards a room at the end of the sheds. It contained a table, a drier, a refrigerator, and a micro-wave. "Put your clothes in the drier and get something to eat from the 'fridge. I heard the guards talking as if no-one would be back until morning, but just in case, I'll keep watch."

Ridge looked steadily at her.

She added, "I will—really."

"Just keep watch," Ridge muttered. "No secret phone calls."

An hour later, with dry clothes, and after sharing two TV dinners, and making sure they'd left no trace of their visit, apart from the missing meals, they were ready to leave.

They slipped outside and scuttled away from the lights around the sheds. They were on the harbor front promenade, near the foot of Water Street, in a pool of darkness between the sheds and the bright lights of the street and the store windows. The promenade was crowded and they guessed it was a Friday or Saturday night, when street lights were left on for an extra couple of hours.

"How we going to play this?" Wenden asked.

Ridge shrugged. "Walk to the Centre. Somehow get to Mrs. Winter."

"First we have a call to make," said Isolde. "Wen and me know a couple of people who might help us."

They set off up Water Street. Ridge tucked his slingshot in its usual place in his back pocket. Isolde held her pitchfork close, trying to shield it from view. Meru carried her qilumitautits over her shoulder, and Wenden again carried his iron rod like a pilgrim's staff, limping if a patrol came along as if he needed it to walk.

He realized they were passing the entrance to the City Mall and murmured to Ridge and Isolde, "Wanna go hang out?"

As he spoke, he realized that everything had started there, Ridge transcending to get the ring for Isolde, all of them taking off up Water Street, helping the injured pedestrian with the strange scar, Ridge stealing the car to take him to hospital. It seemed like another lifetime.

He looked at Ridge and Isolde. They smiled wanly and he knew they were thinking the same thing.

31

The old industrial park was as dark and forbidding as Isolde remembered.

They'd made their way out of the city centre without incident, grateful they had the crowds to move through and feel inconspicuous among. The patrols they'd seen had been preoccupied with rowdiness and fighting as people moved in and out of the bars. The streets grew quieter as they approached the industrial zone and now they slunk in the pitch dark along the sides of the old warehouses and factories.

"Stay close," Wenden breathed. "There are some desperate characters around here."

"Like us," said Ridge.

"Worse."

Ridge felt Isolde's hand slip into his.

"These desperate characters," said Speed. "What are they doing here?"

"Trying to survive," said Wenden. "Like Is and me when we were here."

"I thought you said there were people here who might help us," said Meru.

"There are—if they're still around, and if we can find them," said Wenden.

Isolde whispered to Ridge, "They're prickly. They'll challenge us. Don't react."

Wenden realized they were beside the warehouse where he and Isolde had made their hideout. "They live across this alley. Is and me will do the talking. Stay back and be careful. They like shooting people."

"They may be working," said Isolde.

"Shift work?" Meru asked.

"Kind of."

They crossed to the old engine shed.

Isolde tapped at the door and whispered, "Sadie. Liz."

A voice rasped from the darkness behind them. "Who wants to know?"

They turned. The faint beam of a flashlight played over them briefly and disappeared.

The door opened and another voice said, "Now you've got a taser on you front and back. Who's going to get it first?"

Another faint flashlight beam played over their faces. It lingered on Wenden's, stopped on Isolde's. Snapped off.

"Well, well," said Liz. "Didn't think we'd see you two again."

Sadie said, "Best get inside."

They felt their way into the machine shed. Liz closed the door and draped a blanket over it, while Sadie lit a candle stub. In its flickering light they saw two rickety wooden chairs, bedding on the floor, a shopping cart with a dirty blanket thrown over it.

Sadie and Liz surveyed the companions. They still held their tasers, although they'd lowered them.

"Are these friends?" Liz asked Isolde.

"Yes."

"Are you sure?"

"Yes."

"How do you know?"

"They've helped us. We've helped each other. We've been at the Hinterlands Centre together, and escaped together. We've been on the road, on the run, together."

Sadie was eyeing Ridge, head cocked, eyes narrowed. "This one's dangerous."

"No," said Isolde, although she knew Sadie was right.

"Ruthless—right?" Sadie asked Ridge.

He nodded.

"Ruthless—on whose behalf?"

"Depends."

"Your own?"

"And my friends."

Sadie looked back at Isolde. "Do you trust him?"

"Yes."

"With your life?"

Isolde shrugged. "He is my life."

Liz groaned. "You sound like a Harlequin Romance."

"I hope he's worth it," Sadie muttered.

Liz hugged Isolde. Stepped back. "You're gaunt, girl. Hard times, eh? And your face ..." She stroked Isolde's scars.

Sadie patted Wenden's stomach. "You've lost weight, big boy."

Liz eyed Meru. "Who's this little honey with the beaten up face?"

"This is Meru," said Isolde. "And this is Speed. They've been travelling with us, helping us."

Sadie eyed Speed. "You're different."

"Yes."

"Not from here."

"No."

"How did you get hooked up with this crowd?" Liz asked.

"I met Isolde in the Hinterlands."

"What she means is she rescued me from Leigh Dirk's Agents in the Hinterlands," Isolde added.

"Then I'm proud to meet you," said Liz, shaking Speed's hand.

Sadie did the same.

"What are you all doing back here?" Liz asked.

"We need help," Isolde started.

"Don't we all?" said Sadie.

"Leigh Dirk is holding Meru's mother in the Bayport Centre," Isolde went on. "She told her Meru was killed trying to escape from the Hinterlands Centre. We have to let Mrs. Winter know Meru's safe, and we want to get her out, and ..."

Liz held up her hand. "Are you telling us this gal's mother is Amali Winter?"

Isolde nodded.

Liz looked carefully at Meru. "Yeah—you look like her. I hope you're proud of her. She stood up for us when the city passed the Family Values Ordinance, the one that mandates two years retraining and permanent shunning for women in our line of work."

Sadie laughed bitterly. "And half the council coming to us at the same time as they were making that law."

"She was the only one who stood up against Bradford Glut and his cronies," said Liz.

"That's one of the reasons they made up charges and put her in the Centre," said Meru.

"And now you want to spring her from it," said Sadie.

Meru nodded.

Liz looked at Sadie. "The kids are taking over."

"Someone has to," said Sadie. "The adults have either screwed up or given up."

"But what's your mom going to do when—if—you get her out?" Liz asked.

"She'll find my father, who's banished …"

"… Because he went against Glut, too—right?"

Meru nodded. "… And together they'll organize some kind of opposition from outside the city. That's what Mom said before she was arrested, anyway."

"So … you'll help?" Isolde asked.

Liz looked at Sadie and raised her eyebrows.

Sadie shrugged.

"You bet," said Liz.

"Always happy to taser a few guards," said Sadie.

"We don't want to put you in danger," said Wenden.

Sadie laughed. "Doing what we do, we're in danger all the time."

"What do you want from us?" Liz asked.

"We need help getting into the Bayport Centre," said Wenden.

"And out," said Isolde.

"Ain't gonna be easy," Sadie muttered.

"And getting to Mrs. Winter will be hard," Liz added. "You can bet they'll have someone important like her off by herself with extra guards."

"But we'll come up with something," Sadie promised.

They made themselves comfortable in the old machine shop, Liz and Sadie in the chairs, Isolde and Ridge sprawled on the bed, Speed and Meru leaning against the back wall, Wenden on the floor beside Sadie's chair. She pulled him back against her knees and tousled his hair.

Liz and Sadie kept their tasers close to hand.

"If anyone comes, or you hear anything outside, flatten yourselves," Sadie advised. She patted her weapon. "We usually shoot before we ask who's there."

"That's if there's anyone left who can talk," Liz added.

"Where d'you get them?" Ridge asked.

"Lots of our clients are guards," Liz explained.

"So they know where you live," said Ridge.

Liz looked at him scornfully. "We don't bring them here, dummy."

"We take turns relieving them of their weapons while they're otherwise occupied," Sadie added.

She crossed the room and whipped the blanket off the shopping cart. She pushed aside a pile of old newspapers and rags, revealing tasers, stun guns and stun grenades.

Ridge muttered, "You've got quite the arsenal."

"That's why it doesn't pay to mess with us," said Liz.

32

Meru gazed up at the Bayport Education Centre. It was nothing like the Hinterlands Centre, no compound, no separate dormitories and classrooms. A flat fronted building of four storeys, more glass than brick, revolving doors at the centre, it looked like a suite of government offices. It took up one city block, with insurance offices on one side, and the power company's headquarters on the other. A ramp at one end sloped down to a metal door. She'd arrived early enough to watch the door roll up and the road gangs march out in their red uniforms, twenty gangs, six retrainees and two guards in each. She'd watched the blank faces of the retrainees, remembering the crushing effect of the dreary, name denying routine, recalling how she'd felt as one of them.

It had still been dark when she slipped out of their overnight refuge. She didn't think anyone else was awake. She was sure she'd been caught on one of the surveillance cameras as she walked from the industrial estate. She'd half expected to be picked up by the guards.

But they would have guessed where she was going.

They'd be ready for her.

She crossed the road, pushed through the revolving doors, and stepped into a carpeted, wood paneled reception area, dark after the morning sun outside. Hallways led off on both sides. A guard was sitting at a desk in front of her, elevators behind him.

He ordered, "Wait there, please, miss."

Two guards stepped from the shadows behind her and stood, one on each side. They marched her to the elevator. One pressed the button for the fourth floor.

She walked between them along a hallway, noting doors with numbers and names as they passed: 401 M. Peters, 402 S. Tilley, 403 P. Hunter. They stopped at an unmarked door at the end of the hallway. One of the guards knocked. A voice summoned them. Another carpeted, wood paneled space. A woman sat behind a desk, not a guard, at least not in uniform.

"Meru Winter to see the Chief of Security," one of Meru's escorts announced.

"Ms. Dirk is expecting her," the receptionist said. She picked up a phone, repeated the guard's announcement, and told Meru, "You can go in." She pointed to a door behind her. The guards walked Meru to it. One knocked. The door opened by itself, while the guards, staying in the reception room, positioned themselves on each side of it.

Meru took two steps into the room and stopped. It was like walking on pillows, the pale pink carpet was so thick. Soft lighting spilled from an ornate chandelier. Beside her there was a settee in front of a flat screen TV. Above the TV a bank of monitors flickered with images of the city, including the road in front of the Centre. Leigh Dirk would have watched her arrival on it. A huge desk, bare except for two telephones and a lamp, stood slantways across the far corner. Leigh Dirk sat in the other corner, in one of two small wingback chairs set close together, a table bearing a coffee pot and a plate of sugar cookies in front of her. As always, she wore a pale green trouser suit. Meru wondered if she possessed any other clothes.

The door closed automatically behind her.

Leigh Dirk regarded Meru steadily, her face expressionless.

Meru fell to her knees. She covered her face with her hands, sobbing into them.

"I wondered how long it would be before you came crawling back," said Leigh Dirk.

Meru sniffed.

The Chief of Security snapped, "Stop sniveling and pull yourself together. Stand up."

Meru obeyed.

Leigh Dirk wrinkled her nose. "You have been on the road again. Your face is a bloody mess and you smell. Your hair is disgusting and your breath is repugnant." She waved her hand in front of her nose. "Clean yourself up, please, before we talk. You may use my personal washroom. Have a shower and do whatever else you have to do to make yourself presentable. You will find foundation and concealer with which to disguise the bruises your waywardness has brought you, and there is a new toothbrush by the wash-basin. Meanwhile I will find some decent clothes for you."

She pointed to a door behind the desk.

Meru murmured, "Thank you, Ms. Dirk," and stumbled across the room, her head down.

The washroom was almost as big as the office. Everything—tub, shower, toilet, vanity, tiles, towels—was white. The vanity took up one whole wall, and the mirror above it was ringed with spotlights.

When she came out of the shower she found her clothes gone and a new set left in their place. They fitted her perfectly. She looked at herself in the mirror. Dark blue, knee length dress, black tights, white scarf.

She returned to the office.

Leigh Dirk surveyed her. "That is better. Now—would you like coffee, a cookie?"

Meru shook her head.

Leigh Dirk snapped, "Is that the polite way to answer?"

Meru corrected herself. "No, thank you, Ms. Dirk."

Leigh Dirk's voice softened. "Now sit beside me." She patted the empty wingback chair. "What do you have to tell me?"

"I know where Ridge and the others are hiding."

As she spoke, Ridge's face flashed into her mind, his hard eyed, accusing stare, his rare smile. She pushed the image away.

"Of course you do," said Leigh Dirk. "You are one of them, a fugitive, a traitor to the city. Now you want to be a traitor to your friends—again. How many more times do you plan to change sides?"

Meru hung her head. "No more, I promise."

Leigh Dirk patted Meru's knee. Stroked it. "Do not be ashamed, my dear. I am sorry I spoke harshly. I do it because I care about you. I do not want you ruining your life because of some misguided loyalty to a band of renegades bent on destroying the social order Mayor Glut wants so badly for the city." Her hand moved to Meru's chin, lifted her head, stroked her face, her hair. "Where are they?"

"First you have to let me see my mother."

Leigh Dirk laughed. "You are learning! But why should I bother myself with your delinquent friends? I have more important things to do."

"They want to free my mother, find people who oppose Mr. Glut, join up with them, organize opposition. I'm afraid Mom will be hurt if they try."

"So they are graduating from childish antics to genuine opposition, becoming anarchists with no respect for social order and justice and security. Very well. I agree. You may see your mother in return for telling me where they are."

"And I want you to put her under house arrest, with limited freedom, like you promised before."

Leigh Dirk scoffed, "You blew that offer when you betrayed me at the Hinterlands Centre."

Meru pouted. "My friends made me. I didn't have a choice."

"Do not make excuses. You always have a choice." Leigh Dirk contemplated Meru, her eyes meandering from her face to her ankles, back to her knees, lingering there, back to her face. "How about this? You can live here with your mother in exchange for your telling me where to find your friends. You will find her rooms comfortable, and you, like her, will be well cared for. You will have the freedom to go around the city, as long as you do not associate with anyone of whom I would not approve. If you do, I will know, of course."

Meru nodded.

Leigh Dirk went on, "You will earn your keep by working as my personal assistant and companion."

"Yes, Ms. Dirk."

She took Meru's hand and led her through the reception room, along the hallway, past the elevator and a door marked Stairs. At the end of the hallway she stopped at a door with a sign, Guest Suite A.

"These are your mother's rooms. Remember—your arrival will be a shock because of the lie you forced me to tell her."

A bell rang and the elevator door opened. Agents Watch, Olface, Lister and Miso stepped out. Meru backed away as Miso approached. He smiled at her.

Leigh Dirk laughed. "Do not worry. I will keep him in check—as long as you behave yourself."

She knocked at the door.

"Come in."

Her mother`s voice.

Leigh Dirk opened the door a few inches.

Amali Winter stood in the middle of the room, arms folded, facing the door. She wore the red uniform of a retrainee. She gasped. Held her arms out to Meru.

Leigh Dirk slammed the door and demanded, "Where are they?"

"In the old industrial estate. Block 8, opposite warehouse 14."

Leigh Dirk nodded to the Agents. "Take half a dozen guards. If Meru's former companions resist, use maximum force." She turned to Meru. "I will be back for you in one hour. You will be locked in until then."

"But I may need to go out. My mother may need something from the stores."

"You presume too much, Meru," Leigh Dirk warned. "I said I would allow you limited freedom, but that is a privilege you will have to earn, through the work you will do for me, and by demonstrating your total, unquestioning obedience. If all goes well, I will allow you your first outing at the end of the week."

She opened the door again.

Meru flew to her mother. They hugged. Fell to their knees locked together, tears mingling.

Leigh Dirk closed the door.

33

It was short and brutal.

Waiting on the roof of Liz and Sadie's machine shop home, Ridge thought—the worst that's happened to us so far, excepting Meru's treatment at the hands of Miso, is getting smacked around a bit and tasered a few times.

And the worst we've done to them, so far, is fire a few stones, whack them with a pitchfork and a metal bar, pour sewage and hot blacktop on them.

So far.

How long will it be before someone, one of my friends or one of Leigh Dirk's guards, is more seriously injured?

Killed, even.

He didn't think the Transcenders and guards, most of them, anyway, would have any problem with seriously hurting or killing him and his companions. But he didn't know if he, even when he was Ruthless in Colorland, or any of his friends, could take a life. So far all their encounters with the Transcenders and guards had been like a kind of long drawn out game of extreme paintball, with some extra animosity and risk and danger thrown in. What was the step beyond that? All out war? Were he and his comrades at that point already, now they were planning calculated and strategic violence, disregarding the pain and injuries they were about to inflict?

He told himself they had to fight for what they believed was right. They'd been forced into it.

But he couldn't help thinking—Wasn't it the same for Leigh Dirk and the Agents and the guards? Didn't they, too, think they had to fight for what they believed was right, on behalf of all the people in the city, thousands of them, who agreed with them? Didn't they, too, believe they'd been forced into it?

Then he remembered how at the Centre they had set out to rob him of his sense of self, and how the guards had looked at Isolde as she undressed in the compound, and how the city had alienated Wenden from his parents.

Thinking like that made it personal.

So what choice did he and his comrades have?

The plan was simple. Take out the Transcenders and guards. Allow no chance of escape.

Ridge looked around. He was lying flat so he could watch all sides as Leigh Dirk's forces surrounded the machine shop. They'd been right in their estimate of the time it would take for Meru to betray them, and for Leigh Dirk to send her troops. He'd watched the city transit van park several hundred yards up the road. He hadn't expected ten of them—six guards, as well as Miso, Olface, Lister and Watch—but they'd manage. He was the fourth and final line of attack, as well as the backup if any of the first three lines failed.

They were all in place. He knew, although he hadn't yet transcended, that Isolde and Wenden would be in Colorland already, probably Liz and Sadie, too. The women had assumed the look and manner of desperadoes with nothing to lose before they even took their positions. The night before they'd told stories of their guerrilla warfare against the guards and he wondered again what the city authorities had put them through, for them to become Vendetta and Revenge.

He was saving his transcendence until he really needed it. Isolde had told him again just before they took their positions of her fear he would get himself trapped in Colorland, addicted to the power and excitement and invincibility he felt there.

He'd asked why she was warning him again, and she'd said, "Whatever we're getting into, I've got this feeling you're going to need to transcend more than any of us, and I don't want you to overdo it. I don't want you trapped in Colorland. I don't want to lose you."

He watched the Agents and guards approach at a run. They surrounded the machine shop and rushed it, tasers ready to fire. Miso kicked down the door and barged in, Watch, Lister and Olface on his heels, two guards close behind. The remaining four guards positioned themselves around the shop, one on each side.

Speed jumped from a barrel in the lane behind the shop. She crossed in a blur to the guard stationed at the rear. He heard her and turned a fraction of a second before she was on him. One flying kick to the gut. Another to the head. He lay without moving. She leapt on the roof and lay beside Ridge. At the same time Wenden and Isolde rose from behind a dumpster and rushed the guard stationed on their side of the shop. He just had time to turn and lift his taser before Isolde's pitchfork swept his feet from under him and Wenden swung his staff against his head. He fell. Half rose. Isolde struck him back down with a blow to the ribs. He squirmed. Wenden's staff landed on his head with a sharp crack that made Ridge wince. They stood over the guard, prepared to strike again. He didn't move.

Meanwhile Liz and Sadie, smiling seductively, sashayed up LongWharf toward the guard on the other side. They wore their short working dresses, slit on one side. They'd spent a half hour that morning preparing their hair, while Ridge watched impatiently. Sadie had swept hers to the side, and Liz's was arranged in spikes and ringlets. The guard, trying not to smile back, motioned for them to move along. They strutted to him and stood close, provocatively, still smiling. He made to push them away. Sadie seized and held his arms while Liz took his taser and held it against him.

A shout from inside the shop.

Agent Watch.

"They're outside. They're all around us."

Sadie released the guard and jumped back as Liz fired twice. The guard collapsed. Liz glanced up at Ridge, grinned, and gave him thumbs up.

Only one guard remained outside. He stood at the front of the shop by the open door, where the Agents and guards had rushed in seconds before.

Ridge stood. He chose a large stone and fitted it in the cradle of his slingshot. Moved forward and looked down on the guard.

Time for Colorland.

The guard turns. Looks up. Ridge fires. The stone hits the guard in the centre of the forehead. He takes two steps backwards. Sways. Sits abruptly. Topples sideways. Two guards run from the shed. The first bends over the guard that Ridge has just felled. Ridge calls, "Hey!" The guard looks up. Another stone in the middle of the forehead. The guard drops to his knees beside his comrade. Sprawls across him. Speed launches herself from the roof. She kicks the second guard in the side of the head as she passes him on the way down. Cracks his knee with another kick as she lands. He turns slowly on one leg towards her, trying to lift his taser. She lifts one foot high and smashes her heel into his face. He drops. Ridge jumps down and turns to face the door of the shed as Wenden and Isolde run around one corner and Sadie and Liz stroll around the other, Liz with a taser under each arm, Sadie holding a taser in one hand and pushing the shopping cart with the other.

The Transcenders pour single file through the narrow door, Watch in the lead. Sadie tasers him twice. He collapses. Olface comes next. Ridge fires. Olface's cheek seems to explode. He drops to his knees, holding his face. Lister follows. He runs at Ridge, cudgel raised, as Ridge reloads his slingshot. Wenden and Isolde step in front of Ridge. Lister lashes the cudgel at Wenden's head. Wenden parries with his staff. Lister tries again. Isolde catches the cudgel between the tines of her pitchfork, wrenches it from his hand. Wenden smashes his staff against the side of his head. He falls sideways in the doorway. Ridge has fired at Olface again, this time striking him on the side of the head. He staggers backwards into the shed. Miso barges past him, pushes Lister aside. He bellows as he hurls himself at Ridge. Before he can land his cudgel four taser blasts rip into him, two from each side. He sprawls on his back, his eyes open, staring. Liz and Sadie saunter forward and stand over him. Ridge joins them. Isolde and Wenden stand slightly apart with Speed.

"Give him another blast," says Ridge. "Put him right out."

"I've got something better," says Sadie.

She produces the stun gun from the shopping cart and leans over Miso.

He snarls, "Bitch."

She smiles. Holds the stun gun against his neck and fires.

They dragged Leigh Dirk's fallen Agents and guards into the machine shop, collected all their weapons, cell phones and radios, and stripped three guards of their uniforms. Sadie locked the door and pulled an iron grille across the front of the shop. She padlocked it and threw the key away.

"Why don't we just burn the shop with them in it?" Sadie grumbled. "It'd be a lot less trouble."

"But the fire would raise the alarm," Liz said.

Speed, Sadie and Liz put the guards' uniforms on over their clothes. Liz and Sadie slung a taser over each shoulder. Sadie tucked the stun gun in her pocket. Wenden fetched the city transit van.

34

They parked near the entrance to the Centre, on the opposite side of the road. They waited restlessly for a few minutes, scanning the front of the building.

"How long do you think we have?" Wenden asked.

"Ten minutes for Miso and the others to break out of the shed and contact the Centre. Ten to get transport. Another ten to get here," said Ridge.

"We can't sit in the van too long," said Liz. "It looks suspicious."

A few people hurried in and out of the office buildings on each side of the Centre. No-one entered or left the Centre itself.

"Let's go," said Ridge. "But take your time."

As Wenden climbed out he caught Isolde's eye and nodded towards the cliff that rose where Portage turned sharply two hundred yards ahead. She smiled, recognizing the vantage point from which they'd watched for Ridge months before.

They stood on the sidewalk, Sadie, Liz and Speed in the stolen uniforms with tasers under each arm pointed at their pretend prisoners, Ridge, Isolde and Wenden. Speed carried Wenden's staff and Isolde's pitchfork, and had Meru's qilumitautits slung over her shoulder. Ridge's slingshot was tucked in his back pocket.

They set off across the road. They were half way across when a banner unfurled from a window set so high in the building it was almost under the eaves. They struggled to read it as the wind caught it and swirled it around.

"Floor 4," Isolde read.

"Take elevator and go left," Speed added slowly.

"Guest Suite A," said Wenden.

"Gotta be Meru," said Isolde. "She's telling us where to go."

"Or leading us into a trap," said Ridge.

They stopped on the sidewalk in front of the Centre.

"So what do we do?" said Wenden.

"We can't stop now," said Ridge. "We're on camera already."

He inclined his head towards two security cameras mounted over the entrance. They were pointed directly at the friends. With Liz and Sadie on each side, Ridge, Isolde and Wenden marched towards the entrance. Speed walked behind. Liz led the way through the revolving doors.

A guard, a woman with short blonde hair and a pointed chin, was sitting at the reception desk, watching Bradford Glut on a TV mounted on the wall.

The Mayor announced, "I am making this special broadcast to assure the citizens of Bayport ..."

Wenden thought of school and the Mayor's Message for Young Citizens.

The guard paused the programme with the remote control. "I thought all personnel had been advised that Mayor Glut was making a special announcement and ..."

Liz interrupted her. "We're on urgent business."

The guard held out her hand. "I need to see paperwork, please."

"Guard #47 is bringing it," said Liz. "He'll be along in a minute or two."

"I can't let you proceed without the proper paperwork," the guard insisted.

"I'll make sure Leigh Dirk knows that when we're late reporting to her with these three fugitives."

The guard surveyed Ridge, Isolde and Wenden. She consulted a sheaf of papers on the desk. "It says here six guards went out, as well as Ms. Dirk's Agents, and you were supposed to bring in four fugitives, not three."

"One got away. The Agents went after her."

The guard looked back at her papers. "Guard #47 isn't listed as one of those that went out. I think I'd better call up to Ms. Dirk."

She reached for the phone on the desk.

Sadie glanced around the reception area. One security camera over the elevator, showing the entrance, one over the entrance, showing the reception desk. She stepped to the side, outside the range of both, and tasered the guard, who shuddered and slumped to one side. Her hand, still on the remote, twitched, and Bradford Glut's voice filled the room.

"As I have stated before on numerous occasions, I, as Mayor of the City of Bayport, have worked hard with my colleagues on the city council to create a just, safe and caring community ..."

Liz moved quickly beside the guard and leaned over the desk, as if consulting the papers. She pretended to point something out as she discreetly propped the guard in her chair. Sadie motioned Ridge, Isolde and Wenden towards the elevator. Speed pressed the button for the fourth floor.

When the doors opened, Leigh Dirk was waiting in the hallway. "So the delinquent children are back. I watched your arrival on the monitor. You will regret causing the city so much trouble ..." She broke off, staring at the group. "Where is the fourth fugitive?"

Liz repeated her earlier lie. "She got away. The Agents are in pursuit."

Leigh Dirk looked at Speed and started, "You ..."

Liz and Sadie moved forward in unison and took each of her arms.

She shouted, "Guards."

Only the receptionist appeared, on the run from Leigh Dirk's office. She put her hands to her mouth and stared at Liz and Sadie, who were still holding Leigh Dirk.

"Get back in there and don't do anything," said Liz.

The receptionist scuttled back into the office.

Liz and Sadie marched Leigh Dirk backwards along the hallway. Ridge, following, saw Leigh Dirk's eyes flicker and realized she was transcending. He resisted doing the same, remembering Isolde's warning.

"Let me go this instant," Leigh Dirk ordered Liz and Sadie.

Sadie laughed. "Won't work on us, honey. We're too old and ornery for that crap."

They marched her into the office, past the cowering receptionist. One of Leigh Dirk's TV monitors was tuned to Bradford Glut, who was proclaiming, "… Despite all our efforts, some of our citizens, especially our young people, struggle to conform to the simple rules that underpin a community such as ours …"

Leigh Dirk glared at Ridge. He knew what was coming but could do nothing to resist as her voice rasped, "You and your friends will make these harridans release me immediately."

Ridge grabbed Sadie's arm. She backhanded him and shook herself free. Isolde and Wenden went for Liz. Speed held them back, while Liz and Sadie ran Leigh Dirk backwards across her office, into the bathroom, and threw her in the bath.

Liz, looking around, said, "No windows. No other door. This'll do."

Speed let go of Isolde and Wenden, dragged the receptionist into the bathroom, and pushed her in the bath on top of Leigh Dirk.

Sadie set the door handle in lock position and smashed it with the butt of a taser so it would stay locked. She slammed the door.

"Snap out of it," Liz barked at the friends.

With Leigh Dirk out of sight, Ridge felt her influence disappear.

"Sorry," he said. "I couldn't help it."

Leigh Dirk pounded on the door, demanding, "Children, you will unlock this door immediately."

Speed was peering up and down the hallway from the door of the reception room. "All clear," she called.

She handed Wenden and Isolde their weapons. Ridge drew his slingshot from his pocket and armed it.

They were about to move out when they heard, "Rumors persist of a band of teenage delinquents who have been roaming the city and the Hinterlands, eluding the efforts of our guards to arrest them and bring them to one of our Education Centres in order to protect them from themselves."

Bradford Glut's face was replaced by a series of photographs that flashed up on the screen.

Ridge. A school photo, maybe grade eight. Hands in his pockets, slouching, scowling. The guards must have taken it from his mother's cabin.

Isolde. On a beach, smiling through wet hair. She was thirteen. Ridge remembered taking the photo. It had been pinned to the wall of his room. The guards had helped themselves to it.

Another school photo. Wenden. Smiling falsely in three quarter profile against faux clouds. Wenden thought—thanks, Mom and Dad, for handing it over.

Meru. A soft focus studio shot. It had been on the wall in her aunt's apartment.

Speed. Much younger. In running kit. Speed thought—they've tracked me down, after all these years.

"We're famous," said Wenden.

Bradford Glut was back on the screen. "These delinquents have extensively damaged city property at a time when the city can ill afford the extra and unnecessary expense of repair. They have also assaulted a number of our guards." The Mayor paused before adding, "They have pitched one head first from a fire escape, poured hot blacktop into the face of another, maimed the faces of others."

The friends looked at one another.

"Did we do all that?" said Wenden.

"Doesn't sound like us," said Isolde.

"We gotta keep moving," said Ridge.

They went silently down the hallway and found Guest Suite A. Ridge put his finger to his lips.

Bradford Glut's voice sounded through the door. "Furthermore, let me lay to rest rumors of this ragtag rebel group gathering other gullible misfits to them, and uniting with an opposition movement forming in ..."

Ridge tapped lightly on the door.

"Who's there?"

Meru's voice.

"It's us."

"Leigh Dirk locked us in."

Speed said, "I can open it, but it will be noisy."

"Can't be helped," said Ridge.

Speed called through the door, "Stand clear, Meru and Meru's mother."

She turned, lifted her foot, and drove it against the door. It swung open, dangling from the top hinge, the wood around the lower hinge splintered.

Bradford Glut's voice sounded louder. "I am stating categorically that these rumors are unfounded, that Amali Winter, who seems to be at the centre of them, is currently suffering from emotional instability and is receiving treatment as a guest of the city …"

Meru said, "Mom, these are my friends. This is Ridge, and Isolde, and Wen …"

Ridge interrupted. "What's going on?"

"What d'you mean?"

"You were supposed to meet us out front."

"I didn't know Leigh Dirk was going to lock us in, and I couldn't find a way to get a message to you like we planned, not 'til Mom suggested hang a sign out the window, but Leigh Dirk doesn't allow her writing stuff, so we had to use her sewing kit and cut out letters and sew them on a scrap of material …"

"We have to move."

It was Isolde interrupting this time.

Ridge demanded, "How do we get out of here?"

"First we go to the basement," said Mrs. Winter. "Then …"

"Tell us as we go," said Ridge.

They ran back down the hallway, making for the elevator, the Mayor's voice growing fainter. "I am making this announcement to reassure the citizens of Bayport that no band of misfits will be allowed to upset the peace and good order of the city …"

Liz, in the lead, said, "Whoa. Elevator's coming up."

"Stairs," said Mrs. Winter.

They plunged through the door to the stairs. Ridge was last. He held the door open a crack to see who was in the elevator, at the same time motioning the others to keep going. Six guards burst out. If they turned left, they'd immediately see the door of Mrs. Winter's quarters hanging open. He prepared to transcend, to hold them while his friends kept moving. The guards turned right, towards Leigh Dirk's room. She must have found a way to summon help. They had only a few seconds before she raised the alarm. He raced down the stairs after his friends. By the time he caught up with them Isolde was peering from the stairwell into the basement hallway. Speed, Liz and Sadie had thrown aside their guard uniforms.

Isolde gave thumbs up. All clear.

Mrs. Winter whispered, "A tunnel at the end of this hallway goes under the road and comes out in the council chamber. The Centre used to house the council offices, and the councilors used it as a short cut. There's an exit from the top tier of the chamber to a mall. If you go down two floors, you come out on Water Street, just a few blocks from the harbor."

She set off running down the hallway. She slowed as she approached the end, pointing to a steel door. "Through there."

As she spoke, a harsh buzzer started.

"Just like school," Wenden muttered.

At the same time, a metallic clunk came from the door. Mrs. Winter tried to open it.

She said, "It's always open."

"The alarm's triggered the lock," said Ridge. "We're trapped."

Speed examined the door. "Maybe not."

"You can't kick this one open," said Isolde. "It's a steel door in a steel frame."

"I will need space, everyone," Speed warned.

"You'll injure yourself," said Isolde. She looked at her friends. "We can't let her."

Ridge said, "We got no choice—not if we're going to have any chance of getting out of here."

Speed muttered, "It may be a steel frame but the frame is set in wood. Stand aside, everyone, please."

They made room for her as she trotted back down the hallway. She crouched as if at the start of a race. Hurtled forwards. Passed the friends in a whirl of pumping arms and legs. Launched herself. Flew feet first at the door. Struck it by the lower hinge. A crack like a gunshot echoed up and down the hallway. Speed collapsed on her back. Isolde looked at the door. It hadn't budged. She could see no sign of Speed having struck it.

Speed picked herself up and stood with her hands on her knees, breathing heavily. "One more kick will do it," she said.

"That's enough, Speed," Isolde pleaded.

Speed didn't seem to hear. She backed up along the hallway. Shot forward and launched herself feet first at the door again. Another sharp, echoing crack, this one followed by a drawn out crackle, like a flame eating into wood. The bottom of the door slowly sagged inwards a few inches.

Speed, struggling up, said, "One more."

Wenden said, "I've got it." He ran forward, jammed his iron staff in the gap and levered the door inwards and upwards until the opening was big enough to crawl through.

Speed stood. Staggered sideways. Isolde supported her.

"My right foot hit the door at an angle, instead of square on," she said. "It is sprained, I am afraid."

"Can you walk?" Ridge asked.

"I will manage."

They crawled through the gap. Ridge went last. He looked back along the hallway. No sight or sound of pursuit, only the clamor of the alarm.

The tunnel had white walls and was brightly lit. A janitor's cart loaded with cleaning equipment had been left near the door. Speed took a broom to use as a crutch. Wenden and Ridge jammed the cart against the door and piled the equipment on top.

"It won't hold them up for long, but at least we should hear them coming," said Ridge.

Mrs. Winter led the way through the tunnel.

"Where are we?" Isolde asked after a few minutes.

"We've gone under the road, and we're near the council chamber. We come out in what they call the well. That's the space in the centre of the chamber, at the bottom of the three tiers of seats, where councilors make speeches from."

35

Ridge, in the rear, stops to look back, straining to hear against the alarm that still blares. A distant tramp of feet. He can't tell how many. Liz sees him and stops, too. She has one of her tasers ready to fire, the other over her shoulder. Ridge has his slingshot in his hand. They take turns guarding the back of the little band, one crouching ready to open fire as the other overlaps.

Mrs. Winter slows and points ahead. "We're here."

Isolde whispers, "No more talking."

She approaches the door to the council chamber with Wenden. They wait while Ridge and Liz complete a final overlapping maneuver and catch up.

The alarm at the Centre, still loud in the tunnel despite the distance they've travelled, stops. They look at one another in the sudden silence. Hear the door at the end of the tunnel behind them wrenched open and a clatter as the janitor's cart is kicked aside. The tramp of feet. Ridge nods to Isolde. She tries the door to the council chamber. It's ajar. She looks back. Eases it open.

Bradford Glut's voice pours out, filling the tunnel. "This misguided band of rebels is currently under surveillance, and our chief of security assures me that, even as I address you, arrests are imminent."

Isolde slips inside with Wenden, motioning the others to wait.

Wenden gazes up at the ornate, painted ceiling, hung with chandeliers. He's been here once before, on a school field trip, a lifetime ago. The chamber is round, with three tiers rising from where he stands. The walls are hung with portraits of former mayors. Ahead of him, stairs lead up to a dais containing a throne-like chair, a cloth canopy over it, where he remembers the tour guide saying the Mayor sat for council meetings. A curtain hangs behind it. Above it a banner bears a picture of the harbor, with City of Bayport written across it in old fashioned script. More stairs lead up through the tiers of seats on each side of him.

A huge screen filled with Bradford Glut's face takes up half of one wall. Wenden looks around. Sees a remote control on a table in the well. Grabs it and presses Power. Nothing happens. He tries Mute.

Silence.

He beckons the others. They slip inside, the tapping of Speed's makeshift crutch on the floor, and the tramp of feet in the tunnel, the only sounds. They stand in the well, looking around. Bradford Glut harangues voicelessly.

Mrs. Winter points up the stairs on her left, to a sign at the top, Exit.

Ridge returns his slingshot to his back pocket, murmuring, "So far so good."

A rumble like distant thunder sounds from all around the upper tier as guards step forward, their tasers pointing into the well.

Leigh Dirk, in her transcendent form of Ephebiphobia, flanked by Miso, Lister, Watch, and Olface, appears from behind the curtain and stands on the Mayor's dais. She looms above the fugitives. Bradford Glut's face flickers beside her.

Her voice booms. "You are surrounded by fifty armed guards, as well as my Transcenders. You will now give yourselves up. If you do not, I will order my guards to fire on you without regard for the consequences."

Ridge looks at his companions.

Isolde smoulders.

Wenden watches her. Whatever she does, he will do. He is Devotion.

Meru cowers at the back of the well. Speed puts her arm around her.

Liz and Sadie exchange looks.

Liz murmurs to Ridge, "Your call, honey."

He turns his head away from where Leigh Dirk and the Transcenders stand and mouths to his friends, "Up the left stairs to the exit."

He looks up at Leigh Dirk. Shrugs. "We give up."

"That is the first sensible decision you have made," Leigh Dirk sneers. "Lay down your childish weapons. Guards, hold your fire."

Ridge looks around at his companions. He nods. Wenden lays down his staff, Isolde her pitchfork. Liz and Sadie lay down their tasers. Meru lets her qilumitautits slide from her shoulder to the floor.

Speed is leaning on her makeshift crutch.

"And the broomstick, horse face," Leigh Dirk barks.

Speed lets the broom fall. She staggers to one side, her support gone. Meru and Isolde hold her.

Ridge's head is down and his eyes are closed against Leigh Dirk's overpowering stare.

On the screen, Bradford Glut finishes his address. He tidies a sheaf of papers, like a newsreader.

Leigh Dirk motions to the Transcenders to collect the weapons. They saunter down the steps. Lister and Olface have bandages wrapped around their heads under their stocking caps. Olface's cheek is a pulpy mess of blood. Miso's eyes are fixed on Meru.

Ridge's head still down, eyes still closed. Resigned stance. Right hand behind him, left hand in his pocket. Right hand easing out the slingshot, left hand gathering stones. When the Transcenders are ten yards away, and Miso blocks his view of Leigh Dirk, his right hand snakes from behind his back with the sling, his left from his pocket with a handful of stones. He fits one into the cradle. Pulls back the elastic. Looks up at the last fraction of a second to aim.

The first stone flies into Watch's left eye. The second smashes Olface's nose.

In the silence that follows Ridge's disregard of his promise to lay down his weapon, the guards on the upper tier look at Leigh Dirk for direction, Miso and Lister look from their comrades to Leigh Dirk, Watch and Olface cover their faces as blood trickles between their fingers, and Speed shrugs off the support of Meru and Isolde, pushes off with her good foot and lands one third of the way up the stairs on the left. She gasps with pain as she lands on both feet but pushes off again. Lands two thirds of the way up. Pushes off again and with a final bound lands at the top. Swivels to the right as she lands, broken foot extended, and punches her heel into the chest of the nearest of the guards who stand around the upper tier. He crashes into the guard next to him, who staggers into his neighbor, and the circle of guards starts to fall like dominoes. Speed sprawls on the ground. As soon as Speed takes off, Isolde grabs her weapon. It takes her six pitchfork propelled bounds to land beside Speed. She spins left and kicks the first guard on that side in the chest, sending the guards beside him tumbling around the circle. The first guards to fall, recovering, move in. One punches Isolde and she falls beside Speed. The

guards cover them with their tasers as they wait for Leigh Dirk to give the order to fire.
All they hear is a bellow from Wenden, who has grabbed his staff and is scrambling up
the stairs, holding his weapon like a baseball bat ready to swing.

Bradford Glut is still on TV, but now the scene has shifted from the studio to a
school, where he is reading to a primary class. The students gaze at him adoringly.

Leigh Dirk roars, "You, fat boy. Look at me!"

Wenden obeys.

"Stand still!"

He can't resist. He stops on the stairs.

Leigh Dirk turns on Ridge. "Lay down your slingshot, boy!"

But Ridge still has his eyes closed against her authority. As Miso lurches towards
him, drawing back his cudgel, Ridge uses him to shield Leigh Dirk's glare and fires a
stone between his eyes, reopening the wound left from the encounter in the church. Miso
staggers back. Lister makes to follow Miso but Liz and Sadie fall to their knees and
grab their tasers and fire as they kneel. Lister staggers and falls on his face. Ridge, still
using Miso to shield himself from Leigh Dirk's enervating glare, sends a stone slicing
through one of the ropes hanging from the ceiling and holding the canopy over the dais. He
fires again and the second rope gives way. The heavy canopy falls, draping itself over Leigh
Dirk.

Meru has picked up her qilumitautits but still cowers with her mother against the
door from the tunnel. They stagger forwards as two guards push through it. Liz swings
around and tasers them. Two more guards appear. She shoots them, too. She kicks the
door shut, grabs the table, jams it under the door handle, and tells Meru, "Brace yourself
against it. Don't let them through."

Sadie sprays her taser at the circle of guards on the upper tier as they pick themselves
up. They fall back out of range. Liz joins her and they coolly survey the chamber, picking
off any guard that comes forward.

Sadie beckons Mrs. Winter. "Let's go!"

Mrs. Winter protests, "But Meru ..."

"Ridge will take care of her."

Liz and Sadie start to mount the stairs, shepherding Mrs. Winter between them, Liz in the lead, Sadie walking backwards.

Wenden, freed from Leigh Dirk's power, bounds the rest of the way up the stairs and hurls himself at the guards standing over Isolde and Speed. He swings his staff and three fall. He spears another two in the stomach. Smashes a taser aimed at Isolde. He stands guard over her and Speed. As a taser bolt rips into his back and another into his chest, he just has time, before he loses consciousness, to savour the realisation that he is falling on Isolde, and she is lying under him, as she has in a thousand daydreams.

Bradford Glut is bending down to listen to an old lady in a nursing home. He nods understandingly.

Liz, Sadie and Mrs. Winter are half way up the steps. A guard on the upper tier points his weapon at them. Liz tasers him. He pitches forwards down the stairs. Another appears and she picks him off. Two more confront her and, with a taser under each arm, she shoots them simultaneously. Sadie, climbing the steps backwards, picks off three guards who threaten them from the upper tier on the other side of the chamber. One of them topples over the parapet.

Isolde and Speed have struggled up and are dragging Wenden's lifeless form through the exit, Speed hopping on one leg. Liz, at the top of the steps now, sprays taser fire around to keep the guards away.

Leigh Dirk thrashes under the canopy. She calls, her voice muffled, "Get this off me."

Ridge is picking off guards who threaten to fire at the trio mounting the steps. He has only one stone left.

Lister lies face down, and Watch and Olface are still reeling, but Miso is recovering. Ridge faces him as he stalks towards him, cudgel raised.

Leigh Dirk's voice again, muffled but strident. "Someone get this off me—now!"

Meru jumps clear of the tunnel door as the table splinters. She runs forward to hold the door but it flies open and slams into her face. She staggers back and falls, her nose and mouth bloody.

Ridge cradles his last stone, a big one. He fires it into Miso's crotch. The Transcender's eyes bulge. He grunts and doubles over. Straightens and launches himself at Ridge, swinging his cudgel. Ridge tries to parry it with his arm but it smashes into his shoulder. He falls to his knees. Miso stands over him, his cudgel raised. It falls from his hand as he grabs at his neck, trying to loosen the qilumitautit that has wrapped itself around there. He turns on Meru. Takes one step towards her but falls as her second qilumitautit also wraps itself around his neck and two of the heavy plastic weights smash into his face, one splintering as it lands in his eye, the other smashing into his teeth.

A guard steps through the door from the tunnel, taser at the ready.

Meru is sitting on the floor in front of him, blood running down her face.

Ridge, nursing one arm, his slingshot empty and no stones left, stands and faces him.

His eyes are drawn to a curious scar in the shape of a cross on the right side of the guard's forehead.

Ridge and the guard stare at one another.

Tramp of feet in the tunnel.

The guard lowers his taser and says quietly, "Take your friend and run. I'll cause a diversion."

He opens a panel behind the tunnel door and pulls a lever. A fire alarm blares and water pours from sprinklers in the ceiling. Within seconds everything in the chamber is soaked, including the curtain still draped over Leigh Dirk, which grows even more heavy and unwieldy. Bradford Glut, who is at a day nursery, holding a plump, smiling baby, disappears as the TV fizzes and crackles and the screen goes blank.

"They've got all the roads covered, and you were caught on a hidden security camera in the boatshed so they know you took the keys for the boat," the guard warns.

"You'll be in trouble for helping us."

The guard shakes his head. "I'm out of view of surveillance cameras here in the well, and the Agents aren't seeing anything, thanks to you and your friends."

Watch and Olface are sitting on the stairs to the dais, their hands still covering their faces, trying to staunch the blood oozing from their wounds. Lister lies where Liz and Sadie tasered him. Miso is on his knees, spitting blood and broken teeth and choking as he paws at the qilumitautits still wrapped around his neck.

"They won't see me—if you're quick," the guard with the scar concludes.

Meru stands unsteadily. She sways and the guard holds her. Ridge bends so she falls over his good shoulder. He holds her there.

The guard says, "You know they'll follow you. They won't ever give up."

Ridge nods.

"Go now. Quick."

"Thank you."

Water sluices down the steps like a waterfall as Ridge runs up with Meru over his shoulder.

Two guards, their tasers useless in the drenching spray, stand in Ridge's way. Sadie and Liz, who are standing each side of the exit as Speed and Isolde drag Wenden through, run forward and push them down the stairs. Ridge dodges them as they tumble past him. Mrs. Winter holds the door open and he runs through. Sadie slams it behind him and jams Wenden's staff against it. Liz and Sadie throw their spent tasers beside the door. They run down the hallway to the mall entrance, Speed hopping on one leg, Mrs. Winter and Isolde supporting her, Wenden stumbling between Sadie and Liz, Ridge with Meru in his arms.

36

Ridge set Meru down and said, "Split up. Go through the mall and downstairs and out on to Water Street fast. Guards will be at the exit in a few minutes and any second now they'll break through the door behind us."

As he spoke, a furious hammering sounded from the council chamber.

He turned to Mrs. Winter. "We need food and blankets for the road. Do you have any money?"

"I still have my account at the grocery store in the mall, but they'll recognize me, might be a scene."

"Give me the account number," said Wenden. "I'll go."

"I better come with you," Sadie offered. "You still look shaky."

Ridge said, "Meet on Water Street, but not in a group. Stay among people as much as you can and keep your head down, especially you, Mrs. Winter. You don't want a crowd gathering around you."

"Come with me," said Liz. "We'll make like we're on the job."

She linked arms with Mrs. Winter and they hurried into the crowded mall. Speed leaned on Isolde's shoulder and they set off together. Ridge put his arm around Meru to support her as they followed.

Water Street was busy with four lanes of slow moving traffic, while pedestrians inched their way along both sides of the street. The sun glinted on the harbor in the distance.

Ridge glanced around. Isolde and Speed looking in a shop window a few meters to his right. Liz and Mrs. Winter in a crowd watching a juggling busker on the other side of the street. No sign of Wenden and Sadie. Guards everywhere. He'd heard them crash from the council chamber and clatter through the mall as he and Meru reached the exit. Now more guards were converging on the mall from up and down Water Street. Two were approaching the entrance. Meru's face was still bloody. Ridge pushed her against the wall beside the doors and pressed himself against her, muttering,

"Put your arms round me." From the corner of his eye he watched the guards walk past and enter the mall. He backed away from Meru. Her eyes were closed. He took her hand and led her towards where Isolde and Speed still gazed in the shop window. Isolde saw his reflection in the glass. He slowed and muttered, "Seen Wen and Sadie?"

Without looking around Isolde said, "In the grocery store. Watching."

Ridge kept moving. "Follow, but keep back."

A few seconds later Isolde and Speed turned from the shop window and sauntered behind. Across the street, Ridge saw Liz and Mrs. Winter walking parallel to him.

He told Meru, "Pretend to whisper in my ear and look behind. See if Wenden and Sadie are there."

She nuzzled his ear and murmured, "Just leaving the store. Loaded with shopping bags. Heading this way."

Ahead, guards were stopping pedestrians and checking ID. Behind, a horse drawn wagon full of tourists was holding up the traffic. A horn blared and the horse shied, sidestepping awkwardly, the tourists swaying as the carriage lurched. The driver shouted, "Steady," as he pulled fiercely on the reins and struck the horse with a long thin whip. A few yards further on, beside a café, he hauled on the reins again. The horse, a grey Percheron, slowed. Before it came to a complete halt the driver struck it again and called, "Whoa." The tourists alighted. The driver climbed from his seat at the front of the wagon and started taking off the frock coat and top hat he'd worn to conduct the tour.

Ridge stopped in a shop doorway and pulled Meru to him. He glanced back towards the mall. Isolde and Speed were approaching, watching him. He nodded at the wagon. Speed uttered a soft, whinnying sound. The horse pricked up its ears. Speed snorted. The horse snickered with an upward, questioning inflection. Speed snorted again. The horse shook itself violently, like a dog emerging from water, and the reins slipped from the driver's seat and landed on the ground between the carriage and the horse. The driver swore and struck it on the rump as he went to pick them up. When he was behind the horse, it kicked him. The man hopped to the side of the road, cursing loudly. A crowd gathered around him.

"I'll be okay," he insisted. "Just help me into the café. I'm on a break. Next ride's not for a half hour."

"What about the horse?" someone asked. "Shouldn't it be tied?"

"He won't go anywhere," the driver snapped. "Not if he knows what's good for him."

Two men helped him into the café.

Speed whinnied softly again. The horse moved slowly ahead. When it was alongside, Speed and Isolde climbed in. Ridge watched the café. No sign of the driver. He climbed in with Meru. Wenden and Sadie followed, clutching shopping bags. A few meters further on Liz and Mrs. Winter swung themselves up into the wagon. None of them acknowledged one another.

Speed, on the front seat, donned the driver's coat and hat, and asked, without looking around, "To the boat sheds?"

Ridge muttered, "Right."

Speed clucked her tongue. "Forward, Horace."

They reached the checkpoint where guards were stopping pedestrians. A group of tourists standing at the side of the road waved the wagon down.

"Pick 'em up," said Ridge.

Speed clucked her tongue and Horace stopped. The tourists climbed aboard and sat among the friends. Ridge stayed close behind Speed. The guards were busy checking pedestrians. Speed shook the reins and Horace plodded forwards. A patrol van overtook, siren wailing. At the end of Water Street, Speed turned Horace towards the boat sheds on the harbor front promenade. The patrol van had stopped at the sheds and guards were climbing out. Beyond the sheds, at the end of the breakwater, another group of tourists waited.

Wenden risked a glance at the guards from under the brim of his hat. He looked down quickly. One of them was his father. Had he spotted Wenden? Would he even recognize him, now he was thinner, and his face was dirty and weather beaten, and his hair long and unkempt? He knew Ridge and Isolde, too. Isolde had changed, was scrawny rather than slender, her hair long and wild, her face tanned and drawn and scarred, but Ridge looked the same as always.

Horace plodded past the sheds. Some of the tourists on the wagon waved to the guards. They waved back. The waiting tourists signaled for the wagon to stop.

Ridge thought—If Watch and Lister and Olface have recovered and are anywhere near, they'll be on us in seconds. He muttered to Speed, "Better keep moving."

Speed pretended not to see the tourists. Horace plodded past them.

A shout came from behind. "Tour wagon. Halt!"

Wenden recognized his father's voice.

Speed clucked her tongue. Horace stopped. Speed pulled the top hat low on her forehead.

Wenden's father marched to where Speed sat and demanded, "Are you a new driver?"

Speed nodded. "Yes, sir."

"You missed some customers."

Speed mumbled, "Sorry, sir."

"If I see any more inefficiency I'll report you."

Speed repeated, "Sorry, sir."

Wenden's father surveyed the passengers. "Having a good day, folks?"

Wenden stared at the floor. The tourists nodded and smiled.

"Enjoy your visit to the City of Bayport."

Speed said, "Thank you, sir." She shook the reins and Horace moved ahead.

Wenden risked a glance behind.

His father was staring at him. He raised his hand in a discreet salute. Wenden gave a tiny nod.

As soon as they were out of sight of the boat sheds, Ridge called, "Last stop, folks. We hope you enjoyed the ride."

They were on the edge of the Greenway, a wide belt of fields and woods protected from development by former city councils in order to provide easy access to open countryside for people living in the big housing developments and apartment blocks that surrounded the city centre. Ridge, Isolde and Wenden had played there as kids, hung out there as teenagers. Bradford Glut planned to sell building plots in the Greenway to provide revenue for city services.

The tourists, some of them grumbling at the abrupt end to their ride, climbed from the wagon and began to drift away.

Ridge jumped down. Isolde and Wenden followed.

Isolde said, "You okay, Wen? You look like you've seen a ghost."

"Just tired," he said.

Ridge looked at Speed, grinning. "I thought we'd just hitch a ride on the wagon. I didn't know you'd commandeer it."

Speed smiled. "Horace was happy to help."

"Why d'you call him Horace?" Wenden asked.

"It is his name."

"How d'you know?"

Speed smiled again.

Ridge looked at the strip of countryside that stretched away beside the road.

"Keep the wagon and go through the Greenway," he said. "Then pick up one of the woods roads on the other side. Keep travelling cross country because they're watching the roads."

"Where are you going?" Isolde asked.

"Back to the boat sheds."

"No! They're crawling with guards. They must have found out we were planning to steal the boat."

"They did."

"So let's just keep going."

"You just keep going. I'm going to try and fool them into thinking we've escaped by boat, the way we planned …"

"No!"

"… Otherwise they'll keep coming after us. You know what it was like when they were after you, Is. Between them, the Transcenders will find us wherever we go, unless we can throw them completely off our track."

"What do you plan on doing?"

Ridge shrugged. "Dunno yet."

"I'm coming with you."

"Me, too," said Wenden.

"We are all coming," said Speed.

Ridge shook his head. "Get Mrs. Winter out of the city. I'll catch up with you as soon as I can."

"But how will you find us?" Isolde asked.

"There's a sandy beach outside the harbor, where the bay widens, just before you get the swell of the open sea."

"Where Is and me fetched up when we escaped in the old boat," said Wenden.

Mrs. Winter said, "If you need supplies, there's a store called Sam's Variety just up the street. They know me and will let you charge anything you need to my account. You can at least get something to eat."

Isolde stepped close to Ridge and pulled him to her by the lapels of his jacket. "You can't transcend again. I know what you're like. You're hooked on it, and you're going to get yourself trapped in Colorland if you're not careful."

She kissed him, released him, and stepped back, crying.

Wenden caught Ridge's eye. He realized how rarely he and his friend really looked at one another. Ridge's eyes were a kind of metallic blue. Wenden had never noticed it before.

"Been quite the trip, hasn't it?" he said.

Ridge nodded.

"More exciting than school, anyway," Wenden mumbled.

"Look after Is."

Isolde said, "I don't need looking after."

"You watch yourself," Wenden told Ridge.

"I'll see you," said Ridge.

Mrs. Winter had been restraining Meru.

Isolde noticed and said, "It's okay."

Meru jumped from the wagon and hugged Ridge.

Speed clicked her tongue and Horace set off.

Wenden took Meru's hand and pulled her gently away from Ridge and walked behind the wagon, still holding her hand.

Isolde lingered.

Ridge said, "Go on."

She brushed at her eyes. "I wish you wouldn't fucking make me cry."

"Sorry."

"I'll be waiting for you on the beach. I'll be looking for you."

She turned abruptly and ran after Wenden and Meru.

Ridge watched as Horace pulled the wagon across the fields of the Greenway, Isolde, Wenden and Meru walking behind. When they reached a thinly wooded hillside, the others climbed out and walked beside the wagon as Horace started up the slope.

Isolde turned and waved and blew a kiss.

He watched until they disappeared among the trees, then started back towards the boat sheds, slipping through the crowds enjoying the late afternoon sun on the promenade, and replenishing his supply of stones for the slingshot as he went. He began to form a plan. Maybe, if he could get to the patrol boat, he could take off in it, as Leigh Dirk expected, feign some kind of accident, a collision, followed by a fire, an explosion, even, bodies never found. Would it be enough to convince Leigh Dirk and the Agents there was no need to continue the hunt? Even if it was not, by the time the guards had searched the wreckage, his friends at least should be well on their way, beyond even the hypersenses of Watch, Lister and Olface. He imagined the spin the city would put on the incident. A group of misguided, desperate fugitives ... spurned all the city had done to help them ... inexperienced boaters ... tragic accident ... an example to all of the need to live peacefully and responsibly ...

He slowed, looking ahead warily at the rock breakwater, and the boat sheds on the other side, one end opening on to the road, the other to the harbor. He could slip into the water unnoticed near where he stood. Swim to the breakwater. Climb over it or swim around it. But he'd have to wait until dark. And Isolde was right. Already he was looking forward to the thrill of the power and confidence and sense of inviolability transcending gave him. It was addictive. He'd have to be careful, but he knew he couldn't pull off his plan unless he was in Colorland.

He pretended to gaze across the harbor at the distant light on the huge, jagged rock that marked the channel to the open sea, all the while surreptitiously scanning the area around the sheds, thinking, planning. The guards had disappeared but he was sure they were still there and had the sheds surrounded. The Transcenders could already have arrived. If they had, it would take them only a few seconds to know he was nearby.

He retraced his steps, went past the Greenway, and found Sam's Variety, a little convenience and souvenir store, bars on the window, shatter proof glass in the door. He bought a long paddle board, matches, a box of firestarters, a small, watertight box, a survival blanket with a reflective, mirror like surface, and a snack.

He had his plan.

He returned to the Greenway and found a hollow in a field where he could sit out of sight of the road. He ate his snack, then lay back, wondering how far his friends had travelled, and remembering a spring afternoon when he'd lain in the same hollow with Isolde.

As dusk fell he left the safety of the fields and stalked back along the promenade, carrying his purchases. The tide was high and on the turn. He took it as a good omen. It would be on his side. It was the quiet between the daytime bustle of tourists and pedestrians strolling beside the harbor and the night time scene of the bars along the waterfront filling and revelers spilling from them with their drinks. As he prowled along the deserted promenade he noticed through the gloom something new in the water beside the sheds. A power boat, long, sleek, shining, two big outboard motors on the back. The sort of boat Miso would revel in driving in pursuit. It might complicate the plan.

Ridge stopped and watched as an early evening drunk lurched from a bar opposite the sheds, crossed the street, and stood at the end of the causeway, unzipping his pants and preparing to urinate.

A voice came from the causeway. "Move along, buddy."

One guard.

"Just have to pee."

"Not here—unless you want me to taser your dick."

Another voice. Laughter.

Two guards on the causeway.

"So where am I supposed to take a piss?"

"Go back in the bar and do it."

A new voice, from below the causeway.

Three guards, two on the causeway, one in the power boat.

The drunk zipped himself up and moved away, grumbling.

Ridge fitted a stone in his sling. Drew back the elastic. Aimed at the first guard on the causeway. He had to be fast and silent. A shot to the head, face, crotch or knee would slow the guard down, maybe incapacitate him for a few minutes, but it wouldn't still his voice, prevent him shouting a warning. It had to be the throat. Maybe do permanent damage to his larynx.

Ridge lowered the slingshot.

He couldn't do it.

Not unless he was Ruthless.

He knew he had to be careful, and it would be a long time in Colorland, but he had no choice.

37

He raises the slingshot again. Aims. Fires. The first guard on the causeway clutches his throat, gurgles, and falls. The second guard looks around. Gasps and falls as a stone hits his throat. The guard in the boat says, "What's up with you two?" and looks up to see Ridge on the causeway above him. He manages, "Who ..?" before collapsing as a stone lands between his eyes. Ridge jumps down into the speed boat. Heaves the stricken guard over the side onto the breakwater. He inspects the boat. It's all aluminum, nowhere to set a fire. He takes a rope coiled neatly at the back and wraps it around the motors. He leans over the side of the boat, feeling underwater, and finds one of the stanchions underpinning the sheds. He ties the rope to it. He doesn't know what effect it will have, just hopes it will delay the powerful boat at least for a few seconds. The guards are stirring and groaning. He'll have to move fast.

He takes the waterproof box and paddles on the board to the back of the sheds. The doors of the nearer bay are open. The doors of the further shed, the one housing the patrol boat for which he has the key, are closed. He hopes the boat can smash through them. He can see no guards, but hears voices from the office on the other side of the boat he plans to steal. He pulls himself up on the slipway alongside the nearer boat and opens the waterproof box. He takes out fire starters and sets them along the side of the shed. Lights them. He reaches down into the boat and partly unscrews the cap of the gas tank. He sets it on its side so that fuel seeps slowly out and pools in the bottom of the boat. He sets fire starters on its wooden seats. Lights them. The only other light is from the office. He wonders how long he has before the guards see the flickering light of the fires in the darkness on the far side of the sheds, or the guards from the breakwater recover enough to sound the alarm. He can't afford it to be too soon. The fires need time to take hold and spread.

A guard appears, strolling towards the back of the first boat. Ridge crouches on the slipway, his sling loaded. The guard prepares to urinate in the water. He glances across the shed in the direction of the fires. Ridge sees his face register surprise and alarm. Sees his mouth open to shout a warning. A stone smacks into his throat. He staggers towards the water. Ridge runs and grabs him and lays him out on the slipway. He can't risk a splash alerting the other guards.

He runs back for the paddle board, returns along the slipway, keeping low, and slips into the second boat. He unties the paddle boats, keeping one length of rope. Uses it to lash the board to a dinghy tied with its nose slanting upwards on the stern deck of the patrol boat. Sets fire starters on the wooden seats at the rear. Opens the spare can of gas he remembers seeing on his first visit to the boat sheds and douses himself. Puts the stolen key in the ignition and lies flat in the boat.

A shout. "Fire!"

Guards pour from the office.

At the same time the roadside doors open.

Leigh Dirk's voice. "He's here!"

Watch, Lister and Olface must be with her. He wonders which of them detected him first. Miso will be there, too.

The fires are licking up the side of the shed and the seats are burning in the other boat. Ridge reaches for the ignition. A guard carrying an extinguisher and heading for the fires sees him. Ridge has his slingshot ready. As he aims, he realizes the guard is Wenden's father. He'd recognized him earlier when he stopped the wagon. He was ready then to take him out. He thinks Wenden saw his father, too, from the way he looked when they stopped at the Greenway. Ridge thinks—Sorry, Wen, but it can't be helped. One shot to the throat. Wenden's father collapses, triggering the extinguisher as he falls. Foam gushes out in an arcing fountain, covering the guards following him. They stumble, blinded, falling over one another.

Ridge starts the boat. He stands to steer it.

Leigh Dirk and the Transcenders are beside the roadside door. She points to him. "You! Foolish boy!"

He looks away carefully, determinedly. Feels the lash of the steel ruler against the back of his legs. Stumbles but hangs on to the steering wheel to keep himself upright. He has to convince Leigh Dirk and the Agents that all the fugitives are with him, so that at the conclusion of his plan they can disappear, presumed burned, drowned or both. He's trusting the darkness and confusion to help.

He shouts, "Keep down, all of you!"

Leigh Dirk rants, "You will turn off the ignition immediately."

Ridge calls, "Wenden, look after Mrs. Winter."

Another lash against the back of his legs. They burn.

Leigh Dirk shouts, "Mrs. Winter! Children! Come to your senses."

He rams the boat into reverse. Feels it brush the paddle boats aside and hit the shed doors, which bend but don't give way. Shoves it into forward gear and noses ahead as far as the boat will go.

Leigh Dirk and the Transcenders are still by the roadside door. Olface, Lister and Watch are focused on him, ready to track his course, and track him down. He takes quick but careful aim.

The first stone slices into Olface's nose. The second smacks into Watch's right eye. The third thuds into Lister's left ear and lodges there.

Leigh Dirk doesn't flinch, instead screams, "I order you to stop!"

Ridge finds reverse again. Miso runs at the boat as it pulls away. Ridge fires at his right knee. He stumbles, keeps going, dragging one leg. Ridge fires at his left knee. Miso buckles but launches himself over the water, his arms flailing. He grabs the boat's prow with two hands. Starts to haul himself up. Two more stones, one at each hand, and Miso slips out of sight.

Ridge sends the boat backwards at full throttle. It smashes through the doors. He wrenches the wheel around. The fire in the shed is spreading. The gas in the other boat ignites in a whoosh of flame. Guards are running from the sheds. Taser fire from more guards running out on the breakwater, trying to stay alongside. As the boat turns, its front rising as it gathers speed, Ridge glimpses the Transcenders making for the speed boat, Watch and Lister supporting Miso, dripping wet. Leigh Dirk, framed in the burning, splintered doors, shakes her fist.

He guns the boat out into the harbor, outpacing the guards still running along the breakwater firing at him. Looks back to see Miso starting the twin motors. The power boat leaping forwards. The prow lurching, rising in the water. The boat swinging sideways, broadside with the sheds, as the rope Ridge tied to the stanchions holds it. Miso at the wheel fighting for control. Watch, Lister and Olface watching the burning sheds looming beside them. Miso manages to turn the boat away from the sheds, out into the harbor. The front rises again as the boat strains, the motors churning the water behind. A grinding sound, and the boat moves forward, slowly at first, wrenching the burning sheds from their stanchions, gathering speed, the burning sheds ploughing through the water behind it, guards leaping from them. Ridge is half way across the harbor, the channel marker, the stone mounted light, directly before him. He aims for it. The fires he set in the boat are gaining hold, licking forwards along the seats. He can't let them get too close. If they get within range of his gas soaked clothing he'll be a pillar of flame. He's closing in on the light. When he is sure the boat will hit the rock plinth, leaving it as late as he dares, he locks the steering wheel, assesses the height of the fast approaching rock, wraps himself in the survival blanket, reflective side outwards, glimpses Miso gunning the speed boat in pursuit, the burning sheds a spectacular conflagration churning through the water behind, makes sure the throttle is fully open, scuttles between the burning seats to the back of the boat, lies on the paddle board, unties it, grips its sides tightly.

The patrol boat slams into the jagged rock plinth at full throttle. The paddle board catapults forward, clears the patrol boat as it upends, sending fire roaring upwards. The board just clears the light, soars beyond it as the patrol boat flies upwards and over the light, upside down, flying after Ridge for a few seconds before slamming back into the water at the same time as the fire reaches the gas spilling from the tank and the boat erupts in a mass of flame.

He can't help himself.

He roars, "Whoo-eee!" as he soars, strength and confidence surging through him, exultant at the success of his plan, his ruthlessness exemplified in his destruction of the boat sheds and wounding of Transcenders and guards, his thwarting of Leigh Dirk.

Ridge is welded to the paddle board as it careens into the water and sloms forwards. As he steers the board towards the beach at the edge of the harbor, and starts to paddle, he makes sure the blanket is over him, hoping the Transcenders will not detect his survival. If Olface seeks him by smell, all he will receive through his shattered nose will be the gas fumes from Ridge's clothing, fumes he will assume come from the burning boat. If Watch seeks him by sight, all he will see in the darkness of the harbor will be sky and water reflected in the survival blanket, nothing of Ridge. If Lister seeks him by sound, all *he will hear is the lapping of water against the rock plinth, Ridge's stroking of the paddle board blending with it.*

He sculls steadily towards the open sea on the outgoing tide, while behind him the patrol boat burns, and Miso, Lister, Olface and Watch circle it, the burning sheds behind them.

38

Wenden woke just before the sun tipped the horizon. He watched its gold band strike the tops of the trees in the woods that fringed the beach where he'd slept with his friends, Horace standing nearby, snuffling occasionally. The strip of gold slid down the trees until it fell on the far end of the beach, and on Isolde, who stood motionless, looking across the harbor.

She'd started pacing there as soon as they arrived at the beach after an uneventful journey in which they had seen no-one. He'd carried food to her when she refused to join them for supper, saying she had to watch for Ridge. When they settled down for the night, he'd begged her to rest, and when she refused, offered to keep watch for her, and to wake her if Ridge appeared. Twice during the night he'd gone back to her with the same offer and she'd refused him again.

The second time, realizing she was crying, he'd said, "He'll come. You know Ridge."

She moaned, "I've lost him."

He rose, watching her. Her eyes were fixed on something in the harbor. She walked into the water, her arms outstretched. He followed her gaze. Saw Ridge on a paddle board stroking towards the beach.

He was aware of the others stirring, rising, Meru starting forwards, looking back to say, "It's Ridge!"

Wenden said, "Give Isolde a few seconds with him."

Meru said, "But …"

Mrs. Winter said, "Wait, Meru."

As they watched, Ridge rose from his board, threw it aside, and ran through the shallows, sun flecked water droplets falling behind him, a meteor, a falling star, trailing light.

Isolde waiting for him, her arms reaching for him.

He ran past her.

She turned and watched him, ululation of grief pouring from her, echoing from the woods at the top of the beach, rolling back across the harbor.

Wenden, watching Ridge, hearing Isolde's lament, knew instantly what had happened. He wanted to run to Isolde, console her, slap Ridge, bring him back, but he stayed with his arms held out, protectively, to keep the others back, to give Isolde a few seconds alone with what was left of her Ridge.

He heard her call, "Ridge, it's me."

Ridge turned back to her. "Yeah, right. Hi, Is. You should have seen me. I took 'em out, one by one. I took out Miso and Lister and Watch and Olface, left Leigh Dirk shaking her fist, nothing she could do." His words poured out and his arms flailed, gesticulating. "We're safe. They won't find us, not for a while, leastways. They came in a speed boat, the Transcenders, but I fooled them, they think we're all out there in the harbor somewhere, blown up or drowned."

Isolde knew she had lost him. She knew he didn't mean to hurt her, knew when he was Ruthless she became irrelevant to the focus of his ruthlessness, even when the impetus of his transcendence was his defense of her. When he entered Colorland, all that mattered to him was the intoxicating, ruthless pursuit of those who would hurt her. She knew he did it for her, for all of them, but especially for her, for love of her, although they never spoke of love.

She ran to him. Grabbed his shirt. Shook him. Slapped him. Said, "I saw fire on the water. I thought you were burning." She wrapped her arms round him. Slithered to her knees, her arms still around him, moving down his body.

He said, "Whoa, what's up, Is?"

He disentangled himself, leaving her on her knees at the edge of the water, and strode up the beach, calling, "Hey—here's everyone, and good old Horace."

They ran to him, Meru in the lead. She flung her arms around his neck, hugged him. The others crowded around, peppering him with questions, listening as he recounted his escape.

Isolde stood apart. Wenden went to her. Put his arm round her. She laid her head on his shoulder. She was still crying.

Ridge's words tumbled out. "So that'll throw them off the scent at least for a few days, enough for us to get a good start on them, get clear away, maybe stop 'em coming after us for good. So let's get this show on the road. Let's move, guys. Hitch up ol' Horace. I'm starving. What's for breakfast?"

Wenden called, "Ridge."

He didn't seem to hear. He was marching towards Horace.

Wenden called again. "Ridge."

He stopped. "What?"

Wenden inclined his head towards Isolde.

Ridge walked back. "What's up, guys?"

Wenden took Isolde's hand, placed it in Ridge's, folded his fingers around hers. "Talk to Is, Ridge."

"Why?"

"Because she's missing you."

"I'm here."

"Kind of."

Wenden moved away.

Ridge said, "What's the matter, Is?"

"I told you not to transcend."

"I had to, Is. I couldn't have pulled it off without crossing over."

"But you haven't come back. You're still in Colorland. I want you to come back."

Ridge shrugged. "Can't. Sorry." He turned to Wenden, who waited a few yards away. "Come on, Wen. Help me get things moving."

Wenden looked back as he walked with his friend to join the others.

Isolde was crying again.

Speed and Meru hitched Horace to the wagon, while Ridge and Wenden conferred with Mrs. Winter, and Sadie and Liz disguised all evidence of their stay on the beach, using boughs to erase their footprints and the tracks of the wagon.

Isolde sat alone at the end of the beach.

"We should get going," said Ridge. Before Wenden or Mrs. Winter could answer, he went on, "What was the trip out here like, anyway? Seems to have been smooth, no trouble, thought you'd be okay coming out on the Greenway. I should have thought of it when Meru and me were on the run."

He danced from foot to foot as he spoke and his words were a torrent.

"Are you always going to be like this?" Wenden asked.

"Like what?" said Ridge, still hopping from foot to foot.

"Jesus," Wenden muttered.

"So what's the plan?" said Ridge. "Where we headed?"

"Speed says we should make for her place," said Wenden. "She says we'll be safe there."

"And the route will take us close to the border with Ocean City," said Mrs. Winter. "That's where my husband is. Speed knows a safe place for me to cross. Once I'm over the border I know how to contact him. We have friends there, others who, like us, had to flee Bayport and who are working to replace Bradford Glut and return Bayport to sensible government. Isolde's father is among them. Liz and Sadie are coming with me, to join our movement."

They breakfasted on fruit and cheese.

Ridge and Wenden sat together to eat. Ridge saw Wenden twice glance at him. The second time he demanded, "What?"

Wenden mumbled, "Jus'—glad you're okay, and stuff. I was worried about you." He glanced up and grinned. "Should have known better, of course."

Ridge muttered, "Thanks."

He wondered whether to tell his friend he'd fired a stone at his father's throat. He decided not to. It was collateral damage, one of those things you had to do. Wenden would understand. He would have done the same if he'd been Ridge, in Colorland.

39

They travelled for two days, heading north east on woods roads and across fields. Their route took them over the undulating hills where Isolde and Wenden had wandered in their search for Ridge, and across the road where they had first sighted the retrainees. In the distance they saw the dense woods that sheltered the Hinterlands Centre. There was no sign of pursuit, and no sign of life at all, except for a solitary moose that watched them from a bog, and a herd of caribou in the distance.

Isolde trailed behind them. Wenden walked with her for long stretches. He tried to talk to her but she answered in monosyllables or not at all.

"He'll come back," he said.

Isolde shook her head.

Her distress hung over them and they travelled mostly in silence, Speed walking alongside Horace, Meru and her mother talking quietly, Ridge foraging restlessly ahead, seeking the safest route, Liz and Sadie marching each side of the wagon, watching the woods and the fields on either side all the time, Wenden watching the countryside behind.

Towards the end of the third day Speed pointed to a grassy, tree lined path and said, "You see the bend in the trail up there, Mrs. Winter. That is the border with Ocean City. There is a village only a half mile further on. You can contact Mr. Winter from there."

Mrs. Winter shook hands with Ridge, Isolde, Wenden and Speed in turn, saying, "Thank you all for rescuing Meru, and for looking after her, and for freeing me. When we set up a new government in Bayport, I'll make sure your contribution to it is recognized. I'll give your father your love, Isolde, and tell him you'll soon be together." She hugged Meru and said, "You understand why it's better that you, like Isolde, stay with your friends. I don't know where I'm going, or how long it will take for us to organize opposition to Mayor Glut. But in the meantime your father and I know where you are, and your father has friends who often cross the border and can bring a message to you, and I know you'll be safe with Speed and your friends."

Sadie hugged Isolde as she said, "We have friends who were Colorland junkies and made it back."

Liz whispered as she embraced her, "Don't give up, girl."

They shook hands with Ridge, and Liz said, "You better get back, action man." She grinned at Wenden. "It's been a blast, big boy. Keep on looking out for Isolde, won't you?"

"'Course," Wenden muttered.

"Got no choice, have you?" Sadie whispered, hugging him.

Wenden blushed and hung his head.

Liz told Meru, "Don't worry about your ma, darling. We'll look after her."

Mrs. Winter set off, Liz and Sadie on each side of her. At the bend in the trail she turned and waved. Liz and Sadie saluted, one arm in the air, fist clenched.

They slept in the woods near the border, on the edge of the eastern plains. Horace lay down and Speed rested her head on his flank. Ridge took a blanket and stretched out on a mossy bank. Isolde sat by herself for a long time, until Wenden wandered over to Ridge and whispered to him, and Ridge waved Isolde over, and she lay with him. He seemed hardly to notice her. Wenden settled down in the back of the wagon. Meru, who had been watching Ridge all the time he lay alone, sighed and climbed up after him. He held his blanket open for her.

He murmured, "You know Ridge and Is have been together, like, for ever, since they were little kids, since long before I knew them, like it's their destiny or something. He may not show he loves her while he can't get back from Colorland, but nothing's changed."

She sniffed. "I know." She burrowed against him. "But you don't know what it's like."

Wenden put his arm round her and gazed up through the trees at the stars and thought—I do.

Soon after they set off the next morning they were walking through the pampas grass and low bracken of the plains and could see for miles in every direction. An hour later, just before noon, they saw a low building in the distance, the plains all around it.

"Home," said Speed, pointing.

"How long for?" Meru wondered.

"For as long as you like," said Speed. "There is plenty of room, and lots of food. We will be safe, and we have one another."

"And Horace," said Wenden.

They hurried on across the plain, except Isolde, who still trailed behind.

Wenden stopped and held his hand out to her. "Come on, Is."

She was crying again.

www.ingramcontent.com/pod-product-compliance
Lightning Source LLC
Chambersburg PA
CBHW032032240626
47154CB00003B/879